Our Missing Hearts

ALSO BY CELESTE NG

Everything I Never Told You

Little Fires Everywhere

Our
Missing Hearts

A Novel

CELESTE NG

PENGUIN PRESS   NEW YORK   2022

PENGUIN PRESS
An imprint of Penguin Random House LLC
penguinrandomhouse.com

LIBRARY OF CONGRESS CATALOGING-IN-PUBLICATION DATA
Names: Ng, Celeste, author.
Title: Our missing hearts : a novel / Celeste Ng.
Description: New York : Penguin Press, 2022.
Identifiers: LCCN 2022017272 (print) |
LCCN 2022017273 (ebook) | ISBN 9780593492543 (hardcover) |
ISBN 9780593652763 (international edition) |
ISBN 9780593492550 (ebook)
Subjects: LCGFT: Novels.
Classification: LCC PS3614.G83 O97 2022 (print) |
LCC PS3614.G83 (ebook) | DDC 813/.6—dc23/eng/20220414
LC record available at https://lccn.loc.gov/2022017272
LC ebook record available at https://lccn.loc.gov/2022017273

Printed in the United States of America
1   3   5   7   9   10   8   6   4   2

CJKV

Designed by Amanda Dewey

For my family

In the terrible years of the Yezhov terror I spent seventeen months waiting in line outside the prison in Leningrad . . .

Standing behind me was a woman, with lips blue from cold . . . Now she started out of the torpor common to us all and asked me in a whisper (everyone whispered there):

"Can you describe this?"

And I said: "I can."

Then something like a smile passed fleetingly over what had once been her face.

• Anna Akhmatova, "Requiem, 1935–1940"

But PACT is more than a law. It's a *promise* we make to each other: a promise to protect our American ideals and values; a promise that for people who weaken our country with un-American ideas, there will be consequences.

• from Let's Learn About PACT:
A Guide for Young Patriots

Our Missing Hearts

I

The letter arrives on a Friday. Slit and resealed with a sticker, of course, as all their letters are: *Inspected for your safety—PACT.* It had caused confusion at the post office, the clerk unfolding the paper inside, studying it, passing it up to his supervisor, then the boss. But eventually it had been deemed harmless and sent on its way. No return address, only a New York, NY postmark, six days old. On the outside, his name—Bird—and because of this he knows it is from his mother.

He has not been Bird for a long time.

We named you *Noah* after your father's father, his mother told him once. *Bird* was all your own doing.

The word that, when he said it, felt like him. Something that did not belong on earth, a small quick thing. An inquisitive chirp, a self that curled up at the edges.

The school hadn't liked it. Bird is not a name, they'd said, his name is Noah. His kindergarten teacher, fuming: He won't answer when I call him. He only answers to Bird.

Because his name *is* Bird, his mother said. He answers to Bird, so I suggest you call him that, birth certificate be damned. She'd taken a Sharpie to every handout that came home, crossing off *Noah*, writing *Bird* on the dotted line instead.

That was his mother: formidable and ferocious when her child was in need.

In the end the school conceded, though after that the teacher had written Bird in quotation marks, like a gangster's nickname. *Dear "Bird," please remember to have your mother sign your permission slip. Dear Mr. and Mrs. Gardner, "Bird" is respectful and studious but needs to participate more fully in class.* It wasn't until he was nine, after his mother left, that he became Noah.

His father says it's for the best, and won't let anyone call him Bird anymore.

If anyone calls you that, he says, you correct them. You say: Sorry, no, that's not my name.

It was one of the many changes that took place after his mother left. A new apartment, a new school, a new job for his father. An entirely new life. As if his father had wanted to transform them completely, so that if his mother ever came back, she wouldn't even know how to find them.

He'd passed his old kindergarten teacher on the street last year, on his way home. Well, hello, Noah, she said, how are you this morning? and he could not tell whether it was smugness or pity in her voice.

He is twelve now; he has been Noah for three years, but *Noah* still feels like one of those Halloween masks, something rubbery and awkward he doesn't quite know how to wear.

. . .

So now, out of the blue: a letter from his mother. It looks like her handwriting—and no one else would call him that. *Bird*. After all these years he forgets her voice sometimes; when he tries to summon it, it slips away like a shadow dissolving in the dark.

He opens the envelope with trembling hands. Three years without a single word, but finally he'll understand. Why she left. Where she's been.

But inside: nothing but a drawing. A whole sheet of paper, covered edge to edge in drawings no bigger than a dime: cats. Big cats, little cats, striped and calico and tuxedo, sitting pert, licking their paws, lolling in puddles of sunlight. Doodles really, like the ones his mother drew on his lunch bags many years ago, like the ones he sometimes draws in his class notebooks today. Barely more than a few curved lines, but recognizable. Alive. That's all—no message, no words even, just cat after cat in ballpoint squiggle. Something about it tugs at the back of his mind, but he can't quite hook it.

He turns the paper over, looking for clues, but the back of the page is blank.

Do you remember anything about your mother, Sadie had asked him once. They were on the playground, atop the climbing structure, the slide yawning down before them. Fifth grade, the last year with recess. Everything too small for them by then, meant for little children. Across the blacktop they watched their classmates hunting each other out: ready or not, here I come.

The truth was that he did, but he didn't feel like sharing,

even with Sadie. Their motherlessness bound them together, but it was different, what had happened to them. What had happened with their mothers.

Not much, he'd said, do you remember much about yours?

Sadie grabbed the bar over the slide and hoisted herself, as if doing a chin-up.

Only that she was a hero, she said.

Bird said nothing. Everyone knew that Sadie's parents had been deemed unfit to raise her and that's how she'd ended up with her foster family, and at their school. There were all kinds of stories about them: that even though Sadie's mother was Black and her father was white they were Chinese sympathizers selling out America. All kinds of stories about Sadie, too: that when the officers came to take her away she'd bitten one and ran screaming back to her parents, and they'd had to cart her off in handcuffs. That this wasn't even her first foster family, that she'd been re-placed more than once because she caused so much trouble. That even after she'd been removed, her parents kept on trying to overturn PACT, like they didn't care about getting her back; that they'd been arrested and were in jail somewhere. He suspected there were stories about him, too, but he didn't want to know.

Anyway, Sadie went on, as soon as I'm old enough I'm going back home to Baltimore and find them both.

She was a year older than Bird, even though they were in the same grade, and she never let him forget it. Had to repeat, the parents whispered at pickup, with pity in their voices. Because of her *upbringing*. But even a new start can't straighten her out.

How, Bird had asked.

Sadie didn't answer, and after a minute she let go of the bar and slumped down beside him, a small defiant heap. The next year, just as school ended, Sadie disappeared—and now, in seventh grade, Bird is all alone again.

It is just past five: his father will be home soon, and if he sees the letter he'll make Bird burn it. They don't have any of his mother's things, not even her clothes. After she'd gone away, his father burned her books in the fireplace, smashed the cell phone she'd left behind, piled everything else in a heap at the curb. Forget about her, he'd said. By morning, people living rough had picked the pile clean. A few weeks later, when they moved to their apartment on campus, they'd left even the bed his parents had shared. Now his father sleeps in a twin, on the lower bunk, beneath Bird.

He should burn the letter himself. It isn't safe, having anything of hers around. More than this: when he sees his name, his old name, on the envelope, a door inside him creaks open and a draft snakes in. Sometimes when he sees sleeping figures huddled on the sidewalk, he scans them, searching for something familiar. Sometimes he finds it—a polka-dot scarf, a red-flowered shirt, a woolen hat slouching over their eyes—and for a moment, he believes it is her. It is easier if she's gone forever, if she never comes back.

His father's key scratches at the keyhole, wriggling its way into the stiff lock.

Bird darts to the bedroom, lifts his blankets, tucks the letter between pillow and case.

He doesn't remember much about his mother, but he remembers this: she always had a plan. She would not have taken the trouble to find their new address, and the risk of writing him, for no reason. Therefore this letter must mean something. He tells himself this, again and again.

She'd left them, that was all his father would say.

And then, getting down on his knees to look Bird in the eye: It's for the best. Forget about her. I'm not going anywhere, that's all you need to know.

Back then, Bird hadn't known what she'd done. He only knew that for weeks he'd heard his parents' muffled voices in the kitchen long after he was supposed to be asleep. Usually it was a soothing murmur that lulled him to sleep in minutes, a sign that all was well. But lately it had been a tug-of-war instead: first his father's voice, then his mother's, bracing itself, gritting its teeth.

Even then he'd understood it was better not to ask questions. He'd simply nodded, and let his father, warm and solid, draw him into his arms.

It wasn't until later that he learned the truth, hurled at him on the playground like a stone to the cheek: *Your mom is a traitor.* D. J. Pierce, spitting on the ground beside Bird's sneakers.

Everyone knew his mother was a Person of Asian Origin. Kung-PAOs, some kids called them. This was not news. You could see it in Bird's face, if you looked: all the parts of him that weren't quite his father, hints in the tilt of his cheekbones, the shape of his eyes. Being a PAO, the authorities reminded everyone, was not itself a crime. PACT is not about race, the president was always saying, it is about patriotism and mindset.

But your mom started riots, D. J. said. My parents said so. She was a danger to society and they were coming for her and that's why she ran away.

His father had warned him about this. People will say all kinds of things, he'd told Bird. You just focus on school. You say, we have nothing to do with her. You say, she's not a part of my life anymore.

He'd said it.

We have nothing to do with her, my dad and me. She's not a part of my life anymore.

Inside him his heart tightened and creaked. On the blacktop, the wad of D. J.'s spit glistened and frothed.

By the time his father comes into the apartment, Bird is sitting at the table with his schoolbooks. On a normal day he'd jump up, offer a side-armed hug. Today, still thinking about the letter, he hunches over his homework and avoids his father's eyes.

Elevator's out again, his father says.

They live on the top floor of one of the dorms, ten flights up. A newer building, but the university is so old even the newer buildings are outdated.

We've been around since before the United States was a country, his father likes to say. He says *we* as if he is still a faculty member, though he hasn't been for years. Now he works at the college library, keeping records, shelving books, and the apartment comes with the job. Bird understands this is a perk, that his father's hourly wage is small and money is tight, but to him it doesn't seem like much of a benefit. Before, they'd had a whole house with a yard and a garden. Now they have a tiny two-room dorm: a single bedroom he and his father share, a living room with a kitchenette at one end. A two-burner stove; a mini fridge too small to hold a carton of milk upright. Below them, students come and go; every year they have new neighbors, and by the time they get to know people's faces, they are gone. In the summer there is no air-conditioning; in the winter the radiators click on full blast. And when the balky elevator refuses to run, the only way up or down is the stairs.

Well, his father says. One hand goes to the knot of his tie, working it loose. I'll let the super know.

Bird keeps his eyes on his papers, but he can feel his father's gaze pause on him. Waiting for him to look up. He doesn't dare.

Today's English assignment: *In a paragraph, explain what PACT stands for and why it is crucial for our national security. Provide three specific examples.* He knows just what he should say; they study it in school every year. The Preserving American Culture and Traditions Act. In kindergarten they called it a promise: *We promise to protect American values. We promise to watch over each other.* Each year they learn the same thing, just in bigger words. During these lessons, his teachers usually looked at Bird, rather pointedly, and then the rest of the class turned to look, too.

He pushes the essay aside and focuses on math instead. *Suppose the GDP of China is $15 trillion and it increases 6% per year. If America's GDP is $24 trillion but it increases at only 2% per year, how many years before China's GDP is more than America's?*

It's easier, where there are numbers. Where he can be sure of right and wrong.

Everything all right, Noah? his father says, and Bird nods, makes a vague gesture at his notebook.

Just a lot of homework, he says, and his father, apparently satisfied, goes into the bedroom to change.

Bird carries a one, draws a neat box around the final sum. There is no point in telling his father about his day: each day is the same. The walk to school, along the same route. The pledge, the anthem, shuffling from class to class keeping his head down, trying not to attract attention in the hallway, never raising his hand. On the best days, everyone ignores him; most days, he's picked on or pitied. He's not sure which he dislikes more, but he blames both on his mother.

There is never much point in asking his father about his day, either. As far as he can tell, his father's days are unvarying: roll the cart through the stacks, place a book in its spot, repeat. Back in the shelving room, another cart will be waiting. *Sisyphean*, his father said, when he first began. He used to teach linguistics; he loves books and words; he is fluent in six languages, can read another eight. It's he who told Bird the story of Sisyphus, forever rolling the same stone up a hill. His father loves myths and obscure Latin roots and words so long you had to practice before rattling them off like a rosary. He used to interrupt his own sentences to explain a complicated term, to wander off the path of his thought down a switchback trail, telling Bird the history of the word, where it came from, its whole life story and all its siblings and cousins. Scraping back the layers of its meaning. Once Bird had loved it, too, back when he was younger, back when his father was still a professor and his mother was still here and everything was different. When he'd still thought stories could explain anything.

These days, his father doesn't talk much about words. He is tired from the long days at the library that grind his eyes into sand; he comes home surrounded by a hush, as if it's soaked into him from the stacks, the cool sweet-stale air, the gloom that hovers at your shoulder, barely pushed back by the single light in each aisle. Bird doesn't ask him, either, for the same reason his father doesn't like to talk about his mother: both of them would rather not miss these things they can't get back.

Still: she returns in sudden flashes. Like scraps of half-remembered dreams.

Her laugh, sudden as a seal's bark, a raucous burst that threw her whole head back. Unladylike, she'd called it, with pride. The way she'd drum her fingers while she was thinking, her thoughts so restless she could not be still. And this one: late at night, Bird ill with a rasping cold. Waking from a sweaty sleep, panicked, coughing and crying, his chest full of hot glue. Certain he was going to die. His mother, draping a towel over the bedside lamp, curling up beside him, setting her cool cheek to his forehead. Holding him until he fell asleep, holding him all night. Each time he half woke, her arms were still around him, and the fear that rose in him like a ruffled thing grew smooth and sleek again.

Together they sit at the table, Bird drumming a pencil against his worksheet, his father studiously combing through the newspaper. Everyone else in the world gets their news online, scrolling through the top stories, pulling phones from pockets at the ding of a breaking-news alert. Once his father had, too, but after they moved he'd given up his phone and his laptop. I'm just old-fashioned, he said, when Bird asked. These days he reads the newspaper, front to back. Every word, he says, every single day. This is as close as he comes to bragging. Between problems, Bird tries not to look toward the bedroom, where the letter lies in wait. Instead he studies the headlines on the front page that screens him from his father. SHARP EYE OF NEIGHBORHOOD WATCH FOILS POTENTIAL INSURRECTION IN DC.

Bird calculates. *If a Korean car costs $15,000 but lasts only 3 years, while an American car costs $20,000 but lasts 10 years, how much money would be saved over 50 years by purchasing only American cars? If a virus spreads exponentially through a population of 10 million, and doubles its rate of growth every day—*

Across the table, his father inverts the newspaper.

There is only the essay left. Haltingly, Bird picks his way through the assignment, building a lopsided paragraph word by word. *PACT is a very important law that ended the Crisis and keeps our country safe, because—*

He is relieved when his father folds the paper and checks his watch, when he can abandon the essay and set his pencil down.

Almost six thirty, his father says. Come on, let's get something to eat.

They cross the street to the dining hall for dinner. Another alleged perk of the job: no one has to cook; handy for a single dad. If, through some unforeseen delay, they miss dinner, his father scrambles—a blue box of macaroni from the cupboard, perhaps; a scanty meal that leaves them both hungry. Before his mother left, they'd eaten together, a circle of three at the kitchen table, his parents chatting and laughing as they ate, afterward his mother singing softly as she washed the dishes and his father dried.

They find a spot in the back corner of the dining hall where they can eat alone. Around them, students cluster in twos and threes, the low murmur of their whispered conversations like an air current in the room. Bird knows none of their names and only a few of their faces; he's not in the habit of looking people in the eye. Just keep on walking, his father always says if passersby stare, their gazes like centipedes on Bird's face. Bird is grateful that he isn't expected to smile and nod to the students, to make small talk. They do not know his name either, and anyway, by the end of the year, they will all be gone.

They have almost finished eating when there's a commotion outside. A scuffle and a crash, the screeching of wheels. Sirens.

Stay here, Bird's father says. He runs to the window and joins the students already gathering there, peering out onto the street. All around the dining hall, abandoned plates grow cold. Blue and white lights strobe across the ceiling and walls. Bird does not get up. Whatever it is will pass. Stay away from trouble, his father always tells him, which to his father means anything that attracts attention. You see any trouble, his father once said, you run the other way. This is his father: trudging through life, head bowed.

But the murmur in the dining hall grows louder. More sirens, more lights, casting shadows that swell and loom, monstrous, on the ceiling. Outside, a tangle of angry voices and the jostle of bodies, booted feet on pavement. He's never heard anything like this and part of him wants to run to the window, to peek out and see what's going on. The other part of him wants to duck under the table and hide, like the small scared creature he suddenly knows himself to be. From the street comes a scratchy burst of megaphone: *This is the Cambridge Police. Please shelter in place. Stay away from windows until further notification.*

Around the dining hall, students scurry back to their tables, and Peggy, the dining-hall manager, skirts the room, yanking the curtains shut. The air tingles with whispers. Bird imagines an angry mob outside, barricades of trash and furniture, Molotov cocktails and flames. All the photos from the Crisis they've studied in school, come to life. He jitters his knee against the table leg until his father returns, and then the jittering transfers itself inside him, to the hollow part of his chest.

What's going on, Bird asks.

His father shakes his head.

Some disruption, he says. I think. And then, noticing Bird's wide eyes: It's okay, Noah. The authorities are here. They have everything under control.

During the Crisis, disruptions happened all the time; they've learned this over and over in school, for as long as he can remember. Everyone out of work, factories gone idle, shortages of everything; mobs had looted stores and rioted in the streets, lighting whole neighborhoods ablaze. The nation paralyzed in the turmoil.

It was impossible, his social studies teacher had said, to lead a productive life.

He'd flicked to another slide on the smartboard. Streets in rubble, windows smashed. A tank in the middle of Wall Street. Smoke rising in an orange haze beneath the St. Louis Arch.

That, young ladies and gentlemen, is why you are fortunate to be living in an age where PACT has made disruptive protests a thing of the past.

And it's true, for most of Bird's life disruptions have been vanishingly rare. PACT has been the law for over a decade, passed with overwhelming majorities in both House and Senate, signed by the president in record time. Poll after poll still shows huge public support.

Except: over the past few months, strange things have been happening all over—not strikes and marches and riots like the disruptions they've learned about in class, but something new. Weird and apparently pointless stunts, too bizarre not to report, all of them anonymous, all of them aimed at PACT itself. In Memphis, ski-masked figures emptied a dump truck of ping-pong balls into the river and fled, leaving a plume of white orbs in their wake. A miniature red heart drawn on each, above the words END PACT. Just last week, two drones had unfurled a banner across the Brooklyn Bridge, arch to arch. FUCK PACT, it read. Within thirty minutes, the state police had closed the bridge, rolled a cherry picker to the support towers, and taken it down— but Bird has seen the photos, snapped on phones and unleashed online; all the news stations and sites had run them, and even some papers, too. The big banner with bold black lettering, and beneath it, a splotchy red heart like a splash of blood.

In New York, traffic had snarled for hours with the bridge closed: people had posted videos showing long lines of cars, a chain of red lights stretching into the night. We didn't get home until midnight, one driver told reporters. Under his eyes, dark rings bloomed like smudges of smoke. We were basically held hostage, he said, and no one knew what was going on—I mean, it was like terrorism. News reports calculated the gasoline wasted, the carbon monoxide released, the economic cost of those lost hours. Rumor had it that people were still finding ping-pong balls floating in the Mississippi; Memphis police released a photograph of a duck they said had choked, gullet bulging with tumor-like lumps.

Absolutely unacceptable behavior, his social studies teacher had sniffed. If any of you ever get wind of someone planning disruptions like these, it's your civic duty under PACT to report it to the authorities.

They'd gotten an impromptu lecture and an extra assignment: *Write a five-paragraph essay explaining how recent disturbances to the peace have endangered public safety for all.* Bird's hand had curled and cramped.

And here is a disruption right outside the dining hall. Bird is equally terrified and fascinated. What is it: An attack? A riot? A bomb?

From across the table, his father takes his hand. Something he did often when Bird was still small, something he almost never does anymore now that Bird is older, something Bird—secretly—misses. His father's hand is soft and uncalloused, the hand of a man who works with his mind. His fingers wrap warm and strong around Bird's, gently stilling them.

You know where it comes from? his father says. *Dis-* means *apart*. Like *dis*turb, *dis*tend, *dis*member.

His father's oldest habit: taking words apart like old clocks to show the gears still ticking inside. He is trying to calm Bird, as if telling a bedtime story. To distract him, maybe even to distract himself.

Plus *rupt*: to break. As in e*rupt*, to break out; inter*rupt*, to break between; ab*rupt*, broken from.

His father's voice rises half an octave in his excitement, a guitar string coming into tune. So *disruption*, he says, really means *breaking apart*. Smashing to pieces.

Bird thinks of train tracks uprooted, highways barricaded, buildings crumbling. He thinks of the photos they've been shown in school, protesters hurling rocks, riot officers crouched behind a wall of shields. From outside they hear indistinct screeches from police radios, voices swelling in and out of range. Around them, the students bend over their phones, looking for explanations, posting updates.

It's okay, Noah, his father says. It'll all be over soon. There's nothing to be afraid of.

I'm not afraid, Bird says. And he isn't, exactly. It isn't fear that spiderwebs across his skin. It's like the charge in the air before a storm, some immense and shocking potential.

About twenty minutes later another megaphone announcement crackles through the drawn curtains and the double panes of glass. *It is safe to resume normal activities. Please alert authorities to any further suspicious activity.*

Around them, the students begin to trickle away, depositing their trays at the wash station and hurrying off to their dorm rooms, complaining about the delay. It is past eight thirty, and everyone suddenly has somewhere else they wish to be. As Bird and his father gather their things, Peggy begins to open the curtains again, revealing the darkened street. Behind her, other dining-hall workers dart from table to table with dish-cloths and spray bottles of cleaner; another shoves a push broom hastily across the tiles, collecting spilled cereal and scattered bread crumbs.

I'll get those for you, Peggy, Bird's father says, and Peggy gives him a grateful nod.

You take care, Mr. Gardner, Peggy says, as she hurries back into the kitchen. Bird fidgets, waiting, until his father has re-opened each set of curtains, and they can head home again.

Outside the air is brisk and still. All the police cars have gone, and all the people, too; the block is deserted. He looks for signs of the disruption—craters, scorched buildings, broken glass. Nothing. Then, as they cross the street back toward the dorm, Bird sees it on the ground: spray-painted, blood-red against the asphalt, right in the center of the intersection. The size of a car, impossible to miss. A heart, he realizes, just like the banner in Brooklyn. And circling it this time, a ring of words. BRING BACK OUR MISSING HEARTS.

A tingle snakes over his skin.

As they cross, he slows, reading the letters again. OUR MISSING HEARTS. The half-dried paint sticks to the soles of his sneakers; his breath sticks, hot, in his throat. He glances at his father, searching for a glimmer of recognition. But his father tugs him by the arm. Pulling him away, not even looking down. Not meeting Bird's eye.

Getting late, his father says. Better head in.

She'd been a poet, his mother.

A famous one, Sadie had added, and he'd shrugged. Was there such a thing?

Are you kidding, Sadie said, everyone's heard of Margaret Miu.

She considered.

Well, she said, they've heard her poem, at least.

At first it had just been a phrase, like any other.

Not long after his mother left, Bird had found a slip of paper on the bus, thin as a dead butterfly's wing, in the gap between seat and wall. One of dozens. His father snatched it from his hand and crumpled it, tossed it to the floor.

Don't pick up garbage, Noah, he said.

But Bird had already read the words at the top: ALL OUR MISSING HEARTS.

A phrase he'd never heard before but that sprang up elsewhere in the months, then years, after his mother had gone. Graffitied in the bike tunnel, on the wall of the basketball court, on the plywood around a long-stalled construction site. DON'T FORGET OUR MISSING HEARTS. Scrawled across the neighborhood-watch posters with a fat-bladed brush: WHERE ARE OUR MISSING HEARTS? And on pamphlets, appearing overnight one memorable morning: pinned under the wipers of parked cars, scattered on the sidewalk, caught against the concrete feet of lampposts.

Palm-sized, xeroxed handbills reading simply this: *ALL OUR MISS-ING HEARTS.*

The next day, the graffiti was painted over, the posters replaced, the pamphlets swept away like dead leaves. Everything so clean he might have imagined it all.

It didn't mean anything to him then.

It's an anti-PACT slogan, his father said curtly, when Bird asked. From people who want to overturn PACT. Crazy people, he'd added. Real lunatics.

You'd have to be a lunatic, Bird had agreed, to overturn PACT. PACT had helped end the Crisis; PACT kept things peaceful and safe. Even kindergarteners knew that. PACT was common sense, really: If you acted unpatriotic, there would be consequences. If you didn't, then what were you worried about? And if you saw or heard of something unpatriotic, it was your duty to let the authorities know. He has never known a world without PACT; it is as axiomatic as gravity, or *Thou shalt not kill.* He didn't understand why anyone would oppose it, what any of this had to do with hearts, how a heart could be missing. How could you survive without your heart beating inside you?

It made no sense until he met Sadie. Who'd been removed from her home and re-placed, because her parents had protested PACT.

Didn't you know? she'd said. What the *consequences* were? Bird. Come *on.*

She tapped the worksheet they'd been given as homework: The Three Pillars of PACT. *Outlaws promotion of un-American values and behavior. Requires all citizens to report potential threats to our society.* And there, beneath Sadie's finger: *Protects children from environments espousing harmful views.*

Even then, he hadn't wanted to believe it. Maybe there were a few PACT removals, but they couldn't happen much—or why did no one talk about it? Sure, every now and then, you heard of a case like Sadie, but surely those were exceptions. If it happened, you really must have done something dangerous, your kid *needed* to be protected—from you, and whatever you were doing or saying. What's next, some people said, you think molesters and child-beaters deserve to keep their kids, too?

He'd said this to Sadie, without thinking, and she went silent. Then she wadded up her sandwich in a ball of tuna and mayonnaise and smashed it into his face. By the time he wiped his eyes clear, she was gone, and all afternoon, the stink of fish clung to his hair and skin.

A few days later Sadie had pulled something from her backpack.

Look, she'd said. The first words she'd spoken to him since. Bird, look what I found.

A newspaper, corners tattered, ink smudged to gray. Almost two years old already. And there, just below the fold, a headline: LOCAL POET TIED TO INSURRECTIONS. His mother's photo, a dimple hovering at the edge of her smile. Around him, the world went hazy and gray.

Where did you get this, he asked, and Sadie shrugged.

At the library.

It's become the rallying cry at anti-PACT riots across the nation, but its roots are here—terrifyingly close to home. The phrase increasingly being used to attack the widely supported national security law is the brainchild of local woman

Margaret Miu, pulled from her book of poems Our Missing Hearts. *Miu, who is the child of Chinese immigrants and has a young son—*

The words wobbled out of focus then.

You know what this means, Bird, Sadie said. She raised herself onto her toes, the way she always did when excited. Your mom—

He did know, then. Why she'd left them. Why they never spoke about her.

She's one of them, Sadie said. She's out there somewhere. Organizing protests. Fighting PACT. Working to overturn it and bring kids home. Just like my parents.

Her eyes darkened and took on a far-off gleam. As if she were gazing right through Bird to something revelatory just beyond.

Maybe they're together, out there, she said.

Bird had thought it was just one of Sadie's wishful fantasies. His mother, the ringleader of all this? Improbable, if not impossible. Yet there were her words, emblazoned on all those signs and banners to overthrow PACT, all over the country.

What the news calls people who protest PACT: *Seditious subversives. Traitorous Chinese sympathizers. Tumors on American society.* Words he'd had to look up in his father's dictionary, back then, alongside *excise* and *eradicate.*

Every time they spotted his mother's words—in news reports, on someone's phone—Sadie elbowed Bird as if they'd sighted a celebrity. Evidence of his mother, out there, elsewhere, so worried about somebody else's children though she'd left her own behind. The irony of it leached into his veins.

Now it is no longer elsewhere. Here are his mother's words, streaked across his street in blood-red. Her letter upstairs, in his pillow. The same splash of red heart from the Brooklyn Bridge, there on the pavement at his feet. He glances over his shoulder, scanning the dark corners of the courtyard, not sure if the coldness in his throat is hope or dread, if he wants to run into her arms or drag her from her hiding place into the light. But there is no one there, and his father tugs his arm, and he follows his father inside and up the stairs.

Back in the dorm, sweaty and tired from their climb, his father peels off his coat and hangs it on its peg. Bird settles down to finish his homework, but his mind buzzes, unruly. He glances at the window toward the courtyard below, but all he can see is their own shabby apartment reflected in the glass. In front of him, his half-finished essay trails into blank white space.

Dad, he says.

Across the room, his father looks up from his book. He is reading a dictionary, leafing idly from page to page: an old habit Bird finds both peculiar and endearing. Long ago his parents would spend evenings like this, on the couch with their books, and sometimes Bird would drape himself over his father's shoulder, then his mother's, sounding out the longest words he could find. These days, the dictionaries are the only books in the apartment, the only books they'd kept when they moved. From his father's eyes Bird can see he was centuries away, wandering the zigzagging past of some archaic word. He regrets having to call him back from that peaceful golden place. But he has to know.

You haven't—he clears his throat—you haven't heard from her, have you?

For a moment his father's face goes very still. Though Bird hasn't spoken her name, he doesn't need to: both of them know who he means. There is only one *her*, for them. Then his father shuts the dictionary with a thump.

Of course not, he says, and comes to stand at Bird's elbow. Looming over him. He sets a hand on Bird's shoulder.

She is not a part of your life anymore. As far as we're concerned, she doesn't exist. Do you understand, Noah? Tell me you understand.

Bird knows exactly what he should say—*Of course, I understand*—but the words clog in his throat. But she is, he wants to say. She does, I don't, she has something to say, she has something to tell *me*, this is a loose end that needs to be tied off—or unraveled. In this moment of hesitation his father glances over Bird's shoulder at the unfinished essay on the table.

Let me see, he says.

His father hasn't been a professor for years but he can't stop himself from trying to teach. His brain is like a big dog penned in his skull, restless and pacing, aching for a run. Already he's leaning over Bird's homework, tugging the paper from the crook of Bird's arm.

I'm not done yet, Bird protests, and bites the eraser end of his pencil. Graphite and rubber flake onto his tongue. His father shakes his head.

This needs to be much clearer, he says. Look—here, where you say *PACT is very important for national security*. You need to be much more specific, much more forceful: *PACT is a crucial part of keeping America safe from being undermined by foreign influences.*

With one finger he traces a line, smudging Bird's cursive.

Or here. You need to show your teacher you really get this— there should be absolutely no question you understand. *PACT protects innocent children from being indoctrinated with false, subversive, un-American ideas by unfit and unpatriotic parents.*

He taps the paper.

Go on, he says, jabbing at the loose-leaf. Write that down.

Bird stares back at his father with set jaw and angry, liquid eyes. They have never been like this before: two flinty stones striking off sparks.

Do it, his father says, and Bird does, and his father lets out a deep breath and retreats into the bedroom, dictionary in hand.

After he's finished his homework and brushed his teeth, Bird turns out the lights in the apartment and slips behind the curtains. From here he can see across the street to the dining hall, closed now, lit only by the faint red glow of the exit signs inside. As he watches, a truck pulls to the curb and flicks off its headlights. The shadowy figure of a man gets out, carries something to the center of the road, begins to work. It takes Bird a minute to understand what's happening: the something is a bucket of paint and a large roller brush. He is painting over the heart, and by morning it will be gone.

Noah, his father says from the doorway. Time for bed.

That night, while his father snores faintly beneath him, Bird worms a hand into his pillowcase, feeling for the faint edges of the envelope. Carefully he slips out the letter, flattens it out. He keeps a penlight in the top bunk so he can read while his father is sleeping, and he clicks it on.

In the watery light the cats are a tangle of angles and curves. A secret message? A code? Letters in their stripes, perhaps, in the points of their ears or the bends of their tails? He turns the letter this way and that, traces the ballpoint lines with the beam. On a tabby he thinks he spots an *M*; the arched leg of a black cat looks like an *S*, or maybe an *N*. But he can't be certain.

He's about to tuck the letter away when he sees it, the little circle of light bringing it into crisp focus like a magnifying glass. Down in the corner, where a page number would be: a rectangle, the size of his pinky fingernail. Inside it another rectangle, a bit smaller. The cats, of course, ignore it; unless you looked closely, you would miss it between them. But it catches Bird's attention. What is it? A framed picture of nothing, perhaps. An old-fashioned television set, screen blank. A window with a flat plane of glass.

He studies it. A dot on one side, two tiny hinges on the other. A door. A door on a box, a cabinet shut up tight. A faint breeze flutters a page in the back corner of his brain, then settles again. A story his mother told him, long ago. She'd always been telling him stories—fairy tales, fables, legends, myths: a rainbow of different, beautiful lies. But now, seeing the picture, it's familiar. Cats, and a cabinet, and a boy. He can't quite remember it, but he knows it is there. How did it go?

Once upon a time. Once upon a time there was—a boy who loved cats.

He waits, hoping for his mother's voice to come back to him, to fill in the rest of the story. A ball given a shove downhill. But there's only the whispery sound of his father breathing. He can't remember what his mother's voice sounds like. The voice he hears in his head is his own.

After science, his classmates jostle off to the cafeteria for lunch, eager to buy their corn dogs and chocolate milk, to jockey for seats at the best tables. Bird has never liked eating there, all those whispers. For years he took the table in the corner, half hidden in the nook behind the vending machine. Then, near the end of fifth grade, Sadie had arrived, unabashed and unrepentant, elbowing out a space for the two of them. For one glorious year he'd not been alone. The first day they met, she'd grabbed his hand and pulled him outside to the small patch of lawn. Out there, the air was cool and calm and the quiet poured into his ears, magnifying every sound, and as he settled beside her on the grass, he could hear everything, the rustle of the plastic bags they unfurled from their sandwiches, the scrape of Sadie's sneaker against the concrete as she curled her leg beneath her, the murmur of the newly uncurled leaves overhead as the breeze rattled their branches.

The whispers had changed then. There were songs: Noah and Sadie, sitting in a tree.

Kids still sing that? his father had said, when Bird told him about it. That idiotic chant will outlast the apocalypse. When they've burned all the books, that's all we'll have left.

He cut himself off.

Just ignore it. They'll stop.

Then he paused. But don't spend too much time around that Sadie, he said. You don't want people to think you're like her.

Bird had nodded, but after that he and Sadie ate together every day, no matter the weather, huddling together under the overhang when it rained, shivering side by side in the winter slush. After Sadie disappeared, he hadn't returned to the cafeteria but went back to their spot each day. He'd learned, by then: sometimes being alone was the less bad option.

Today, instead of going outside, he lingers in the science classroom, pretending to rummage in his bookbag, until everyone else has gone. At her desk, Mrs. Pollard stacks her papers in an orderly sheaf, gives him an appraising look.

Did you need something, Noah? she asks. From a drawer she removes a brown paper sack, neatly crimped: her own lunch. On the wall behind her, a row of colorful posters beam. IN THIS TOGETHER, one reads, a chain of red, white, and blue paper dolls stretched across a map of the United States. *Every good citizen is a good influence*, says another. *Every bad citizen is a bad influence.* And then, of course, there is the flag that hangs in every classroom, dangling just over her left shoulder like a raised axe.

Could I use a computer? Bird says. I wanted to look something up.

He waves toward the table by the far wall, where a half dozen laptops have been placed for student use. Most of his classmates look things up on their phones instead, but Bird's father won't let him have one. Absolutely not, he says, and as a result Bird is one of the few kids he knows who ever use the school computers. Behind them, empty bookshelves. Bird has never seen books on them, but there they stand, fossils of a long-gone era.

Did you know, their teacher explained the year before, that paper books are out of date the instant they're printed?

The beginning-of-year welcome talk. All of them sitting crisscross applesauce on the carpet at her feet.

That's how fast the world changes. And our understanding of it, too.

She snapped her fingers.

We want to make sure you have the most current information. This way we can be sure nothing you use is outdated or inaccurate. You'll find everything you need right here online.

But where did they all go, Sadie insisted. Sadie, still new to the school then, and fearless. The books, she said. There must have been some before, or there wouldn't be shelves. Where did you take them?

The teacher's smile widened, and tightened.

Everyone has storage limitations, she said. So we've culled the books that we felt were unnecessary or unsuitable or out of date. But—

So you banned all those books, Sadie said, and the teacher had blinked twice at her over her glasses.

Oh no, sweetie, she said. People think that sometimes, but no. No one bans anything. Haven't you ever heard of the Bill of Rights?

The class giggled, and Sadie flushed.

Every school makes its own independent judgments, the teacher said. About which books are useful to their students and which books might expose them to dangerous ideas. Let me ask you something: Whose parents want them to spend time with bad people?

She looked around the circle. No one raised a hand.

Of course not. Your parents want you to be safe. That's part of being a good parent. You all know that I'm a mom, too, right?

A general murmur of assent.

Imagine a book that told you lies, the teacher went on. Or one that told you to do bad things, like hurt people, or hurt yourself. Your parents would never put a book like that on your bookshelf at home, would they?

All around the circle, children shook their heads, wide-eyed. Only Sadie's stayed still, her arms folded, her mouth a thin straight line.

Well, it's like that, the teacher said. We all want our children to be safe. We don't want them exposed to bad ideas—ideas that might hurt them, or encourage them to do bad things. To themselves, or to their families, or to our country. So we remove those books and block sites that might be harmful.

She smiled around at all of them.

It's our job as teachers, she said, her voice soft but firm. To take care of all of you, just like I'd take care of my own children. To decide what's worth keeping and what isn't. We just have to decide on these things.

Her gaze came to rest, at last, on Sadie.

We always have, she said. Nothing's changed.

Now, Bird holds his breath as Mrs. Pollard hesitates. It's only a month into seventh grade but he already likes Mrs. Pollard; her daughter, Jenna, is a year behind Bird, and Josh, her boy, is in first. She has gray-blond hair and wears sweaters with pockets and big, round earrings that look like candy. Unlike his social studies teacher, she never stares at him when PACT comes up, and if she hears one of the kids giving him a hard time, she'll say, *Seventh graders, let's focus on the task at hand, please*, with a rap of her knuckles on the desktop.

Is this for class? she asks.

Something in Mrs. Pollard's voice puts Bird on his guard—or maybe it's the way she peers at him, eyes narrowed, as if she knows what he's doing. He wishes he had that confidence in himself. To believe that what he's after is anything more than a wild-goose chase. On her lapel, a tiny flag pin glints in the fluorescent light.

Not exactly, he says. It's just something I'm interested in. About cats, he adds, improvising. My dad and I—we're thinking of getting a cat. I wanted to look up different breeds.

One of Mrs. Pollard's eyebrows lifts ever so slightly.

Well, she says, brightly. A new pet. That's lovely. Let me know if you need help.

She tips her head toward the row of computers, shining and silver, and begins to unwrap her lunch.

Bird seats himself at the computer farthest from her desk. On each, a small brass plaque reads: *A gift from the Lieu family.* Two years ago Ronny Lieu's family had purchased them for every classroom, upgraded the whole school to high-speed internet. Just part of giving back to society, Mr. Lieu had said at the unveiling ceremony. He was a businessman—some kind of real estate—and the principal had thanked him for this generous gift, said how grateful they were to private citizens for stepping in where the city budget still fell short. He'd praised the Lieus for being such loyal members of the community. It was the same year Arthur Tran's parents had donated money to renovate the cafeteria and Janey Youn's father had given the school a new flagpole and flag.

He jiggles the mouse and the screen snaps to life, a photo of Mount Rushmore under cloudless blue. A tap of the browser and a window opens, cursor blinking slow and lazy at its top.

What to type? *Where is my mother.* Is it too much to hope the internet can tell him this?

He pauses. At her desk, Mrs. Pollard scrolls on her phone as she nibbles her sandwich. Peanut butter, by the smell. Outside, a brown leaf drifts from treetop to pavement.

Story about boy with many cats, he types, and words flood the screen.

The Black Cat (short story). List of Fictional Cats in Literature. He clicks one link after another, waiting for something familiar, that jolt of recognition. *The Cat in the Hat. The Tale of Tom Kitten. Old Possum's Book of Practical Cats.* Nothing he recognizes. Gradually he wanders farther and farther afield. *Amazing and True Cat Stories. Five Heroic Cats in History. Care and Feeding of Your New Cat.* All these stories about cats, and none of them his mother's. He must have imagined it. But still he digs.

Finally, when he is too tired to resist, he pecks out one more search, one he has never dared to try before.

Margaret Miu.

There's a pause, then an error message pops up. *No results*, it says. Somehow he feels her absence more, as if he's called out for her and she hasn't come. He peeks over his shoulder. Mrs. Pollard has finished her lunch and is grading worksheets, ticking check marks down the margins, and he clicks the back button.

Our missing hearts, he types, and the page stills for a moment. *No results*. This time, no matter how many times he clicks, it won't reset.

Mrs. Pollard, he says, approaching the desk. I think my computer froze.

Don't worry, dear, she says, we'll fix it. She rises and follows him back to the terminal, but when she sees his screen, the search at the top, something in her face shifts. A tenseness in her that Bird can feel even over his shoulder.

Noah, she says after a moment. You're twelve?

Bird nods.

Mrs. Pollard squats down beside his chair so they are eye to eye.

Noah, she says. This country is founded on the belief that every person gets to decide how to live his own life. You know that, right?

To Bird, this seems like one of the things adults say that do not require answers, and he says nothing.

Noah, Mrs. Pollard says again, and the way she keeps saying his name—which is not his name, of course—makes him clench his teeth so tightly they squeak. Noah, honey, listen to me, please. In this country we believe that every generation can make better choices than the one that came before. Right? Everyone gets the same chance to prove themselves, to show us who they are. We don't hold the mistakes of parents against their children.

She looks at him through bright, anxious eyes.

Everyone has a choice, Noah, about whether they're going to make the same mistakes as the people who came before them, or whether they're going to take a different path. A better path. Do you understand what I'm saying?

Bird nods, though he's fairly sure he doesn't.

I'm saying this for your own good, Noah, I really am, Mrs. Pollard says. Her voice softens. You're a good kid and I don't want anything to happen to you and this is what I'd tell Jenna and Josh, truly. Don't make trouble. Just—do your best and follow the rules. Don't stir things up. For your dad's sake, if not your own.

She rises to her feet, and Bird understands that they're finished here.

Thank you, he manages to say.

Mrs. Pollard nods, satisfied.

If you decide on a cat, be sure to find a good breeder, she says as he heads into the hall. Adopting a stray—who knows what you'll get.

A waste of time, he thinks. All afternoon, through English and math, he berates himself. On top of it all, his lunch is still in his bag, uneaten, and his stomach rumbles. In social studies, his mind wanders and the teacher calls him sharply to attention.

Mr. Gardner, he says. I would think you, of all people, would want to pay attention to this.

With a blunt nub of chalk he taps the board, leaving white flecks beneath the letters: WHAT IS SEDITION?

Across the aisle Carolyn Moss and Kat Angelini glance at him sideways, and when the teacher turns back to the chalkboard, Andy Moore throws a ball of wadded-up paper at Bird's head. What does it matter, Bird thinks. Whatever this cat story is, it has nothing to do with him, nothing useful or purposeful. Just a story, like everything his mother had told him. A pointless fairy tale. If he even remembers right, if there was even a story like that at all.

He's on his way home when he sees it. First the crowd, then a cluster of navy uniforms in the center of the Common—then a second later, all he can see are the trees. Red, red, red, from roots to branches, as if they've been dangled and dipped. The color of cardinals, of traffic signs, of cherry lollipops. Three maples standing close, arms outstretched. And strung between their branches, woven between the dying leaves: a huge red web, hanging in the air like a haze of blood.

He's supposed to walk straight home, to stay on the route his father has prescribed: cutting across the wide courtyard between the university's lab buildings, then through the college yard with its red brick dorms. Staying off the streets as much as possible, staying on university land as much as he can. It's safer, his father insists. When he was younger, he'd walked Bird to and from school every day. Don't try to take shortcuts, Noah, his father always says, just listen to me. Promise me, he'd said, when Bird began walking to school alone, and Bird had promised.

Now Bird breaks his word. He darts across the street to the Common, where a small group of onlookers has gathered.

From here he can see it more clearly. What he'd thought was

red paint is yarn, a giant red doily fitted round each tree, all the way up the branches in a tight red glove. The web, too, is yarn, chains of red stretching twig to twig, crisscrossing, thickening in some places to clots, thinning in others to a single thread. Knotted in the strands, like snared insects: knit dolls the size of his finger, brown and tan and beige, fringes of dark yarn framing their faces. Around him passersby whisper and point, and Bird edges closer, into the crowd.

It frightens him, this thing. A monster's knitting. A scarlet tangle. It makes him feel small and vulnerable and exposed. But it fascinates him too, pulling him closer. The way a snake holds you with its eyes even as it draws back to strike.

A group of police officers clusters around the trees in intense conversation, prodding the yarn with their fingers. Discussing the best way to take it all down. It's too late: already passersby are slipping phones from pockets and bags, quietly snapping photos without breaking stride. They will be texted and posted everywhere soon. Beneath the trees, the officers circle the trunks, pistols dangling at their hips. One of them pushes his visor back up over his head; another sets his plexiglass shield down on the grass. They are equipped for violence, but not for this.

Clear out, folks, one of the policemen booms, stepping between the crowd and the trees as if he can hide this strange spectacle with his body. He draws his nightstick, thwaps it against one palm. Active crime scene, here. Move along, all of you. This is an unlawful gathering.

Overhead, the breeze flutters and the dolls bob and sway. Bird gazes up at them, the dark shapes they make against the innocent blue sky. Around him, the onlookers drift obediently away, the crowd thinning, and it is then that he spots it, stenciled on the pavement in white: *HOW MANY MORE MISSING HEARTS WILL THEY TAKE?* Beside it a red blotch—no, a heart.

He knows it is improbable—impossible—but he looks anyway. Over his shoulder, all around him, as if she might be lurking behind a tree or a bush. Hoping for her face in the shadows. But of course, there's no one there.

Let's go, son, the policeman says to him, and Bird realizes the crowd has dispersed, that he's the only one left. He ducks his head—*sorry*—and retreats, and the policeman turns back to his fellow officers. Cruisers, lights flashing, block the street at either end, directing traffic away. Cordoning off the park.

Bird crosses the street but loiters, watching surreptitiously from behind a parked car. Had his mother knitted? He doesn't think so. Anyway, surely one person could not have done this alone: the yarn, the web, the dolls wobbling like overripe fruit, all knitted into place, as if they've sprung fungus-like from the tree itself. How did they put this in place, he wonders, even as he is unsure who *they* might be. Through the windows of the car he can see the policemen debating how to handle this unusual situation. One of them worms his fingers into the web and yanks, and a thin branch snaps with a crack like a gunshot. A single long loop of yarn billows down, unraveling inch by inch. Something inside Bird cracks and unravels too, at the sight of something so delicate and intricate, destroyed. The dolls tremble, trapped in their red net. His skin feels too small for his thoughts.

Then one of the policemen produces a box cutter, begins to

saw his way through the knitting from top to bottom, and yarn falls away in a waterfall of snippets. Another arrives with a ladder, climbs into the branches, pulls down the first doll and tosses it to the ground. Not dolls, Bird thinks suddenly: children. The big heads and snub limbs and dark hair. They had eyes but no mouths, just two buttons on a blank face, and as the small body tumbles down into the mud below, Bird turns away, stomach roiling. He can't bear to watch.

He'd thought Sadie had been an exception. *PACT-related re-placements remain extremely rare.*

Well, they aren't, Sadie said.

But how many, he'd asked once. Ten? Twenty? Hundreds?

Sadie eyed him, hands on hips. Bird, she said, with infuriating pity, you don't understand anything, do you?

People didn't like to talk about it, liked to hear about it even less: that the patriotism of PACT was laced with a threat. But some had tried to say what was happening, to explain it to others, and to themselves. Sadie's mother had been one of them. There is footage of her, on a tidy tree-lined street in Baltimore. It could be any street in America except that it is deserted: no cars, no people walking their dogs or out for a stroll, just Sadie's mother in a yellow blazer, the black foam bulb of her Channel 5 mic held to her mouth.

Yesterday morning, she says, *on this quiet street, Family Services officers arrived at the home of Sonia Lee Chun and took custody of her four-year-old son, David. The reason? A recent post by*

Sonia on social media, arguing that PACT was being used to target members of the Asian American community.

Behind her a pair of police cars pull up—lights off, ominously silent—and park, blocking the street. You can see them at a distance, the four officers emerging from the barricade of cars and approaching slowly, a push broom relentlessly sweeping the pavement clean. The camera is steady, and so is her voice. *We seem to have attracted some police presence. Officer, we are with Channel 5, here is my press badge, we—* Muffled cross-talk and then, to the camera, she says, imperturbably calm: *They are arresting me.* As if she is reporting on things happening to someone else.

The police seize her microphone. Her lips keep moving, but now there is no sound. As one officer pulls her arms back to cuff her, another approaches the camera, hand on holster, his mouth barking silent commands. The unseen cameraman sets his camera on the ground and the horizon tips sideways, a plumb line from sky to earth. As they are led away, the camera—still rolling—catches only their feet, retreating upward, off, then gone.

Bird has seen this video because Sadie kept a copy of it on her phone. Technically it is incriminating evidence—it shows her mother *espousing, promoting, or endorsing unpatriotic activity in private or in public*—but Sadie had managed to get a copy somehow and doggedly transferred it, over the years, from phone to phone. On the dumbed-down smartphone her foster parents have granted her—my leash, she says, sarcastically: so that they can always reach her, so that they can track her by GPS if need be—she hides it in a folder labeled *Games*. Sometimes Bird would find her crouched in the corner of the playground, or under the structure in the cubby where the younger kids played house. Over and over on the screen, her mother. Calm in the chaos around her. Slowly walking off into the sky.

It was the first time she'd been arrested, Sadie said, but it had only made her braver. After that she'd gone looking for other families whose children had been taken under PACT, trying to convince them to speak with her on-camera. Trying to trace where the children had been taken. Trying to film a PACT re-placement in action, pulling on her contacts in Family Services, in the mayor's office, anyone with a lead on who might be next.

Soon after, Sadie's mother got an email from her boss, Michelle: coffee, that weekend. Just a friendly chat. Unofficial. Off the record. Michelle stopped by, two takeout cups in hand, and they sipped them at the kitchen table. Out in the hallway Sadie lurked, unnoticed. She was eleven.

I'm worried, Erika, Michelle said over a flat white, about *repercussions.*

A reporter over at WMAR had recently been fined for saying that PACT encouraged discrimination against those of Asian descent; his story, the state insisted, drummed up sympathy for people who might be dangerous to public stability. The station had paid it, almost a quarter of their yearly budget. In Annapolis, another station had had its license revoked. By coincidence, surely, it also had run a number of segments critical of PACT.

I'm a journalist, Sadie's mother had said. Reporting on these things is my job.

We're a small station, Michelle said. The bottom line is, with budget cuts we're basically at bare-bones operation as it is. And if our funders pulled out . . .

She stopped, and Sadie's mother twisted the sleeve of her paper cup around and around.

Are they threatening to? she asked, and Michelle replied, Two already have. But it's not just that. It's the repercussions for you, Erika. For your family.

They'd known each other for years, these two women: one Black, one white. Barbecues and picnics together, holiday gatherings. Michelle had no children, had never married. This station is my baby, she always said. When Sadie was born, Michelle had knitted her a yellow sweater and booties to match; over the years she'd taken Sadie on outings to the zoo and the aquarium and Fort Henry. Auntie Shellie, Sadie called her.

I'm hearing things, Michelle said. Really scary things. It's not just PAOs and protesters who need to worry about PACT, Erika. It might be best if we assigned you a different beat for a while. Something less political.

What beat would be less political, Sadie's mother asked.

I just don't want anything to happen to you, if you keep pushing this, Michelle said. Or to Lev. And most of all Sadie.

Sadie's mother took a long, slow sip. The coffee had gone cold.

What makes you think, she said finally, that any of us will be safe if I don't?

It was just a few weeks later that they'd come for Sadie.

They came at night: that's what Sadie said. After dinnertime. She'd just taken a shower and was swathed in a towel when the doorbell rang. Her mother was combing Sadie's hair, which was thick and curly and prone to tangles, and downstairs they heard her father, shouting. Then the voices of strangers—a man, two men. Sadie's mother had lifted a section of hair in one hand and gently worked the comb through it, and this is what Sadie remembered most clearly: a stray drop of water trickling down the back of her neck, her mother's steady hand as she coaxed out the knots.

She didn't shake, Sadie said, her voice proud. Not one tiny bit.

Maybe she didn't know what was happening, Bird said.

Sadie shook her head.

She knew, she said.

Her mother wrapped her arms around her, pressed her lips to Sadie's forehead. Sadie hadn't understood, yet, what was going on, but dread seeped into her like a chill against her damp skin. She leaned against her mother, burrowed her face into the soft crook of her mother's neck so hard she couldn't breathe.

Don't forget us, okay? her mother had said, and Sadie was still confused when the bathroom door opened. A man, in a police uniform. Sadie's father was still shouting downstairs.

There were four officers, it turned out. Two stayed with her father downstairs and one stayed with her mother upstairs and one stood guard outside Sadie's room while she got dressed. Unsure what to do, she'd put on her rainbow-striped pajamas, as if she were simply going to bed like any other day. Let her go back and change, her mother had said, when Sadie came out into the hallway, at least let me braid her hair. But the man in the hallway shook his head.

From now on, he said, she's not your responsibility anymore.

He put his hand on Sadie's shoulder and steered her down the stairs, and Sadie understood that something terrible was happening but was positive, at the same time, that it could not be real. She'd tried to look back at her mother for a clue—if she should scream or fight or run or obey—but all she could see was the broad blue chest of the officer behind her, blocking everything but a sliver of her mother's arm from view. And so she remembered what her mother had always taught her: be extra careful around policemen, say please and thank you and ma'am and sir. Whatever you do, don't make them angry. They'd shuttled her into a big black car, and the policeman had buckled her into the back seat, and she'd said: *Thank you.* After they'd driven away, after they'd taken her to the station, then the airport, then a foster home, after she'd realized she wasn't going home again, she'd regretted that thank-you, she'd regretted going so quietly.

Her first foster parents had wanted to rename her. A new name for a new start, they'd suggested, but she'd flat-out refused.

My name is Sadie, she said.

For two weeks they'd tried to convince her, but eventually they'd given in.

So many new things for her in those early days. Some—new family, new house, new city, new life—she could not fight, so she resisted in the few places she could. On the way to school, she'd stopped on the front step and stripped off the flounced, flowered dress they'd given her, left it on the lawn, walked the rest of the way in her underwear. A phone call from the principal;

a stern lecture from her foster parents. The next morning she did it again. You see, everyone said. What kind of parents—? She's practically a savage.

Her second foster mother tried to untangle the dense cloud of her hair. We'll have to have it relaxed, she said, despairing, and that night, after everyone was asleep, Sadie snuck downstairs for the kitchen shears. From then on she kept it clipped to a curly halo around her head. I don't know what to do with her, this foster mother said once to a friend, when she thought Sadie couldn't hear. It's like she takes no pride *at all* in her appearance.

They were kind people who thought they meant well. They'd been government-selected as fit parents, certified as people of *good moral character* who could teach good patriotic values.

There's something wrong with her, Sadie heard her latest foster mother say into the telephone: the weekly check-in with the social worker, pumping for evidence that Sadie would need to stay. She hasn't cried once, all the time she's been here. I even sat outside her room and listened all night. She doesn't cry at all. Now tell me, what kind of child goes through all this and doesn't even cry? Yes. That's what I think, too. What kind of parents she must have had, to make her so cold and unfeeling.

She'd sighed. We're doing what we can, she said. We'll try to repair the damage that's already been done.

A few weeks later, a letter, which Sadie had found in her foster mother's desk: *In light of severe emotional scarring inflicted by child's previous domestic situation, recommend permanent removal. Permanent custody granted to foster parents.*

And it was true, Sadie never cried. A few times she'd given Bird letters to her old address, scribbled on notepaper, but the last had come back stamped RECIPIENT UNKNOWN. Even then, Bird had not seen her cry.

Sometimes, though, when he saw her squatting in the corner of the playground, head leaning against the chain-link fence, he turned away, so she wouldn't have to pretend to be brave. To let her be alone with her grief, or whatever heavier thing she'd put on top to hold it down.

She'd suggested they run away, last May.

We'll go and we'll find them, she said.

Sadie, he knew, had run away before, though they'd caught her every time. This time, she insisted, she would make it. She had just turned thirteen—basically an adult, she insisted.

Come with me, Bird, she'd said. I'm sure we can find them.

Them was her parents and his mother. Her certainty that they were still out there, findable and maybe even together, was unshakable. A comfortable, beautiful fairy tale.

They'll catch you, he said.

No, they won't, Sadie snapped. I'm going to—

But he'd cut her off. Don't tell me, he said. I don't want to know. In case they ask me where you've gone.

He'd watched her on the next swing, pumping and pumping her legs, hard, harder, until her feet cleared the top bar and the chain went slack and bucked beneath her. Then Sadie let out a whoop and catapulted herself free, leaping into the air, into nothing. When he'd been small, he'd loved leaping from the swings that way, swooping into his mother's waiting arms. Sadie hadn't even done anything, Bird thought, she didn't deserve any of it, and he hated her parents for doing this to her. Why didn't they stop, that first time, how could they have been so irresponsible? Sadie sat up and looked back at him from where she'd landed in a tumbled heap in the grass. She wasn't hurt. She was laughing.

Jump, Bird, she cried, but he didn't, just let the swing slow until the toes of his sneakers dragged in the gravel, leaving grubby gray scratches on the canvas.

He thinks about her now: Sadie, poised in midair, arms flung wide, slicing across the sky. After she'd disappeared, no one seemed to know where she'd gone; his classmates and even his teachers simply went on as if she'd never existed. As he stands there, he knows the photos from the Common are already beginning to appear online, the trees holding up little figures in their fingers, raising them to the light. A thousand little Sadies silhouetted against the blue.

The next morning, walking to school, he sees the real trees: stripped bare to rough bark again. As if nothing had ever been there at all. Yet there is the sharp bright gash running down each trunk like a scar; there are the broken spots where the web, roughly yanked, has dragged the branches away. There, in the mud, a single strand of red yarn left behind. Something happened here, and he is determined to find out what, and thinking of Sadie, suddenly he has an idea of where to begin.

After school he is supposed to come straight home. Stay in the apartment, his father says. And do your homework. But today he does not follow the path. He turns onto Broadway, follows it out toward the high school, where he'll have to go in a few years, toward the big public library beside it, where he has never been.

From *liber,* his father has told him. Books. Which comes from the word meaning *the inner bark of trees,* which comes from the word for *to strip, to peel.* Early peoples pulled off the thin strips for writing material, of course.

A fall walk, once. His father's hands had brushed the flaking birch bark, rising paper-white in curls from the slender trunk.

But I like to think of it as peeling back layers. Revealing layers of meaning.

In the science museum, long ago: a giant slice of tree trunk, taller than his father. Rings of caramel against cream-colored wood. They'd counted the rings, bark to core, then back out again. His father's finger tracing the grain. This is when the tree was planted, when George Washington was a boy. This is the Civil War, World War I, World War II. This is when his father was born. This is when everything fell apart.

You see? his father said. They carry their histories inside them. Peel back enough layers and they explain everything.

It's like a castle, Sadie had told him. She'd visited the library daily, a stolen five minutes on the way home from school. Half jogging to get there as fast as she could, sprinting to get home on time after lingering as long as she dared. Sadie, I think you need to start showering more often, her foster mother would say when she arrived home sweaty and rumpled. You'll get caught, Bird warned, but Sadie was unmoved. Her parents had read to her every night and where stories were grit in Bird's memories, in Sadie's they were a rich balm. A castle, she insisted to Bird, her voice swollen with awe. He had rolled his eyes, but now he sees it is more or less true: the library is a huge sandstone building with arches and a turret, though a newer glass wing has been added on, all sharp angles and sparkling panes, and because of this, as he climbs the steps, he feels that he is somehow entering both the past and the future at once.

He's seldom around so many books, and for a moment it is dizzying. Shelves and shelves. So many you could get lost. At the front desk, the librarian—a dark-haired woman in a pink sweater—glances his way. She sizes him up over the tops of her glasses, as if she knows he doesn't belong, and Bird quickly sidles away into the aisles, out of view. Up close, he can see that here and there books have been removed, leaving gaps in the rows like missing teeth. But still he senses that there are answers here, caught somewhere between the pages and filed away. All he has to do is find them.

Placards hang at the ends of the shelves, a list of subjects that live down each aisle, perplexingly numbered and inscrutably arranged. Some sections are still lush and thriving: Transportation. Sports. Snakes/Lizards/Fish. Other sections are dry deserts: by the time he gets to the 900s, nearly everything is gone, just rows and rows of skeletal shelving, slicing the sunlight into squares. The few remaining books are small dark spots against all that bare. *The China-Korean Axis and the New Cold War. The Menace at Home. The End of America: China on the Rise.*

As he roams, he notices something else, too: the library is all but deserted. He is the only visitor here. On the second floor sit rows of bare study carrels and long worktables with wooden chairs, all unoccupied. All the way down to the basement, just empty seats and a forlorn sign reading: CHANGED YOUR MIND? PLEASE PLACE UNWANTED BOOKS ON THE CART BELOW. There is no cart anymore, only a bare stretch of linoleum tile. It is a ghost town, and he, still alive, is intruding in the land of the dead. With one finger he traces an empty shelf, making a clean bright line in the thick fur of dust.

Far downstairs, in the back corner, he finds the poetry section, scans the shelves until he reaches *M.* Christopher Marlowe. Andrew Marvell. Edna St. Vincent Millay. He isn't surprised to find that the shelf jumps straight from Milton to Montagu, but he's sad not to find her name.

Coming here was a mistake, he thinks. This place feels forbidden, the whole undertaking unwise. In his nostrils, the sharp scent of iron and heat. He inches toward the front, where at the desk the librarian sorts through a crate of books with ruthless efficiency. He's afraid to catch her eye again. When she turns around, he thinks, he'll slip out.

Peering through a gap in the shelf, he watches, waiting for an opening. The librarian pulls another book from the blue plastic crate on the desktop, consults a list, makes a check mark. Then—and here Bird is puzzled—she quickly riffles through the book, fanning the pages like a flipbook, before shutting it and placing it on the stack. With the next book, she does the same. Then the next. She's looking for something, Bird realizes, and a few books later she finds it. This time she scans the list once, then again, and sets her pen down. Evidently this book isn't on it. Slowly she flips through the pages, one at a time, pausing finally to extract a small white slip of paper.

From where Bird stands, he can just make out a few lines of handwriting scribbled across it. He leans around the shelf, trying to see more, and it is at this point that the librarian looks up and spots him peeking out.

Swiftly she folds the paper in half, hiding it from view, and marches toward him.

Hey, she says. What are you doing back there? Yes, you. I see you. Up. Stand up.

She jerks him up by one elbow.

How long have you been there, she demands. What are you doing back there?

Up close she's both older and younger than he expected. Long dark brown hair threaded with iron gray. Older, he thinks, than his mother would be. But there's a youthful quality to her, too:

a small flash of silver in her pierced nostril; an alertness in her face that reminds him of someone. After a minute, he realizes who. Sadie. The same glinting dare in her eye.

I'm sorry, he says. I'm just—I'm looking for a story. That's all.

The librarian peers at him over her glasses.

A story, she says. You'll have to be more specific.

Bird glances at the maze of shelves around them, the librarian's hand clamped on his arm, her other fist clenched—around what? His face flushes.

I don't know the title, he says. It's a story—someone told me a long time ago. There's a boy, and a lot of cats.

That's all you know?

Now she'll throw him out. Or she'll call the police and have him arrested. As a child, he understands instinctively how arbitrary punishment can be. The librarian's thumb digs harder into the crook of his arm.

Then she half closes her eyes. Thinking.

A boy and a lot of cats, she echoes. Her grip on his arm slackens, then releases. Hmm. There's a picture book called *Millions of Cats*. A man and a woman want the prettiest cat in the world. Hundreds of cats, thousands of cats, millions of cats. Ring a bell?

It doesn't sound familiar, and Bird shakes his head.

There's a boy in this story, he repeats. A boy, and a cabinet.

A cabinet? The librarian bites her lip. There's a sudden light in her eyes, an alertness to her, as if she is a cat herself, on the hunt with ears pricked and whiskers twitching. Well, there's a boy in *Sam, Bangs and Moonshine*, she says, but no cabinet, that I can recall. Lots of cats in Beatrix Potter, but no boys. Is it a picture book, or a novel?

I don't know, Bird admits. He has never heard of any of the books the librarian is describing, and it makes him slightly dizzy, all these stories he hadn't even known existed. It's like learning there are new colors he's never seen. I never actually read it, he says. I think it might be a fairy tale. Somebody just told it to me, once.

Hmm.

The librarian pivots on her heel with startling alacrity. Let's take a look, she says, and marches off, discreetly sliding the folded slip of paper into her pocket.

She walks so briskly that he nearly loses her. Shelf by shelf, the world rushes by in microcosm: Customs & Etiquette. Costumes & Fashion. This is a world, he realizes, she knows forward and backward, a map she's traveled so many times she can draw it from memory.

Here we are, she says. Folklore.

Drumming her fingers along the spines, she skims the shelf, appraising and ticking off each book in her mind.

I know there's a story called Cat-skin, she says, pulling down a volume and handing it to Bird. On the cover, gilt letters and a cluster of golden-haired ladies and knights.

And there's one in there called The Cat and Mouse in Partnership, too. Ends how you'd expect. Nothing about a boy, though. Of course there's Puss in Boots, but I don't know that I'd call the miller's son a boy—and there's no cabinet, for sure. And only the one cat.

Before Bird can reply, she's already moved on.

Let's see: Hans Christian Andersen? No, I don't think so. There's an old legend about a cat calming baby Jesus in his cradle—that's sort of like a cabinet. Or maybe it's a myth? There's Freyja and her chariot cats, and of course there's Bastet, but no cabinets or boys. And I don't remember the Greeks saying much about cats.

She rubs her temple with one bony knuckle. It's almost, Bird thinks, as if she's forgotten about him, as if she's talking to herself. Or to the books themselves, as if they're beings of their own who might answer back. To his great relief, she seems to have forgotten about him spying, about the mysterious slip of paper.

You don't remember anything else? she says.

I can't, he says. I mean, I don't.

He looks down at the book of fairy tales in his hands, turns it over. On the back: a slain dragon, borne on a pole, red tongue lolling like a dangling rope. His throat goes hot and sticky, and he closes his eyes and swallows, trying to clear it.

My mother told it to me, he says, a long time ago. It's okay. Never mind.

He turns to go.

You know, I think I remember an old picture book, the librarian says. She lowers her voice. A Japanese folktale.

She pauses a moment, glances at the shelf, then the search terminal at the end of the row.

But it won't be in there.

Then she snaps her fingers, points at him. As if he himself has figured out the answer.

Come with me, she says.

Bird follows her between the shelves to an office marked STAFF ONLY. The librarian lifts a key from her lanyard, unlocks it. The room beyond is full of stacks of books, a desk piled high with papers. Filing cabinets, a rotary fan. Dust. But they walk straight past the desk to a rusty metal door the gray-green color of mold. She shoulders it open, tugs a wastepaper basket toward her with her foot, wedges it behind the door to keep it from shutting. From the dent in the basket, it's clear that this has been its job for years.

There's one more place we might look, she says, and beckons him through.

It's a kind of loading dock, separated from the outside by a roll-down metal grate. Once, trucks must have dropped off their cargo here: books, he supposes, from other libraries. From the piles of crates and boxes on the sides of the dock he can see it hasn't been used in some years; there's no way a truck could even approach it.

Fewer loans these days, the librarian says. Just a crate or so a week. Easier to just bring it in the front.

She begins to lift them down, and when Bird goes to help, he sees that they're stacked on something: a huge wooden cabinet, bigger than his dresser at home, made of dozens of little drawers.

We stopped using this years ago, when we converted the catalog to digital, the librarian says, clearing the last of the boxes away. Moved it out here to save space. Then the Crisis hit. Now they still haven't restored our budget. The city won't take it and we don't have the funds to have someone haul it away.

She runs her fingers along the brass labels of the drawers and hooks her finger into the pull.

Here, she says. Let's take a look. The book I'm thinking of is quite old.

Inside, to Bird's astonishment, the drawer is jammed with small cards covered in neat typing. With deft flicks the librarian riffles through, so quickly he can barely make out the words. *Cats—literature. Cats—mythology.* Every one of these cards, he realizes, is a book. He had no idea there could be so many.

Ah, the librarian says, with a sigh of satisfaction. It's the tone of someone who has solved a puzzle, of someone who's decoded a riddle and found the treasure beneath the X. She extracts a single card and holds it out to him.

Cats—folklore—Japanese—retellings. The Boy Who Drew Cats.

Recognition chimes in him, setting him aquiver like a tuning fork. A strangled noise rises in his throat.

That's it, he says. I think—I think that's it.

The librarian turns the card over and scans the back.

I was afraid of that, she says.

You don't have a copy? Bird asks, and she shakes her head.

Removed. Three years ago, it says. Someone complained, probably. That it encouraged pro-PAO sentiment, or something. Some of our donors have—opinions. On China, or in this case, anything that vaguely resembles it. And we need their *generosity* to keep this place open. Or just as likely, someone got nervous and got rid of it preemptively. Us public libraries—a lot of us just can't take the risk. Too easy for some concerned citizen to say you're promoting unpatriotic behavior. Being overly sympathetic to potential enemies.

She sighs and slides the card back into its place in the stack.

There's another book I wanted to find, Bird says cautiously. *Our Missing Hearts.*

The librarian's eyes snap toward him. For a long moment she studies him. Appraising.

I'm sorry, she says curtly. That book I know we don't have anymore. I doubt you'll find it anywhere.

With a bang, she pushes the long thin drawer shut again.

Oh, Bird says. He'd known it was unlikely and yet deep down, he'd still nursed a flicker of hope, and it goes out in a small sooty puff.

What did they do with them, he asks after a moment. All those books.

He remembers a picture from history class: heaps of books in a town square, set ablaze. As if she can tell what he's thinking, the librarian gives him a sideways glance and chuckles.

Oh no, we don't burn books here. This—this is *America.* Right?

She raises an eyebrow at him. Serious, or ironic? He can't quite tell.

We don't burn our books, she says. We pulp them. Much more civilized, right? Mash them up, recycle them into toilet paper. Those books wiped someone's rear end a long time ago.

Oh, says Bird. So that's what happened to his mother's books. All those words ground up into dingy gray, flushed down into the sewer in a mess of shit and piss. Something goes hot and liquid behind his eyes.

Hey, the librarian says. You okay?

Bird snuffles and nods. Fine, he says.

She doesn't ask any more questions, doesn't press him or ask why he's crying, only pulls a tissue from her pocket and hands it to him.

Fucking PACT, she says softly, and Bird is speechless. He can't remember ever hearing an adult swear.

You know, she says, after a minute or two. It's possible some library might have a copy of that cat book still stored away. A big library, like the university's. Sometimes they can get away with keeping things we can't. For *research* purposes. But even if they did, you'd have to ask for it at circulation. Present credentials and a reason for requesting access.

Bird nods.

Good luck, she says. I hope you find it. And Bird? If there's anything I can help with, just come back and I'll try.

He is so touched by this that it doesn't occur to him until much later: to wonder how she knows his name.

When his father gets home, Bird decides, he will ask. He'll ask him to look at work for a copy of the book. He is certain that somewhere in the university library is a book of Japanese folktales with this story in it. They still have thousands of Asian texts, he knows, because every so often, there are petitions to purge all of them—not just those from China and Japan and Cambodia and other places, but those about them, too. The news calls China *our greatest long-term threat*, and politicians fret that Asian-language books might contain anti-American sentiments or even coded messages; sometimes angry parents complain if their children choose to study Mandarin, or Chinese history. *I sent him to get an education, not to be brainwashed.* Each time it makes the college paper, then the news; a congressman or sometimes a senator delivers an impassioned speech about universities as *incubators of indoctrination*; the provost issues another public statement in reply, defending the library's collection. Bird has seen it in the newspaper as his father turns the pages. *If we fear something, it is all the more imperative we study it thoroughly.*

He'll ask his father just to check. Just to see if this book still exists, and if it does, if he'll bring it home so Bird can see it. Just for a day. He doesn't need to tell his father about the letter, or about his mother. It's just a book he's interested in; it's just a story, just a folktale about a boy and some cats, surely there's no harm in it. It's not even Chinese, after all. When his father gets home, he will ask.

But his father doesn't come, and he doesn't come, and doesn't come. They don't have a telephone; no one has a landline anymore, the dorms ripped out all those wires years ago, so all Bird can do is wait. Six o'clock arrives, then seven. They've missed dinner; in the dining hall the workers will be lifting the pans from the steam baths, tipping dried-out leftovers into trash cans, scouring the stainless steel clean. Through the window Bird watches the lights of the dining hall turn off, one by one, and a thin tentacle of dread slithers through him. Where is his father? Could something have happened? As eight o'clock ticks by, he thinks suddenly of his trip to the library that afternoon, of the computer at school blinking *No results*. Of Mrs. Pollard, clicking her pen over his shoulder; of the librarian pocketing her mysterious note. Of the policeman at the Common, tapping his baton against his palm. Of Sadie, and her mother, asking questions, nosing into dark corners. There is always someone watching, he realizes, and if someone has seen him, might his father be blamed, might his father—

It's almost nine when he hears the stairwell door creak open and slam shut—the elevator still not working, after three days—then footsteps in the hall. His father. Bird has a sudden impulse to run to him, the way he did as a small child. When his arms barely circled his father's knees, when he still thought his father was the tallest man in the world. But his father looks so tired, so sweaty and defeated from all those stairs, that Bird hesitates. As if he might knock his father down.

What a day, his father says. The FBI came in just after lunch.

Bird flashes hot, then cold.

They're investigating a professor over at the law school. Wanted a list of every book she's ever borrowed. And then, once they had the titles, they wanted to take every single one. Took me six and a half hours to pull them all. Four hundred and twenty-two books.

Breath rushes into Bird; he hadn't known he was holding it.

Why did they want them, he asks cautiously.

It is a question he would not have asked a week ago; a week ago, he would not have found this ominous, let alone unusual. Maybe, he thinks suddenly—maybe it isn't unusual at all.

His father sets his bag on the floor, drops his keys with a clatter on the counter.

She's writing a book on the first amendment and PACT, apparently, he says. They think she might be funded by the Chinese. Trying to stir up unrest over here.

Slowly he pulls the noose of his tie free from his collar.

Is she? Bird asks.

His father turns toward him, looking more tired than Bird has ever seen. For the first time he notices the gray threading through his father's hair, the lines etched from the corners of his eyes, like tear tracks.

Honestly? his father says. Probably not. But that's what they think.

He checks his watch, then opens the cupboard, which contains nothing but a half-empty jar of peanut butter. No bread.

Let's get some dinner, he says to Bird.

They hurry down the stairs and out to the pizza place just a few blocks away. Bird's father doesn't care for pizza—too greasy, he tells Bird, all that cheese—but it is late and they are hungry and this is the closest place, open until nine.

The man behind the counter takes their order and slides four slices into the oven to heat up, and Bird and his father lean against the sticky wall, waiting. His stomach is growling. Cool dark air wafts in through the propped-open door, and the handful of notices taped to the store's window flutter in the breeze. Found cat. Guitar lessons. Apartment for rent. Down in the corner, right above the health inspection sticker, a star-spangled placard: GOD BLESS ALL LOYAL AMERICANS. The same placard nearly every store displays, sold in every city, proceeds benefiting neighborhood-watch groups. The few stores that don't hang it are viewed with skepticism. *Aren't you a loyal American? Then why the fuss over a little sign? Don't you want to support the neighborhood watch?* The huge steel oven ticks and steams. Behind the counter, the pizza guy rests one elbow on the cash register, scrolling on his phone, smirking at a joke.

It is 8:52 when the old man comes in. An Asian face, white button-down and black pants, silvering hair neatly clipped.

Chinese? Filipino? Bird can't tell. The man sets a folded five on the counter.

Slice of pepperoni, he says.

The pizza guy doesn't even look up. We're closed, he says.

You don't look closed. The man glances over at Bird and his father, who half steps in front of Bird like a screen. They're here, he says.

We're closed, the pizza guy repeats, louder. His thumb flicks upward across the phone, and an endless river of pictures and posts whizzes by. Bird's father jostles him on one shoulder. The same jostle as when they pass a policeman, or roadkill in the street. It means: Turn around. Don't look. But this time Bird doesn't turn. It's not curiosity; it's a need. A morbid need to know what's been crouching behind him, unseen.

Look, I just want a piece of pizza, the old man says. I just got off work, I'm hungry.

He slides the bill across the counter. His hands are leathery and tough, the fingers knobbled with age. He looks like someone's grandfather, Bird thinks, and then the thought arrives: if he had a grandfather, he might look like this man.

The pizza guy sets his phone down.

You don't understand English? he says calmly, as if commenting on the weather. There's a Chinese restaurant over on Mass Ave. Go get yourself some fried rice and spring rolls, if you're hungry. We're closed.

He folds his hands like a patient teacher, and stares squarely at the old man. *What are you going to do about it?*

Bird is frozen in place. He can only look and look: at the old man, jaw set, one leg squared behind him as if braced for a push. At the pizza guy, the oil spots speckling his T-shirt, his large meaty hands. At his father, the lines on his face making whiskery shadows, his eyes fixed on the flyers on the window, as if nothing is happening, as if this is just an ordinary day. He wants the old man to deliver a biting comeback, he wants the old man to punch the pizza guy in his smirking face, he wants the old man to back away before the pizza guy says—or does—something worse. Before he lifts those hands that pound and flatten thick dough into compliance. The moment tautens and tightens, like an overtuned string.

And then the old man plucks the money from the counter again, wordlessly, and tucks it back into his pocket. He turns, away from the pizza guy's grin, and looks at Bird instead, a long hard look, then at Bird's father. And then he murmurs something to Bird's father, something Bird doesn't understand.

He has never heard these words before, has never even heard this language before, but it is clear from the look on his father's face that his father has, that he not only recognizes the language but understands it, understands what this man has said. He has the feeling, somehow, that they're talking about him, the way the man looks at him and then at his father, that meaningful gaze that cuts right through Bird's skin and flesh to scrutinize his bones. But his father doesn't reply, doesn't even move, just quickly glances away. Then the old man strides out, head held high, and is gone.

A timer dings and the pizza guy turns to open the oven. The hot smoky air shrivels Bird's throat.

Some people, the pizza guy says. I mean.

He slips the long wooden paddle into the scorching oven and extracts their slices, slips them into a waiting box. For a moment he stares through narrowed eyes at Bird, then at his father, as if trying to place their faces. Then he slides the pizza across the counter.

Have a good night, Bird's father says, and he takes the box and guides Bird toward the door.

What did he say, Bird says, when they're back on the sidewalk. That man. What did he say?

Let's go, his father says. Come on, Noah. Let's get home.

At the corner, a police car glides by, lights off, nearly silent, and they wait for it to pass before crossing. They reach the dorm just as the church tower across the way begins to strike nine.

It's not until they're back in the apartment that his father speaks again. He sets the pizza down on the counter and pries off his shoes and stands there, his eyes very far away.

Cantonese, his father says. He was speaking Cantonese.

But you understood him, Bird says. You don't speak Cantonese.

Even as he says it, he realizes he does not know this is true.

No, I don't, his father snaps. And neither do you. Noah, listen to me very carefully. Anything that has to do with China, Korea, Japan, anything like that—you stay away from it. You hear someone talking in those languages or talking about those things, you walk away. Understand?

He pulls a slice from the box and hands it to Bird, then takes one himself and settles wearily into a chair without even getting a plate. It is the second time, it occurs to Bird, that his father has climbed all those steps in the past hour.

Eat your dinner, his father says gently. Before it gets cold.

He knows then: even if he asks, his father won't track down this book. He'll have to find another way.

It is difficult to sneak into the university library; it always has been. There are old books in there, valuable books. A Gutenberg Bible and a first folio of Shakespeare, Bird's father told him once, though Bird has only a hazy idea what this means. Countless irreplaceable old documents. Even—his father wriggled his fingers creepily in the air—an anatomy book bound in human skin. He had just transferred over—linguistics professor to book shelver—and Bird, age nine and newly cynical, had decided all of this was an attempt to make his job sound more impressive, and had ignored it.

What he does know is that he needs a keycard to enter the building, huge and impressive, a marble paperweight pinning down one end of the college yard—and even then, only staff are permitted to pass further into the warm labyrinth of shelves where all the books are kept. But when he was younger, on days off school, he'd trotted along after his father into the reshelving room, where carts of books sat waiting to be set back in place. You can help, his father had suggested, and once or twice Bird had, pushing the cart through the narrow aisles until they found the right one, pressing the antique switch in the corridor to flick on the lights. While his father scanned the shelves, sliding the books one by one into the gaps from which they'd come, Bird ran his fingertips over the embossed spines where gilt lettering had long been rubbed away, breathing in the peculiar smell of the library: a mix of dust and leather and melted vanilla ice cream. Warm, like the scent of someone's skin.

It soothed him and unsettled him at the same time, the murky hush like a wool blanket thrown over everything. Underneath, something large lying in wait. It never ended, the stacks of books needing to be set back in place, the constant insistent reiteration of order, and the thought was dizzying: that just beyond this shelf there were hundreds more, thousands of books, millions of words. Sometimes after his father had nestled one book into its spot, lining up the spines, Bird had the impulse to sweep the whole rack clear with one arm, to send the whole shelf dominoing into the next and the next and the next, to shred the smothering silence. It frightened him, and he made excuses for not coming into the stacks. He was tired, he would rather sit in the staff room and have a snack, he would rather stay home and play.

He hasn't come to the library in years; the last time, he was ten.

That evening, while his father is brushing his teeth, Bird rifles through his briefcase. His father is a creature of habit; after he comes back to the apartment he always stores his keycard in the outside pocket of his bag, ready for the next day. Bird slips the card into his back pocket and zips the bag shut again. His father never checks for it in the morning: for the past three years it's been right there when he arrives at work, exactly where he put it the night before. Tomorrow, just this once, it won't be. But the security guard knows him, has seen him every day for years, will let him in for the day, just this one time. Tomorrow evening, when Bird's father arrives home and does a thorough search for the keycard, he'll find it right there on the floor beneath the table, right where his briefcase always sits. Must have slipped it next to the bag rather than into it, he'll think, and that will be that.

At first the plan works perfectly. After school, Bird heads to the college yard, climbs the huge mountain of stairs to the library's front entrance. In the lobby, he copies the impatient and vaguely annoyed look the students always wear and swipes his father's card quickly through the reader. The turnstile turns green and he passes through without stopping and without looking back. As if he has somewhere to be, on the trail of important knowledge. The security guard doesn't even glance up from his monitor.

The next problem: how to get into the stacks. Long ago, his father told him, they'd been open to anyone. You could go in and wander, exploring whatever came your way. Now they don't let just anyone in. Now you have to fill out a slip of paper at the counter, explain why you need the book, show your ID. And if your reason is good enough—a treatise on the failures that led to the Crisis, perhaps, or new strategies for detecting internal enemies—someone, like his father, will venture into the stacks and retrieve it for you. He doesn't say what changed, but Bird understands: it is PACT, of course, that changed everything. That deemed some books dangerous, to be kept only if they were kept out of reach.

Bird heads into the circulation room and eyes the entrance to the stacks at the other end. A squeaky cart comes around the corner and he recognizes the woman pushing it: Debbie, one of the other shelvers. Long ago she'd given him gold-wrapped butterscotch candies, those times he'd come to work with his father. In fact, she looks exactly the same—long billowy dress, frizzy gray hair pinned in an improbable cloud around her head—and though he's older and taller now, he's sure she'll recognize him, too. Quickly he darts behind one of the computer carrels, and Debbie and her cart squeak their way past, leaving a lingering smell of cigarette smoke in their wake.

This reminds him of something. Debbie is a chain smoker; the minute she came into the room, sometimes, the other librarians would lift their heads, sniffing, as if suddenly remembering the possibility of fire. Officially, smokers must leave the premises and stand at least fifty feet from the building before lighting up, but no one ever seemed to do this. Instead Debbie and the other smokers ducked out the side door of the stacks and then out a side door of the building, propping each open with a brick, huddling beside the huge library until their furtive cigarettes were gone, then ducking back inside. His father often complained about the smell drifting into the hall, had combined it with a lecture on the evils of smoking. *You see what a slippery slope it is? Once you start, you can't shake free.*

After Debbie and the cart have gone, Bird heads downstairs, where the side door to the stacks lets out. Despite the lack of a sign, he's certain this is the right place. There, just across from it, is an emergency exit, clearly marked KEEP CLOSED.

Most tellingly, just beside it is an old, weatherworn red brick. All he has to do is wait and hope for a stroke of luck. He stations himself around the corner, where—if anyone comes by—he might conceivably be heading into or out of the men's room nearby.

For twenty minutes no one passes, and he understands why the staff use this spot for smoke breaks: upstairs people come and go, but down here, it's practically deserted. Then, just as he's debating giving up, he hears a hinge creak, the scrape of brick on stone flooring, the soft thud of a heavy door coming to rest. A second later, another clicks open and the faint sounds of the outside rush in: a whoosh of wind, birds chirping, someone laughing far off in the distance, across the yard.

Bird peeks around the corner. The door to the outside is propped open: someone must be out there, sneaking a quick smoke, and just as he'd hoped, the one leading back into the stacks is propped open, too. He doesn't have much time. As quietly as he can, he creeps down the hallway and pries the stacks door farther open. It emits a faint creak, and he glances back over his shoulder to see if the smoker has noticed. No movement. Bird takes a deep breath and slips inside.

It takes him a minute to get his bearings. All the titles around him are in a language he doesn't know, in words he has no idea how to say: *Zniewolony Umysł. Pytania Zadawane Sobie.* He darts into one of the aisles and heads upstairs, away from the door. Whoever is out there smoking will be finished soon, and he shouldn't be anywhere nearby when they return. The stacks are incredibly silent—an absorbent, watchful, almost predatory quiet, waiting to suck away any noise you dared to make. A staffer comes by, paper in hand, one book lodged in her armpit as she scans the shelves for the next. Bird waits for her to turn away before he passes. Somewhere there must be a search terminal, and eventually he finds one in a corner, taps at the keyboard. *The Boy Who Drew Cats.* A long pause, and then a number pops up on the screen. He scribbles it on a slip of paper and consults the charts posted beside the monitor, running his finger down the list of call numbers: D level, the bottom floor. Four levels below ground. Southwest corner.

Before he leaves, he can't resist typing in one more search. *Our Missing Hearts.*

Another pause, longer this time, and then instead of a number, a notice: DISCARDED. Bird swallows and clears the screen. Then he grabs the slip of paper and sets off for the stairs.

The stairs bring him down on the wrong end of the library, northeast instead of southwest. But at least D level is deserted. Only the main corridors are lit, and those dimly; the aisles criss-crossing them are pitch black. He's never appreciated before just how big the library is: a full city block, hundreds of feet by hundreds of feet with miles of shelves in between. Something his father once said comes back to him: the shelves around him are not just book holders but the iron skeleton of the building itself, holding the library upright. The easiest way, he decides, will be keeping to the edges; zigzagging his way across, he'll get lost for sure. Cautiously he picks his way along the wall, heading south. It isn't as straightforward as he'd hoped. Sometimes, a stack of old chairs or tables looms up in his path and he has to turn aside, go over a few aisles, and then find his way back. Somewhere, overhead, footsteps thump across C level. A furnace clicks on and a breath of warm air, like a thermal geyser, flows through the grated floor.

Bird passes shelf after shelf, slotting his fingers into the spaces where removed books once stood. There are fewer missing here than at the public library, where some shelves had been more gap than books. But still nearly every shelf is missing one, sometimes more. He wonders who decided which books were too dangerous to keep, and who it was that had to hunt down and collect the condemned books, like an executioner, ferrying them to their doom. He wonders if it is his father.

At the correct shelf he slows, then pauses, tracing the call numbers along the neatly squared spines as they count down, fraction by fraction. And then: there it is. Slim and yellow. Hardly a book at all, barely bigger than a magazine. He'd nearly missed it.

With one finger he tips it from the shelf. *The Boy Who Drew Cats: A Japanese Folktale.* He's never seen this particular book before, but as soon as he sees the cover he knows it's the same story. A Japanese folktale, but his Chinese mother had heard it or read it somewhere, had remembered it and told it to him. On the front is a watercolor drawing of a boy, a Japanese boy, holding a brush. Painting a huge cat on a wall. The boy looks a bit like Bird, even: dark hair grown shaggy over his forehead, the same dark eyes and slightly rounded nose. It's coming back to him, the way his mother told it, a story buried in Styrofoam packing long ago that he's digging out, pulling back into the light. A boy, wandering alone and far from home. A lonely building, in the darkness. Cat after cat after cat springing from the bristles of his brush. His fingers shake, struggling to peel the cover from the cloth-soft pages beneath. Yes, he thinks. It's almost there, like something edging out of the shadows, just starting to take its shape; as soon as he reads it, he'll remember it, remember what happens, this story from his mother, in a moment he'll understand everything.

It is at this point that someone sets a hand on his shoulder, and he whirls around to find his father.

They let me come to find you, his father says, instead of security.

He should have known: of course the library has security cameras, of course they would have noticed that someone swiped in with his father's card just hours after his father—responsible and rule following as ever—had reported his card was lost.

Dad, Bird begins, I just needed to—

His father turns around without responding, and Bird follows his straight, angry back all the way through the stacks and up the stairs to the staff room with its endless rows and rows of carts, where two security guards are waiting. In the instant before the guards turn around, he shoves the book into the back waistband of his jeans, beneath his T-shirt.

It's okay, Bird's father says, before the guards can speak. Just my son, like we thought. I left my card in his bookbag by mistake, and he came in trying to find me to give it back.

Bird studies the linoleum floor, holding his breath. His

father has not asked him a single question about what he's doing there, and to him this story sounds implausible. Why would he search for his father in the stacks, how could he possibly expect to find one man in that labyrinth of shelves? The security guards hesitate, teetering on the edge of belief. One of them leans closer, squinting at Bird's face. Bird blinks, trying to look innocent, and inside his balled-up fists, his fingernails bite into his palm.

His father lets out a chuckle, a loud, insincere whinny that gallops around the room and then vanishes. Just trying to be responsible, right, Noah? he says. But don't worry. He understands now.

He claps Bird on the shoulder, and grudgingly, the security guards nod.

Next time, one of them says to Bird, just stop at the front desk, okay, son? They'll call your dad down for you.

Bird's legs go quivery in relief. He nods, and swallows, and squeaks out *Yes, sir,* because from his father's taut grip on his shoulder, he understands this is what he needs to do.

When the security guards have gone, Bird reaches to the small of his back, plucks the book from beneath his T-shirt.

Dad, he whispers. His voice quivering. Dad, can I—

His father barely glances at the book. In fact, he doesn't look at Bird at all.

Put that on the cart, he says quietly. Someone will reshelve it. Let's go.

Only once has Bird ever been in trouble. Mostly, he listens to his father's advice: Don't attract attention. Keep your head down. And: If you see any trouble, you go the other way, understand?

It had driven Sadie crazy. Sadie, at the first scent of trouble, would follow it like a bloodhound to its source.

Bird, she'd said. Don't be such a pussy.

It was the posters that caught her eye that time, the ones that hung and still hang all around town, in grocery-store windows and on community bulletin boards and sometimes even in the windows of houses, reminding everyone to be patriotic, to watch over each other, to report the merest sign of trouble. Each designed by a famous artist to be eye-catching and collectible. A red-white-and-blue dam over a huge yellow-brown river, with a hairline fracture: *Even small cracks widen.* A blond woman peeking through curtains, cell phone at her ear: *Better safe than sorry.* Two houses, side by side, a pie passing hand to hand over a white picket fence: *Watch over your neighbor.* At the bottom of each, four bold capitals: PACT.

That afternoon, Sadie had paused by a row of posters pasted to a bus shelter, ran her fingers over the glue. It flaked away under her fingers like chalk.

That evening, a pair of policemen arrived at their apartment.

We were told, said one, that your son was part of a group defacing public-safety posters earlier this afternoon.

Sadie, pulling a Sharpie from her jeans pocket. Scribbling out the slogans of watchfulness and unity.

A group, his father said. What group?

Naturally we're very concerned, the officer said, about why he might have felt the need to do this. What kind of messages he's getting at home that make him feel this kind of unpatriotic and, frankly, dangerous behavior is appropriate.

It was that Sadie, wasn't it? his father said, to Bird this time, and Bird swallowed.

Mr. Gardner, the officer said, we've looked into your file, and given your wife's history—

His father cut them off.

That woman is no longer part of this family, he said brusquely. We have nothing to do with her. We have had nothing to do with her since she left.

It was as if his father had struck his mother, right there in front of him.

And we have absolutely no sympathies for the radical stances she supported, his father went on. Absolutely none.

He gave Bird a look, and Bird stiffened his spine into an iron bar and nodded.

Noah and I both know PACT protects our country, he went on. If you doubt my sincerity, just take a look. I've made steady donations to security and unity groups for the past two and a half years. And Noah is a straight-A student. There are no unpatriotic influences in this house.

Be that as it may, the officer began, your son *did* deface a sign advocating for PACT.

His gaze rested on Bird's father, as if waiting for a reply, and then Bird spotted it: the quick flick of his father's eyes to the kitchen drawer, where they kept their checkbook. The pay at the library wasn't much, he knew; at the end of each month his father spent a good hour hunched at the table over the check register, painstakingly tabulating the balance. How much, he could see his father calculating, would it take to make them go away? Already he knew it was more than they had.

It's the influence of that girl, his father said. The re-placed one. Sadie Greenstein. I understand she's a tough case.

Shock sizzled through Bird.

We've encountered her before, the officer admitted.

That's where it's coming from. You know how boys start to get around this age. Girls can get them to do anything.

He put a hand on Bird's shoulder, firm and heavy.

I'll make sure it comes to an end. There are no questions about loyalty in this household, officer.

The officer hesitated, and Bird's father sensed it.

We're very grateful to folks like you who are protecting our security, he said. After all, if it weren't for you, who knows where we'd be.

Not anywhere good, the police officer said, nodding. Not anywhere good, that's for sure. Well. I think we're all set here, sir. Just a misunderstanding, obviously. But you keep out of trouble, son, okay?

When the police had gone, Bird's father put his fingers to his temples, as if he had a migraine.

Noah, he said, after a long, long pause. Don't ever do that again.

He opened his mouth, as if he wanted to say more, but all the air seemed to have gone out of him, like a tent whose poles had collapsed. Bird wasn't sure what *that* was: Destroy posters? Talk to the police? Get in trouble? At last his father opened his eyes again.

Stay away from that Sadie, he said, as he headed into the other room. Please.

So Bird didn't sit with Sadie the next day, and he didn't have lunch with her the next day, and a week later he still wasn't speaking to her when she stopped coming to school and didn't come back, and no one seemed to know where she'd gone.

Today his father doesn't say anything all the way down the steps of the library, all the way out of the college yard to the street. Bird follows him home in silence, though it's the middle of the afternoon and his father would usually be at work for another two hours at least. Even from behind he knows his father is furious from the rigid rectangle of his back. His father only walks like that—stiff, angular, as if his joints are rusted—when he's too angry to speak. Bird lags behind, letting the distance between them stretch out to a few yards, then half a block. More. If he slows down enough, maybe they'll never reach home, they'll never have to talk about this, he'll never have to face his father again.

By the time they reach the Common, his father is nearly a full block ahead, so far distant that from where Bird stands, he could be a stranger. Just some man in a brown overcoat, carrying a briefcase. No one he knows. There was something else in his father's voice in the library, not just anger but an acrid thing Bird can't quite name, and then, suddenly, he knows. It's fear. The same loud, blustering fear that he'd heard that day with the posters, when his father spoke to the policemen. A hot metallic musk, the hiss of claws drawn.

Bird's eyes go again to the three big trees that just days before had been red, to the jagged scars running down their lengths. A wound like that, his father had once told him, will never fully heal. The bark will grow over, but it'll stay there, under the skin, and when they cut the tree down, you'll see it there, a dark mark slicing through the rings of the wood.

He's so busy thinking about this he runs smack into someone coming the other way. Someone large, and in a rush, and angry.

Watch where you're fucking going, chink, he hears, and a big hand catches his shoulder, shoves him to the ground.

It happens so quickly then that he doesn't piece it together until later. It only becomes clear in the aftermath, as he lies there on the damp grass, winded, cold smudges of mud caked to his palms and knees. There is the man who pushed him, running away, one hand clutching his bloody nose. There on the sidewalk is one fat red droplet, like a splash of paint on the concrete. There, standing over him, is his father, looking down at him as if from a very great height.

You okay? his father says, and Bird nods, and his father reaches down a hand, its knuckles red and raw. His father, he realizes, is a big man, too, though he doesn't seem it: soft voiced, bashfully stooped, he seems smaller than he is, but in college he ran track, he's broad and tall and sturdy. Fast enough to race back to a son in danger. Strong enough to punch someone threatening his child.

Let's go home, his father says, helping him to his feet.

Neither of them speaks until they're back at the dorm.

Dad, Bird says, as they enter the lobby.

Not now, is all his father says, heading for the stairwell. Let's get upstairs first.

.   .   .

When they reach their own floor, his father shuts and bolts the door of the apartment behind them.

You have to be careful, he says, grabbing Bird by the shoulders, and Bird bristles.

I didn't do anything. *He* pushed me—

But his father shakes his head. That man, he says, he's not the only one like that out there. They'll see your face and that's all the provocation they need. And this library stunt—

His father stops.

You usually follow the rules, he says.

It was just a book.

I'm responsible if you get in trouble, Noah. Do you know how bad this could have been?

I'm sorry, Bird says, but his father doesn't seem to be listening. He has braced himself for shouting, for parental rage, but his father's voice is a seething hiss and somehow Bird finds this more terrifying.

They could have fired me, he says. The library isn't open to just anyone, you know. You have to be a researcher. They have to watch who they let in. The university gets a lot of leeway because of its reputation, but they're not immune. If someone caused trouble and they traced it back to a book they got here—

He shakes his head.

And if I lost my job we'd lose this apartment, too. You know that, right?

Bird hadn't, and a chill washes over him.

Worse than that. If they realized *you* got it, and decided to take a closer look at us—at you—

His father has never hit him, not even a spanking, but he stares at Bird with such violent intensity that Bird flinches, preparing for a blow. Then with a jerk his father yanks Bird into his arms, so hard the breath flies out of him. Holds him tightly in a shaking embrace.

And suddenly, a door clicks open in Bird's mind. Why his father is always so cautious, why he's always nagging Bird to follow this particular route or that, to not go off on his own. How his father reached him so fast. It isn't just dangerous to research China, or go looking for Japanese folktales. It's dangerous to look like him, always has been. It's dangerous to be his mother's child, in more ways than one. His father has always known it, has always been braced for something like this, always on a hair trigger for what inevitably would happen to his son. What he's afraid of: that one day someone will see Bird's face and see an enemy. That someone will see him as his mother's son, in blood or in deed, and take him away.

He puts his arms around his father, and his father's tighten around him.

That man in the pizza place, Bird says, slowly. What did he say?

He's one of us. His father's voice is half muffled against Bird's hair and buzzes inside Bird's skull. And he's right. What he meant was, these kinds of things—they might happen to you, too.

His father's arms loosen, and he holds Bird at arm's length.

Noah, he says. That's why I keep telling you, keep a low profile. Don't do anything to call attention to yourself.

Okay, Bird says.

His father goes to the sink, begins to run cold water over his bruised knuckles. And because it feels like the door between them is still ajar, Bird sets his palm against it. Pushes.

Did my mother like cats? he asks.

His father stops. What, he says, as if Bird has spoken in another language, one of the few he doesn't know.

Cats, Bird repeats. Did she like them.

His father shuts off the water. Where is this coming from? he says.

I just want to know, Bird says. Did she?

His father glances quickly around the room, his habit whenever Bird's mother comes up. Outside, all quiet, only the occasional siren passing.

Cats, he says, looking down at his raw and reddened hand. She did. She adored them.

He looks at Bird searchingly, with a gaze more pointed than Bird has seen in a long time. Like he's spotted something unusual in Bird's face, like a sheath has been removed.

Miu, his father says slowly. Her surname.

He writes the character in the dust on the top of the bookshelf: a square crisscrossed to represent a field, two smaller crosses sprouting from the top.

$$苗$$

It means seedling, or sometimes crops. Something just beginning to grow. But it sounds like a cat's meow, doesn't it? *Miu.*

And, he says, his voice warming the way it does when he grows excited, when he's talking about things that he loves, like words. It has been a long time since this happened.

And, his father goes on, if you put this, which means *beast*, in front of it—

He adds a few more strokes, a pared-down suggestion of an animal sitting at attention:

貓

—this whole thing means cat. The beast that makes the sound *miu*. But of course you could think of it as the beast that protects the crops.

His father is in his element, as Bird hasn't seen him in years. He has almost forgotten his father could be like this, that his father had this in him. That his eyes and his face could light up this way.

The story, his father says, is that once there were no cats in China. No house cats, anyway. Only wildcats. Classically, cat was written like this—he sketches another character—

貍

—which really meant a wild creature, like a fox. Then Persian traders taught them to domesticate their wildcats, and they added this—

He begins to write a third character, made of two halves. First, the character for woman. Then beside it, so close they almost overlap, the symbol for hand.

奴

Slave, his father says. Wildcat plus slave, a domesticated cat. See?

Together they look down at the characters written in the dust. *Miu.* His mother. Beast plus seedling meant cat. What kind of beast would she have been? A cat, for sure. Woman plus hand meant slave. Had his mother ever been domestic, or domesticated?

With one swipe of his palm his father wipes the top of the bookshelf clean.

Anyway, he says. We used to talk about these kinds of things, your mother and me. Long time ago.

He rubs his palm against the thighs of his pants, leaving a faint gray streak.

She liked that idea, he says after a moment. That the only thing separating her from a beast was a few little strokes.

I didn't know you knew Chinese, Bird says.

I don't, his father says absently. Not really. But I can understand some Cantonese. I studied it, for a while. With your mother. A long time ago.

He turns to go, and then, just as suddenly, turns back.

That book.

And then, after another long pause: Your mother used to tell you that story, didn't she.

Bird nods.

I remember, his father says.

And as he begins to speak, it comes back to Bird, all of it: not the words on the pages of the book, not the few bare-bones sentences his father uses to tell it to him now, but the way he remembers hearing it, in his mother's voice. Painting a picture with words on the blank white wall of his mind. Long buried. Crackling as it surfaced in the air once more.

Once, long ago, there was a boy who loved to draw cats. He was a poor boy, and most of the day he worked in the fields, planting rice with his parents and the others in his village in the spring, harvesting the paddies beside them in the fall. But whenever he had a spare moment, he would draw. And what he most liked to draw, what he drew most often of all, were cats. Big cats, little cats, striped and calico and spotted. Cats with pointy ears and skinny eyes, cats with black paws and black muzzles, cats with white patches on their chests like eagles. Shaggy cats, smooth cats, cats leaping, cats stalking, cats sleeping or cleaning their fur. On the flat rocks by the river, he sketched them with a burnt stick. He scraped them into the sand on the shores of the nearby lake where the fishermen pulled in their nets. On dry days, he scratched them into the dust of the path to his house, and after the rains he carved them into the thick mud where puddles had once glistened.

The others in his village thought this was a waste of time. What use is it to draw cats, they scoffed. It doesn't put food on the table or bring in the grain. The richest man in town had beautiful scrolls on the walls of his house: paintings of fog-tipped mountains and elegant gardens, far-off things no one in their village had ever seen. But you could simply step outside and see a cat; they were everywhere. They had never heard of an artist choosing to draw cats. What was the point?

The boy's parents, however, did not agree. Although they had to work many hours in the field—and the boy often had to help—they were proud of his talent. After the day's work was done, the father collected pieces of bamboo the length of his hand and gave them to his son for brushes. The mother cut the tips of her own hair and bound them into tufts for the bristles. The boy gathered stones—every color he could find, from deep red to pure black—and ground them to dust to make his paints. And every night, he painted cats—on flat pieces of bark, on scraps of paper and worn-out rags—until it was time for bed.

One year, sickness struck the village, and the boy's parents died. No one in the village would take him in: he had a reputation. A boy who wasted time, a boy who did useless things. Besides, the villagers had little to spare. They had been sick, too; there was little food, nothing left for one who wasn't their own. Each family took a handful of rice from their stores, bound it all in a cloth, and gave it to the boy. Good luck, they said. May fortune smile on you. He thanked them and shouldered the bundle, tucked his brushes in his pocket, and set off on his way.

It was winter, and bitterly cold. The boy wandered for hours through the dark until he came to a small village, where every door was shut tight. Though he could see the glow of firelight through the windows, no one would answer his knock. A harsh wind began to blow; snow began to whirl around him in the air like ghosts clawing at his face. At the last house, an old woman peered out. I'm sorry, she said. If I let you in, my husband will kill me. We dare not take in strangers. This whole town is afraid. Afraid, the boy said, afraid of what? But the woman simply shook her head.

In desperation, the boy looked around the deserted street. At the end, just past the outskirts of town, he spotted a small building he hadn't noticed before. What about that, he said, that deserted house? Surely I can stay there just for the night.

The old woman seized his hands. That place is dangerous, she said. Cursed. It is said that a monster lives there. No one who enters at night ever returns.

I am not afraid, the boy said, and anyway, I may as well be eaten by a monster as freeze to death out here in the street.

The old woman bowed her head and gave him a torch lit from her cooking fire. Take this, she said. And keep to the small. Then she blessed him and wiped a tear from her cheek. May you see tomorrow, she said. And if you do, I beg you forgive us.

The boy made his way to the deserted house. Snow had begun to stick to the ground and to the bare branches of the trees, and when he reached it he found a small drift just beginning to form at its door. But it was unlocked, and he let himself inside. He lit a fire in the fireplace and looked around. There was only one room, with only one piece of furniture: a small cupboard, the kind that his mother had once kept their blankets in. There were no carpets on the floor, no decorations on the walls: only whitewashed walls, a plain dirt floor swept clean.

Well, he thought, this place may be cursed, but at least it's dry and warm. He was about to unroll his blanket on the floor and go to sleep when the white walls caught his attention. They seemed so bare, so empty. Like a face without features. He dug into his pocket and pulled out his brushes, and before he had thought it through, he had painted a cat on one of the walls. Just a little one, a small striped gray-and-white thing. A kitten, really. There, he thought, that's better. And again he prepared to go to bed.

But the cat seemed lonely, all by itself on the wall— and there was so much wall. He painted it a friend, a bigger cat, a tabby sitting beside it, licking its paw. Then he forgot himself completely. He painted another cat, a big orange tom, asleep by the fire. A black cat ready to pounce, a white cat watching with big blue eyes, a calico clambering among the rafters. He painted cats until all the walls were covered, a whole coterie of cats to keep him company, and only when he ran out of space—and the fire was sputtering down to embers—did he put his brushes away.

The boy was tired—who wouldn't be, after conjuring a hundred cats out of nothingness? He unrolled his blanket, but despite all the cats, he was lonely. He missed his parents, and he wished he were at home again, in his own house, in his own bed, with his parents sleeping beside him. He thought of his brushes, made from his father's bamboo, his mother's hair. He remembered the small gestures about them he missed the most: the way his mother raked her hand through his hair, smoothing it from his face; the way his father had hummed while he worked in the field, so quietly it might have been the buzzing of bees. He felt small, and suddenly he remembered the old woman's words: keep to the small. He took his blanket and opened the cupboard and made his bed inside it. It was as close to his own little bed as he could get, and he crawled inside, with all of his things, and pulled the door shut behind him.

In the middle of the night he awoke to a terrible wordless wailing. It was an unearthly shrieking: like the groaning of old trees splintering as they fell, like the howling of a hundred winter winds, like the screeching of the earth as it shifted and tore itself apart. Even his eyelashes stood on end. He put his eye to a tiny crack, but all he could see outside was a ghastly red light, as if the whole room were full of blood. He shut his eyes and held his breath and pulled the blanket over his head. Whatever you do, he thought, don't make a sound.

After a long time—he didn't know how long—it was quiet again. Still he waited in silence. An hour passed. Two. He put his eye to the crack again and this time, no red: only a faint sliver of sunlight. Hands shaking, he pushed his way out of the cupboard. His cats were still there, on the walls, just as he'd painted them. But every cat's mouth was red. All over the floor: the prints of hundreds and hundreds of cat feet, pressed into the dirt, scrapes and smudges and marks of a battle. Flecks of blood and foam sprayed on the walls. And there, in the corner—a huge dead shaggy thing. Still now, clawed half to shreds. A rat the size of an ox.

So what does it mean, Bird thinks, as he lies in his bunk that night. It's well after midnight and below him his father snores once, then turns to one side, and is still. Outside, the city is quiet, except for an occasional siren wailing its way through the dark. *We promise to watch over each other.*

Bird tiptoes into the living room, pushes the edge of the curtain aside, slips behind it, and looks out. All he sees are the hulking forms of buildings, the far-off specks of streetlights. The flat dark band of the street. Newly blackened, but somewhere beneath it, a painted heart still blooms. So risky, he thinks, and what was the point? When a few hours later all trace of it was gone.

But the truth is: it isn't gone. He can't see that bare stretch of ground without thinking of it, the bright splotch flashing into his mind, sharp as a wildcat's snarl.

Hadn't they been afraid?

He tries to imagine what it had felt like, to be that painter. Tiptoeing into the street. Breath dragon-hot beneath a mask, heartbeat a deafening roar. Slapping stencil to pavement with shaking hands, spraying a sizzling cloud of red. And then running, lungs aflame with fear and fumes, finding a small sheltered corner to hide. Red paint like smears of blood on his hands.

And then it floods him. Rushing in as if someone has unstopped a plug.

A game they played, he and his mother, when he was very small. Before school, before he had any other world but her. His favorite game, one he'd begged her to play. Their special game, played only when his father was at work, kept as a secret between just them.

You be the monster, mama. I'll hide, and you be the monster.

She'd taped sheets of paper to the walls and Bird drew cat after cat: with crayons, half-dried markers, pencil stubs. Simple cats, scrawls with ears, but still. Cats. Cats, all over his room. And then, when he tired of drawing, came the second part of the game. Inside his closet was a crawl space his parents had discovered when they'd fixed up the house. Too small, under the eaves, for anything practical, but his mother had kept it. For him. A perfect boy-sized cubby she'd furnished with a sliding panel, a pillow and a blanket and a flashlight. A dragon's cave. A bandit's lair. And sometimes, the cabinet in which the boy hid.

He would crawl inside and slide the panel shut and yawn loudly, then flop down and begin to snore. From outside would come a growl that peppered goose bumps up and down his arms. A series of snarling meows. Inside, Bird pulled the blanket over his head and shivered deliciously. After a few minutes it grew quiet, and he would crawl from the hot cubby back out into the closet and then the light of the room, and there, on the carpet:

his mother on her back, arms curled to her chest. Deadly still. The mouth of every cat he'd drawn smeared with red.

He would run to her then and throw himself on her chest and she would catch him in her arms, warm and strong, and tickle him and laugh. Always, a moment of terror at seeing her there, and a hot rush of relief when she came back to life. Over and over they played it, this game, his mother indulging him again and again. So long ago that he'd forgotten. Kindergarten, new friends, new games arrived and swept it away. And then, after she'd gone, he'd packed that memory up, along with everything else he could, and left it behind in the house they'd once shared. Where maybe—just maybe, though he doesn't even dare to think the words—perhaps he might find her again.

Something he's never told anyone, even Sadie: he's been there many times, over the years. It is just a few blocks from his new school, and though he's supposed to come directly home, sometimes he detours, just a little, so he can walk past the old house. Just to see it. It is the only time he ever deviates from the path. Construction, he imagines telling his father, the main road was closed, I had to go around. Or: The police were detouring people—I dunno why. His father would never argue with that; he's always reminding Bird to stay away from trouble, to avoid the police.

But his father never even asks. He is so certain Bird will always follow the rules, so confident in Bird's unquestioning obedience, and on those days—standing on the sidewalk, looking up at the house where they no longer live, at its shaded-over windows like closed eyes—Bird resents it, this assumption that there could be nothing off his prescribed path that he wants or misses or needs.

No one has moved into the house in the past three years. His father hasn't sold it—he can't, without his mother's signature, too—and no one seems to want to rent it, once they learn who'd lived there before. Every time Bird visits, it is just the same, windows obscured by blinds, tall back gate always shut tight. None of the houses in this neighborhood have front yards; the houses come right up to the sidewalk like pushy neighbors, elbowing their way in. A scraggly strip of grass runs between sidewalk and street in a threadbare ribbon, and this is the only thing that changes from visit to visit: first overgrown and tufty, then knee high and gone to seed, then buried under a bank of uncleared snow. One spring he visited and found it bristling with daffodils: he had forgotten his mother had planted them there, and their cheerful yellow—her favorite color—pained him so much that he did not come back again for a whole month, until the flowers had shriveled, leaving nothing but splayed stems and wilting leaves.

What he knows from this: the house is still sitting empty. The perfect place to hide.

The next day, after school, instead of heading home, he follows the road along the curve of the river, back toward their old house. As he walks, a smattering of memories flare at each step, small bright stones lighting a path through the forest. There is the huge gray-brown sycamore, like an enormous elephant's foot, which even together their arms could not encircle. There is the lopsided white house, two centuries old and all corners and additions: the mish-mosh house, he'd called it; his mother had called it the House of the Thirty-Seven Gables. There is the monastery behind its high sandstone wall, as impenetrable and imperturbable as ever. Monks live there, she'd told him, and when he'd asked *what's a monk*, she'd answered: a person who wants to escape the world. All the landmarks of his childhood coming back, patiently pointing the way. For a moment he pauses before the great hollow of an old stump, disoriented, until he realizes: the big maple he remembers has been cut down. In the fall it had showered red leaves over the sidewalk, the smallest as big as his face. His mother had plucked one, poked two eyeholes, let him wear it as a mask. One for her, too. A pair of wood spirits, roaming the city. The tree must have been decaying from within all that time, rotting and crumbling like sponge. The tragedy of this nearly crushes him, until he peers inside and sees small green shoots rising deep within the ring of stubborn wood.

On their old street, each house is a different drab shade: tan, dirty cream, the washed-out gray of tattered laundry: as if all the color has leached away since his childhood. Slope shouldered, listing slightly to one side, they resemble old ladies, their clothing grown shabby and loose. There are garbage cans stowed behind fences, here and there a soggy newspaper, still in its plastic sheath, on the sidewalk—but it's quiet. And then there it is again: their house, just as it has always been. Dusty green, like the underside of a leaf. Wooden steps leading to the porch, gracefully sagging, edges rounded with age. The front door, once cherry red, faded to the soft brown of aged brick.

If his father never sold the house, Bird reasons, then it's still theirs. Which means it isn't trespassing. Not, technically, breaking the rules. Still, he glances over his shoulder, scanning the street, as he picks his way through the weeds toward the gate and the backyard. The windows of the other houses glaring at his back.

After his mother left, some of their neighbors had shied away from them. Before, they'd waved, said hello, maybe told Bird how tall he was getting, or commented on the weather. After: tight lips, the merest head nods. Darting inside quickly as if they'd forgotten something, or left the stove on. Once, in Harvard Square, Bird and his father had run into Sarah, who lived two houses down, who had sometimes brought them rhubarb muffins and borrowed Margaret's pruning shears. She'd crossed the street as they approached, casually but quickly, as if there were a bus she needed to catch. The next time they saw her, on their own street, hauling in garbage cans after the truck had gone by, she didn't meet their eyes.

Worse than the neighbors who ignored them: the ones who began to check on them. To see if you needed anything, one would say. Just dropping by, to see how you were doing. To see how you were holding up. What was it they were supposed to be holding up, Bird wondered, though eventually he realized it was themselves. It did feel that way in those early days, on the mornings when he'd learned to eat his cereal dry, because the milk in the fridge always seemed to have curdled: like they were puppets and the strings *holding them up* had gone slack. His mother had done all those things, but she was gone, and they would have to learn to survive on their own: a near impossible thing, those first weeks.

When the smoke alarm went off, the fire department arrived and his father had to explain: no, everything was fine, just the pancakes left in the pan too long. Yes, he knew the stove should never be unattended; Bird had called him into the other room; no, Bird was perfectly safe, everything was under control. Another afternoon, Bird fell off his bike at the corner and skinned both knees and ran back home, screaming, blood trickling down both shins: he was sitting on the closed toilet, sniffling, his father dabbing at him with a damp paper towel—it's okay, Bird, see? just a scrape, not as bad as it seems—when the police arrived. A neighbor had called. The little boy, crying and alone. The bike abandoned, front wheel still spinning. *Just wanted to make sure he wasn't unattended. You know, with his mother gone. Just wanted to be sure someone was watching.*

Someone was always watching, it seemed: when Bird went out without a hat and stood shivering at the bus stop; when Bird forgot his lunch and his teacher asked him if his father was giving him enough to eat. There was always someone watching. There was always someone wanting to check.

It's probably nothing, but—

I just figured I should say something in case—

Of course I'm sure everything is fine, but—

Posters were starting to appear all around town then, all over the city. All over the country. *United neighborhoods are peaceful neighborhoods. We watch out for each other.* Years later, Bird would see Sadie pull a Sharpie from her jeans pocket and scribble over *out for.* Their neighbor across the street, who had never liked them, who said their yard was overgrown and their house needed painting and their car was parked too close to hers, took particular joy in calling in everything. When his father burned his hand on the cast-iron skillet and dropped it on the floor with a loud clang and a shouted oath, a police officer arrived fifteen minutes later. Report of domestic disturbance, they'd said. Was he in the habit of using profanity in front of his son? Would he say he had a temper? And to Bird, privately, out of his father's hearing: Was he ever afraid of his father, had his father ever hit him, did he feel safe at home?

Every few days, menacing items would appear in their mailbox, or on their front steps: broken glass; bags of garbage; once, a dead rat. All-caps notes that his father tore down before Bird could read them. It was not long after that, he realizes, that his father had transferred to his new job, that he'd switched Bird to his new school, that they'd moved to the dorm. For the first time, he considers what might have appeared at his father's work, outside his office, on the desks in his classrooms. What his bosses might have said, or not said, about it all.

Good news, his father had said, the university has agreed to let us use an apartment in one of the dorms.

His new job paid hourly, barely enough for food and clothes, not enough for Cambridge rent. But through favors and kindnesses, he'd managed to negotiate a safe place for them to live. At the top of a tower, buffered by a courtyard, a key-swipe, an elevator. A refuge from prying eyes.

As Bird pushes the back gate open, there's a sudden scurrying, a blur of brown and a flash of white: a rabbit, startled while browsing in the overgrown lawn. It darts to a gap under the fence and disappears, and Bird picks his way through the grass. The weeds are waist high after three years of neglect and nearly cover the path; here and there a branch, grown leggy and bare, plucks at his sleeve like a beggar asking for alms. A story comes back to him: a castle, all covered in a rose briar. *So thick nothing could be seen of it, not even the flag on the roof.* All the princes struggling to fight their way through. When the rightful prince came, after a hundred years, the hedges made a path for him. Once he had loved that story, once his mother had told it to him and he had believed it, every word.

As he looks around, memories hover close before alighting on his shoulders like dragonflies. They'd had flowers here, before: lavender, and honeysuckle, and huge purple puffballs, his father's favorites. White roses the size of his fist that fat golden bees wriggled into. Vines with purple star-shaped blooms. Here there had been vegetables, curling squash with hairy leaves and sprawling tomatoes. His mother's green rubber boots, treads caked with mud. His had been orange. Once he'd been stung and his mother had pulled his wrist to her mouth, sucked the stinger from his skin.

He ventures farther, parting the weeds. There is the pole where beans once twined themselves up a teepee of string. A cool green hideaway, once upon a time. His father had had one as a child and then his mother had grown one for him. Now the strings are bare, gray from the weather, some slack and some frayed. At his feet, a tangle of dry, withered vines.

Somewhere here, he remembers, somewhere in this garden,

there is a key. He is sure of it. Near the back steps, perhaps, or under the porch. A rock with a key buried under it.

They'd been outside. How old had he been? Four? Five? His father at work. His mother tending the garden: pulling weeds, pruning shrubs, tying branches—swollen with ripening fruit—to their stakes. He'd shut the back door and it wouldn't open again and he'd burst into tears. Certain they were trapped outside forever. It's all right, she'd said. Listen, I'll tell you a story. She told him stories often, while she worked, as he dug in the dirt, collected twigs, lay in the grass at her feet. *Once upon a time, there was a witch with a magical garden. Once upon a time, there was a young man who understood the language of animals. Once upon a time, there were nine suns in the sky, and it was so hot nothing could grow on the earth.*

This time, as she wiped the smudge of dirt from his wet cheek: *Once upon a time, there was a boy who found a golden key.* She'd knelt by the bottom of the stairs, flipped over a stone. Presto! There it was.

She was always doing that, telling him stories. Prying open cracks for magic to seep in, making the world a place of possibility. After she left, he had stopped believing all those fantasies. Wispy, false dreams that disintegrated in the morning's light. Now it occurs to him that, perhaps, there might be truth in them after all.

It takes him a long time, but he finds it. Pressed down into the dirt, teeth edged with rust. But it is there, hard and solid and real in his hand. It still fits in the lock, still clicks when he turns it, still draws the bolt back so he can turn the knob and step through.

Inside: the smell of a house long unoccupied. A clamminess, the musty scent of air not mellowed by the warmth of bodies, but he expected this. What he hasn't expected is how familiar it is. The long narrow hallway from kitchen to living room where he and his father had raced wind-up toys, the brick fireplace set into the wall, the staircase rising steeply before him and disappearing into the darkness overhead. Like somewhere he's been in a dream, a place he knows without recognizing, a place he can navigate though he could not draw a map. Everywhere he looks, memories ripple and swell. He remembers the furniture that has vanished, once hulking and solid: his mother's beloved leather armchair, the glass-topped coffee table where the three of them had once played Candyland. He remembers the color of the light in the evenings, when it was nearly time for bed: honey-colored and warm, coating everything in its sweet syrupy glow.

Inside the castle, everything was frozen in time. The maid dozed in the kitchen with a half-plucked chicken on her lap. The cook snored, one hand still raised, about to slap the scullion.

Hello? he calls, but no one answers.

There's nothing here anymore, just speckles of dust hanging in the sunlight that seeps around the drawn blinds. A darker rectangle on the wooden floor, which for years their rug had kept unfaded. A pile of ashes on the hearth, the color of faded bones. His father had stacked his mother's books there, set a match to their corners.

No sign of her anywhere here. Signs of her everywhere here.

He sets his hand on the banister and begins to climb. On each step his feet leave prints in the dust.

. . .

Upstairs, the landing is lit only by slashes of light slicing around pulled-down shades. His parents' room. The bathroom, clawfoot tub now streaked with rust. And there, at the end of the hallway, his room, with its uniquely shaped door: one corner cut off, to fit under the sloped ceiling. He nudges it open, but there's no one there. In the corner stands a frame with no mattress, the skeleton of a bed. By the opposite wall, an bare bookshelf, a dresser with drawers lolling. He peers inside: empty. The husk of his old life. A long-ago memory surfaces, and he runs his hand down the jamb, brushing away the grime, until he finds it. Pencil ticks like the rungs of a ladder, each labeled with a date and two letters. BG. Bird Gardner. His name, once upon a time. Three feet. Three feet, two inches. Three feet six. Creeping ever upward.

The closet's hinges groan as he pulls it open. Empty. Overhead, a solitary wire hanger dangles from the bare rod. There it is, on the back wall: the panel that's actually a door, the secret he'd guarded so fiercely that he'd never even shown his friends, had kept it just for himself. And his mother. Exactly as he remembers it, uncannily so. As if he has imagined it into being.

Carefully Bird lifts up the latch and slides the panel open, revealing a gap that would be tight for a five-year-old. He flops down on the closet floor, wedges his head and one shoulder inside. He can't see anything, but he feels around the cubby with his hands, sweeping his palms over everything he can. In his memory it's a vast space, a huge cave, but the truth is, it's just a nook. If he could squeeze through the opening now, it wouldn't even hold him crouching down.

Inside he finds an old flashlight, flips the switch: the battery, of course, is long dead. A threadbare pillow. A crinkle of cellophane that, when examined, proves to be an empty Twinkie wrapper, caked with dust. Nothing else. He feels foolish now, for ever thinking she might have been here.

Bird wriggles himself backward, hooks his hands in the opening to lever himself out, and then he feels it. A little card, wedged in the backside of the cubby door's frame. No, not a card: a scrap of paper. Dusty, like everything else, as if it has been there a long time. A single word printed in black pen—DUCHESS—and beneath it an address in New York City, on Park Avenue. The handwriting is his mother's.

The next day after school he goes back to the library, the public one, the librarian's words drifting back to him as he nears the entrance: *If there's anything I can help with.* He's not sure if she can, but if there's one thing he remembers from stories, it's that people who offer help along your way—whether directing you to treasure or warning you of danger—should not be ignored.

Today, to Bird's consternation, the library is not quite deserted. There's another visitor: an older Black man in the how-to section, not far from the front desk. Tall and trim, a gray beard, long gray locs neatly tied back at the nape of his neck. Bird dawdles by the cookbooks, out of sight, watching the man flip books open and shut them again, replacing them with no apparent interest in what's inside. He'll simply wait for the man to go away, he decides, and then he can speak to the librarian without being overheard.

But after nearly ten minutes of idle browsing, the man is still loitering there. What was taking him so long? Sometimes people came in off the street, Bird knows, just looking for a place to get warm. It's October; each day the weather gets colder, and a full decade after the Crisis there are still plenty of people living rough—lingering on street corners, hunched on park benches, dodging police and the neighborhood-watch groups. But this man doesn't look like he lives on the street. He wears dark jeans and a tailored tan blazer, shoes of polished leather; there's an ease to his bearing, a comfort in this place—despite his apparent aimlessness—that Bird himself doesn't share. Yet there's a tension, too: as if he's readying himself for a difficult task.

Then the man pulls a small slip of paper from his blazer pocket, inserts it carefully between the pages of a washing machine repair manual, and shuts it again. A bookmark, Bird thinks. Still, something about it catches his attention: the slightly furtive glance the man casts over his shoulder, the way he nudges the neighboring books back into place, lining the spines up so precisely you can't tell that one has disappeared. Suddenly Bird remembers the librarian searching the books at her desk last time, the note she'd retrieved. On his side of the shelf, the man straightens, as if he's made a decision, tucks the book under his arm, and heads for the circulation desk with a new air of purpose.

Excuse me, he says to the librarian. I found this book lying around. I'm not sure but I think—I think it might have been taken out of its place.

Bird can see him more clearly now. The black-brown of his eyes, the clean white collar of his shirt. The precisely trimmed edges of his beard.

The librarian looks up, and when she speaks there's a tightly tethered eagerness in her voice. Thank you, she says. I'll take a look.

The man sets the book on the counter. I'm not sure, you understand, he says. But I *think* someone might be looking for it.

He slides the book toward her, but his hand is still pressed to the cover. As if he can't bear to let it go.

They're probably very, very worried, he says. The words come out thick and sticky, as if he's trying not to cry.

I'll do my best to find out where it belongs, the librarian says.

Bird, peering out from behind the shelf of cookbooks, understands that something is being said that he can't hear. He senses it more than registers it: a faint thrumming felt deep in the bone. No one would cry over a misplaced book.

I won't speak of this to anyone, the librarian is saying. Her voice is so low that Bird has to strain to make out the words. Thank you. For bringing this in.

She smiles at the man then, sets her hand on the cover beside his, not prying the book away, just holding it, waiting for the man to be ready, and at last the man lets it go.

I couldn't live with myself if I didn't, he says quietly. My brother and I grew up in foster care, years ago. They said our parents couldn't provide—I was almost grown up by the time they got us back.

And then he is gone.

The librarian has just pulled out the slip of paper when she spots Bird and swiftly shuts the book again. This time Bird catches a glimpse before she slips it into her sweater pocket: jotted-down notes, what might have been an address, a name. The excitement on her face cools into wariness as she recognizes him.

Well, hello again, she says. You're back. Did you need something else?

You said you could help me, Bird says. Last time I was here. You said—if there's anything you could help with, to come back.

The librarian doesn't say yes and she doesn't say no. With the book still clutched in her hands, she studies him.

I can try, she says. What do you need?

Bird clears his throat.

I need to get to New York, he says. New York City. There's somebody I have to see.

The librarian laughs. That's out of my area of expertise, she says. I meant with another book. Or finding information.

This is finding information, he says. There's someone there I need to talk to.

All last night he'd thought about it. His mother has left him this address for a reason, he is sure of it. No one else would have known about the cubby, let alone left something inside. Her letter, the story, this note: it is too much to be a coincidence. To Bird it has the certainty of a prophecy, or a quest; he feels it with the arrogant confidence only a child can have. This Duchess, whoever she is, will have something to tell him about his mother, and therefore his next step must be to go and hear it.

The librarian rubs a knuckle to her temple. I'm sorry, she says. I can't really help with that.

Please, he says. It's for a good reason. I promise.

But still she shakes her head.

I'm not a travel agent. And even if I were, I can't help a kid run away.

I'm not running away, Bird begins, but she's not listening anymore.

I'm sorry, she says again, and starts to turn away, and he decides to bluff.

I know about what you're doing, he says, though of course he does not quite yet; he knows only that it is something illicit, something shameful or perhaps even illegal, and therefore it is a crowbar: something that can be used to pry, or—if it comes to that—something to swing.

She doesn't answer but pauses, half turned away from him, and from the slight stiffening in her posture he knows she's listening and decides to press further.

I saw that man, he goes on, his gaze trained on her back. And what you were doing the other day. The note in the book.

And then, steeling himself, he takes the plunge: I saw what you put in your pocket, he says.

It works. The librarian turns around, and though her face is calm and still, there's a new tightness in her voice.

Let's talk in my office, she says, and then her hand is on his elbow, pincerlike, and she marches him back through the shelves and to the STAFF ONLY office again. This time, once they're inside, she grabs him by the shoulders, her eyes blazing.

I knew you were spying, she says. That other day. I knew you were going to make trouble. You cannot mention to anyone— anyone—what you've seen. Do you understand?

Bird tries to wriggle free, but can't. I just need your help, he says.

No one can know, she says. People will get hurt—really hurt—if anyone finds out.

Like that man? Bird says. A guess, but a right one. The librarian releases him, leans back against the wall, hugging the book to her chest.

He's trying to help, she says. And risking so much just to try. Most people won't even do that. They'd rather just close their eyes, as long as it's not their kids at stake.

She turns back to Bird.

How old are you? Twelve? Thirteen? You're old enough to understand this, aren't you? People's lives are at stake. Children's lives are at stake.

I'm not trying to cause trouble, Bird says. His tongue is awkward and unwieldy, a fish flopping on the shore. I'm sorry. I really am. Please. You're helping them. Can't you help me, too?

From his jeans pocket, he extracts the paper with the address, now battered and wrinkled.

I'm just trying to find my mother, he pleads, and then it strikes him: this, of all things, might convince her. She'd known his name, before. How else, but through his mother? It is all coming together in Bird's mind, the pieces zippering neatly together. The painting on the street, the banner in Brooklyn, the ephemeral flyers that dot the neighborhoods. His mother's poems, the stolen children, our missing hearts. He can see it all, as clearly as a spider's web misted with dew, the wispy strands crisscrossing into a magnificent, crystalline whole. They're on the same side.

My mother is one of the leaders, he says, proudly. A feeling he's never dared claim about her before, and saying it feels like standing full height after years of crouching.

The librarian gives him a look. A wry look, as if he's about to tell her a joke she already knows.

Your mother, she says.

Bird clears his throat. Margaret, he says, his voice cracking just a bit on the *M*, a hairline fracture. Margaret Miu.

It is the first time he's said her name aloud in as long as he can remember. Maybe ever. It feels like an incantation. He waits—for what? Earthquakes. Lightning strikes. Bolts of thunder. But all he sees is a half smirk at one corner of the librarian's mouth. He'd thought it would be a password that let him through the secret entrance into sparkling rooms beyond. Instead he's smashed his nose into a wall.

Oh, I know exactly who your mother is, the librarian says.

She studies Bird, leaning in closer to him, so close he can smell the morning's sour coffee on her breath, and he sags under her gaze.

You know, I didn't recognize you at first, she says. The last time I saw you, you were a baby. She used to come in, with you in a sling. But when you asked me about her book, I realized who you reminded me of. Why you looked familiar. You look a lot like her, actually, once I made the connection.

Bird has so many questions he wants to ask, but they all jam together in his mind and fall in a muddled heap. He tries to picture it: his mother, here, among these very shelves; himself, snuggled small against her chest.

She used to come here? he repeats. Still processing the idea that once his mother stood in this very spot, touched the same books that stand all around them.

Every day. Borrowing books, back when she was still writing her poems. Before she became the *voice of the revolution.*

The librarian laughs, a short laugh edged with bitterness. She closes her eyes and recites in a singsong.

All our missing hearts
scattered, to sprout elsewhere.

Bird sits with this, lets it soak into him like rain into stone. Leaving a wet dark patch. Not just a book, but a poem, too, and a line in the poem as well.

I've never heard the whole thing, he admits.

The librarian settles back against the wall, hands at her hips. All those posters and banners with her slogan on them. Such good *branding.* All those viral photo ops.

She sniffs.

I guess it's easier, she says, to write brave words than to actually do the work.

So that's what you do, he says. You find the children and bring them back home.

The librarian sighs.

It's not quite that simple, she admits. There's so much fear around it all. Most people won't even publicly say their children have been taken. People are told if they stay silent, they can get their kids back. But—

She stops, pinches the bridge of her nose. We try to convince them, she says. We keep a list: name, age, description. And if we hear about a re-placed child, we try and figure out who it is. Sometimes the leads pan out, sometimes they don't.

Unconsciously, her hand touches her sweater pocket, and the man's note crinkles inside.

It's risky, you know—a lot of people just don't want to get involved. But we try to find people we can trust, here and there.

Like that man, Bird says, and she nods.

A lot of times no one knows where the children have been taken. Some of the younger ones, at least, are re-placed. But some of them are given new names. Some are so young they don't even know their parents' names. And usually they're re-placed far away from home. Not accidentally.

Bird thinks of Sadie, the hundreds of miles between Cambridge and her parents in Baltimore. How impossible it would be for a child to retrace that distance alone.

Then what, he asks.

For now, then nothing, she says, and he can feel how bitter the words are on her tongue. There isn't anything we can do yet, to actually bring them back home. Not as long as PACT is in effect anyway. But we've matched up a few and I think it helps the families, letting them know at least their children are safe, and where. We're just trying to keep track. Of who's been lost, and who's been found. As much as we can.

We?

A handful of us, she says carefully. All over the country. We share notes. She half smiles. It's part of our job, you know: information. Gather it. Keep it. Help people find what they need.

All this time a question has been flickering inside Bird.

But why, he says. When it's so risky. Won't they punish you, too, if they find out?

The librarian's lips tighten.

Of course they could. Me, and everyone else who's trying to find these children. That man and anyone else who passes us information. Of course it's a risk. But—

She pauses, and rubs her temples.

My great-grandfather was at Carlisle, she says simply, as if that explains everything. Then at the sight of Bird's blank face, she snorts. You have no idea, do you, she says. How could you? They don't teach you any of this. Too unpatriotic, right, to tell you the horrible things our country's done before. The camps at Manzanar, or what happens at the border. They probably teach you that most plantation owners were kind to their slaves and that Columbus *discovered* America, don't they? Because telling you what really happened would be espousing un-American views, and we certainly wouldn't want that.

Bird doesn't fully understand any of these things, but what he does understand, suddenly, and with head-spinning force, is how much he does not know.

I'm sorry, he says meekly.

The librarian sighs. How can you know, she says, if no one teaches you, and no one ever talks about it, and all the books about it are gone?

A long silence unwinds between them.

I didn't mean to make trouble, Bird says finally. Honest. I just—I just want to find my mother.

She softens.

I only knew your mother a little, she says. And a long time ago. But I remember her. She was a nice person. And a good poet.

But a bad mother, he thinks.

Only when the librarian replies does he realize he's spoken out loud.

You shouldn't say that, she says. Not about your own mother.

She puts her hand on Bird's shoulder again—gently, this time. A tender squeeze.

I'm not saying there aren't bad mothers, she says. Just that you don't always know. What makes them do something, or not do something. Most of us, we're trying our best.

Something in her voice makes Bird pause. A brittle sound. Something stretched too thin, more cracks than whole.

Do you have kids? he asks.

Two, she says slowly. I had two.

Past tense. Snipping the sentence in two: before, and after.

What happened to them, Bird asks.

My little girl got sick, she says. During the Crisis. We couldn't afford the hospital, hardly anybody could. Then my boy ran out of insulin, toward the end.

Her eyes have drifted away from him, are focused somewhere just over his shoulder, on the wall beyond.

Wherever your mother is, whatever she's doing, the librarian says, I'm sure of this: she'd be happy to know you grew up and stayed well. That you're still here.

Then she blinks, once, twice. Returns to the present, to him.

But look, Bird, she says, if you want to get to New York—you need to find your own way. I can only pass on information. Not people.

Bird nods.

And I can't let you go until you promise not to speak about any of this. Please, Bird. You of all people should understand. Pretend you don't know anything—I mean *anything*—about this. People's lives are at stake.

I would never, he says, the last word half garbled. I could never. And then, to prove to her he means it: My best friend, Sadie, was one of those kids.

A long, startled pause.

You knew Sadie? she says.

And then Bird remembers: of course. Sadie, after school every day, stopping by the library, even just for a few minutes.

We'd talk, the librarian says. Hard not to notice a little girl coming in like that, on her own.

A sudden hot flare of hope sears through Bird.

Is that where she went? he says, excited. You sent her home? Back to her mom and dad?

But the librarian shakes her head.

I couldn't find out where her parents had gone, she says. Nobody could find out anything, except that they weren't home anymore. And then all of a sudden, Sadie was gone, too.

A moment of silence, in which the librarian's eyes on him are gentle and kind. It feels good, surprisingly good, to talk about Sadie with someone who knew her. To remember her.

Listen, the librarian says. I can't take you to New York. I don't know anyone who can. But I can do something.

She leads him back out of the office and through the shelves to a thick maroon binder. Inside: pages and pages of timetables, printed in pale blue columns.

Train schedules and routes, she says. This binder here, this one is buses. At the station, you can go to the counter, but there are also machines that sell tickets. In case you wanted to avoid— questions.

Thank you, Bird manages to say.

She smiles. I told you, she says, that's my job. Information. Passing it on. Helping people find what they need.

She sets the opened binder atop the shelf and slides it across to him.

What you do with this information, she says, is your own business only.

M onday morning, his father is already waiting, work satchel in hand, when Bird emerges from the bedroom. He has hidden his schoolbooks under the blanket on his bed; in their place, the bag on his back holds a change of clothes, a toothbrush, and all the money he has. All the dropped bills he's found and saved over the years, all the lunch money kept from all the days when, rather than eat in the cafeteria, he would sit alone with his thoughts outside. Just enough, according to the timetables in the library, for a one-way ticket to Manhattan. The bus he's selected departs at ten o'clock. Plenty of time.

Though the elevator has been repaired at last, it groans and fumbles as it shudders its slow way downward. Between the mirrored walls, an infinite chain of Bird and his father accordions into the distance.

Bird waits until the numbers tick down from six to five before he speaks.

I forgot my lunch, he announces.

Noah, his father says, how many times do I have to tell you.

The elevator grinds to a halt and opens onto the dorm lobby. Sunlight pours through the plate-glass windows, so bright he feels like an insect on a light table. Surely his father will look at his face and know that he's lying. But his father just sighs and checks his watch.

Staff meeting at nine today, he says. I can't wait for you. Run back up and get it and hurry to school. Don't dawdle, okay?

Bird nods and hits the elevator button again, and his father turns to go. At the sight of his back—so familiar, in his old brown coat—Bird's throat tightens.

Dad, he calls, and his father turns around, gives a soft *oof* as Bird throws his arms around him.

What's this? his father says. I thought you were too old for hugs.

But he's teasing, and he squeezes Bird tight, and Bird snuggles into the comfortable dusty wool of his father's overcoat. He suddenly wants to tell him everything. To say, come with me. We'll find her together. But he knows his father will never let him go, let alone come with him. If he wants to go, he will have to go alone.

Bye, Dad, he says, and his father gives him a wave and is gone.

Upstairs, Bird lets himself back into the apartment and rushes to the window. He ducks behind the curtains and peeks down at the small grassy square of courtyard below. There he is: the dark speck of his father, nearly at the gate.

He's watched his father cross this courtyard before, on snow days when Bird's school closed but his father's work did not. He used to stand by the window, waiting until his father emerged far below, watch him head down the path and out of sight. In the winter, the small dots of footprints that appeared in his father's wake were like magic. Up close, Bird knew, they were jagged holes crushed into the ice. But from where he stood—ten stories up, pinned against and behind glass—they were dainty and precise. Beautiful. Purposeful. Thin stitching on a snow-white quilt; a trail of stones placed to mark the path home, or to show someone the way. How comforting, to know that he could go downstairs, follow the marks his father's feet have made, all the way to wherever he's gone.

Now, as he watches, the lone figure in the brown coat hugs that coat tighter around himself against the chilly fall breeze and steps through the gate. There is no snow, yet, to hold footprints, and in a moment, as his father disappears from sight, it is as if he never passed that way at all. Today it strikes Bird as unbearably sad, to pass by and leave no trace of your existence. To have no one remember you'd been there. He wants to run down all ten flights of stairs and place his feet into the invisible footsteps his father has left behind. He presses his fingertips to the cool glass, as if—if he tried hard enough—he could push the entire window aside and step through into the air above all of this.

He hadn't looked up when she'd said goodbye.

Birdie, she'd said, I have to go out.

Was that it? Or had she said: I have to go? He can't remember. He'd been playing with Legos, building something. He doesn't even remember what anymore.

Bird, she called again. She'd hovered just behind him, and

he'd bristled with irritation. Whatever he was building wouldn't hold together; it kept tipping and falling in a shower of bricks, breaking itself apart again and again. He took two bricks, jammed them together as hard as he could, so hard that the knobs left divots in his skin.

Birdie, she said. I'm—I'm going now.

She was waiting for him, waiting for him to come and kiss her, like he usually did, and he attached one more brick and the whole thing collapsed again with a clatter, and he blamed her, for calling him when he was busy with something else.

Okay, he said. He picked up the bricks again, piecing the thing together once more, and by the time he turned around at last, to see if she was still there, she was gone.

It is nearly nine o'clock: time to go. When his father comes back for dinner, the apartment will be empty, and Bird will be in New York. He's thought about this all weekend, how to tell his father where he's gone. Any mention of his mother is too big a risk, so his note is short and obscure: *Dad, I'll be back in a few days. Don't worry.* Beside it, he places the cat letter in its envelope on the table. Then he rips the paper from the cubby in two: the Park Avenue address he tucks back into his pocket; the last line—*New York, NY*—he sets beside the letter and his note. And last of all, a box of matches. He hopes his father will understand— where he's gone, and why, and most of all, what to do with this information.

He has never traveled out of Cambridge; all night he'd fretted about the dangers that might lie ahead. Taking the wrong train or turning down the wrong street or boarding the wrong bus, ending up who knows where. A ticket agent demanding: where are your parents? Policemen stopping him, loading him into the back of a patrol car, carting him back to his father—or worse, somewhere else. Strangers, so many of them, scrutinizing him. Measuring him with their eyes, gauging whether he is a threat or to be threatened.

Yet none of this happens. Baseball cap pulled down, sunglasses on, he rides the T to the station. The cops on the platform, talking football, don't even give him a second glance. Instead of approaching the ticket window, he heads for the machine: cash in, ticket out, no questions asked. At the bus terminal, no one looks around; everyone here seems to be focused on the ground, avoiding eye contact, and it occurs to him that maybe they, too, are hoping not to be seen. A pact between strangers, all of them agreeing tacitly to ignore one another, to mind their own business, for once. As one fear after another fails to materialize, Bird grows increasingly, absurdly confident. It's as if the universe is signaling he's on the right path, that he's doing exactly what he's meant to be. When his bus pulls in, he takes a seat by the window toward the back. He's made it. He's on his way.

After his mother left, for months he would lie in bed at night, certain that if he could stay awake long enough, she would return. He was convinced, for reasons he could never explain, that his mother came back in the night and disappeared by morning. By sleeping, he missed her each time. Perhaps it was a test—to see how badly he wanted to see her. Could he stay awake? He imagined his mother, each night, standing over his bed, shaking her head. Again he was asleep! Again he had failed the test.

It made perfect sense to him then; it still does. In all the stories his mother had told him, there was an ordeal the hero had to endure: Climb down this well and fetch the tinderbox. Lie beneath this waterfall and let it drum you to pieces. He was sure if he could stay awake his mother would be there. The fact that the test was so arbitrary did not bother him; the tests they had in school were arbitrary, too: circle the nouns and underline the verbs; combine these two random numbers into a third. Tests were always arbitrary; it was part of their nature and, in fact, what made them a test. Separate the peas and the lentils from the ashes before morning's light. Journey beneath the sea and bring back the pearl that shines by night.

He'd pinched his own arm, bruising black and blue down the forearms, trying to stay awake. Night after night he would catch a sliver of flesh between finger-pad and thumbnail, squeezing until white flashes flecked the corners of his vision. In the morning, his mother was still gone and a half-moon of purple blotted his forearm, and his father asked if the other boys at school were bullying him. They were, but not in the way his father meant. It's fine, Dad, he said, and all day his eyelids drooped and sagged, and that evening, he would try, and fail, to stay awake again. It was around then that he stopped believing in stories.

Now, after all this time, he is on his way to find her. Like someone in those very stories she'd told him all those years ago. He will journey to where his mother is waiting patiently for him. As soon as she sees him, whatever spell has kept her away all this time will be broken. In the fairy tales, it happens at once, like a switch flipped: At once she recognized him. At once she knew her true self. He is certain this is how it will happen for his mother, too. She will see him and at once she will be his again and they will all live happily ever after.

The interstate scrolls by as the motor settles into the steady thrum of high gear. The farther they go, the easier Bird begins to breathe. He falls asleep and wakes only when the bus downshifts and merges left, jostling him against the glass. By the roadside: a navy-blue SUV has pulled over to the shoulder, a police cruiser parked behind it, lights flashing. An officer, navy suited, emerges from the driver's seat. Stay away from policemen, his father says in his mind, and Bird tugs the visor of his hat a bit lower, shading his face, as they whip by. He should be scared, but to his surprise, he isn't. Everything beyond the window feels far away, walled off behind glass, and his heart beats with the same slow, steady thump of the wheels beneath them. Outside the bus, trees and scrubby fields blur on and on.

The bus drops him in Chinatown in the midst of a fine drizzle. A different world: more people than he's ever seen, more bustle, more noise. Despite the clamor and commotion, he feels oddly at home, and it takes him a moment to understand why: all around him, suddenly, are people with faces like hers. And a bit like his. He has never been in a place like this, where no one gives him a second glance. If his father was here, he'd be the one standing out, not Bird, and Bird laughs. For the first time in his life, he is unremarkable, and this feels like power.

Before he left he'd studied the map, the librarian nudging it wordlessly toward him. A grid, his father would say, calm and patient. Just count your way up and over. He does the math:

Bowery will turn into Third; eighty-seven blocks up, then two blocks west. Just over five miles. All he has to do is walk in a straight line.

He begins.

He begins to notice things.

That on all the signs here in Chinatown, something has been painted out or taped over or, in some cases, pried away. He can still see the perforations where something was once nailed on, still make out shapes embossed beneath silvery-gray duct tape. He notices that the street signs have been painted over, too: a fat swath of black runs under the feet of neat white letters spelling MULBERRY and CANAL, like a shadow at high noon, like a dark ring beneath the white of an eye. Only when he spots one where the paint has begun to wear away, revealing a thicket of characters beneath, does he understand. He remembers his father's finger, inscribing characters like these in the dust: once, all these signs bore two languages. Someone—everyone—has tried to make the Chinese disappear.

He begins to notice other things.

How the people he passes speak either in English, or not at all, casting quick glances at one another but saying nothing. Only when they duck into a shop can he sometimes catch the low murmur of another language—Cantonese, he guesses. His father would know; his father might even understand. Everyone here seems cautious and edgy, scanning the sidewalks and the street, checking over their shoulders. Poised to run. He notices how many, many American flags there are—on nearly every storefront, on the lapels of nearly every person he sees. In the corner of each store hang the same kinds of posters from home:

GOD BLESS EVERY LOYAL AMERICAN. All the way through China-town, not a single store is without one. Some sport other signs, too, garish in red, white, and blue: AMERICAN OWNED AND RUN. 100% AMERICAN. Only when he's left Chinatown, and the faces around him become Black and white instead of Asian, do the flags become more sporadic, the people here apparently more confident that their loyalty will be assumed.

He walks.

He passes storefronts shielded by graffitied metal grates. New and Used. Bought and Sold. For Lease. A concrete median divid-ing patched concrete streets. Mystifying names: Max Sun. Chair Table Booth. On the curbside, broken pallets splay like desert-bleached bones. No grass, no trees, nothing green, only street lamps the same gray as the sidewalk, the roads, the dirt that streaks its way up the sides of the buildings from the ground. Everything grit-colored, as if trying to escape notice. The people who pass carry heavy plastic bags, roll shopping carts, avoid each other's eyes. They do not linger. Sometimes the crosswalks under their feet are simply spray-painted on, the lines wobbling and uncertain; in other places there are no crosswalks at all. More than a decade after the Crisis ended, so many things still haven't been repaired.

Block by block, the landscape begins to shift around him. Stunted patches of grass fight their way through gaps in the sidewalk. How long has he been walking? An hour? He's lost track already. Has the school already noticed his absence, have they notified his father? Up, up, up. The drizzle slows, then stops. Supermarkets with giant glossy billboards of pizza, intricately ruffled kale, slices of mango that make his mouth water. His stomach growls, but he doesn't stop: he has no money left anyway. Bodegas with tumbling mountains of fruit and buckets of sheathed roses and indifferent, yawning cats stretched across the displays; barbershops where men's laughter floats through the propped-open doors on a wave of aftershave. In their windows, familiar posters: PROUD TO BE AMERICAN. WE WATCH OVER EACH OTHER. Now there are trees, small wispy ones barely above a man's head, but trees, nonetheless. Somewhere a church bell strikes. Three o'clock, or four? The street buzzes with life, and he can't tell chimes from echoes. He should be walking home from school, but instead he is here, his pulse growing faster with each block. Nearly there.

He walks faster and around him the city changes faster, too, like a sped-up video zipping into the future, or possibly the past. The way things used to be, that golden pre-Crisis world he's only heard about. More taxis, nicer ones, newer. Cleaner, as if they've just been washed. The streetlights are shiny black here, taller, sleeker, as if here there is more space to hold their heads high. He passes buildings with crowns of decorative stonework over each window: someone took the trouble, up here, to pick out details in beige against the red, just so that they would be beautiful. Now there are stores with wide glass windows, unafraid of being smashed. Restaurants with awnings. People walking small dogs; trees ringed by neat metal fences no taller than his knee: for show, not for protection.

As the mist clears, he spots patches of green high in the air: rooftop gardens, the peaks of potted evergreens pointing at the sky. The buildings and businesses are no longer trying to hide. YES WE ARE OPEN. Flashy, catchy, quirky names, trying to stand out, trying to catch your attention and stick in your mind: The Salty Squid. Sound Oasis. Chickenosity. His father would have laughed. In each window, the familiar star-spangled placard. Banners advertising the fanciness of what they had, not its cheapness. Higher and higher the cross streets climb, as if he is scaling a ladder: Fiftieth, Fifty-Fifth, Fifty-Sixth. Men in suits. Men with ties. Men in leather shoes with fringed tassels and smooth soles in which you had no need to run. Long ago his father had worn shoes like that. Banks, so many banks—three, four, five in a row, sometimes the same bank on both sides of the street, one across from the other. He had not known it was possible to be so rich you would not cross the street.

A department store the length of an entire block, all sleek dark granite polished to mirror gloss. As if to say: in this place, even stones shine like stars. In its windows, faceless mannequins wear floral silk scarves around their throats. Tall apartment buildings, each window a pocket of reflected sky set into the walls like a gem. He imagines his mother living in one of them, looking down on him, waiting for him. Soon he'll know. Refrigerated trucks idle by the curbs, crammed with grocery deliveries, huffing their frosted breath into the air. Now there are coffee shops, places meant to linger in. Billboards for whitening and straightening teeth; hotels with suited bellhops in hats poised just outside. Here, people hold bags not meant to carry, but to be pretty. Dry cleaner after dry cleaner: a neighborhood of silk, too delicate to wash. At each door, burly men from the neighborhood watch stand guard.

Seventy-Fifth Street. Seventy-Sixth. Older buildings that wore their age gracefully, looking staid, not shabby. Here foreign words are proudly displayed: Salumeria. Vineria. Macarons. A safe and desirable foreignness. Shops labeled *gourmet* and *luxury* and *vintage*. Here—and it does not seem possible that this is the same street he's followed from those painted-over signs and fearful whispers; it must be another world he's journeyed into—the street is wide and lined with trees. He likes the thought of his mother here, in this beautiful place. Blond women in jogging tights puff beside him, ponytails bobbing, as they wait for the signal to change. Nannies push sleek strollers, the babies inside sumptuously dressed. He passes stores that make only picture frames, restaurants that serve only salad, shops selling pink shirts embroidered with tiny, smiling whales. Buildings so tall their tips are invisible, even when he cranes his head so far he nearly falls backward. Anything could happen here, everything does happen here. It is like fairyland, or a fairy tale.

This is the place, he thinks. This is where she is.

And because this is a magical fairyland, where anything can happen, because he is so invigorated by all that he's seen, still swooning on the rich air of possibility inflating his lungs, he isn't surprised when suddenly, there she is: his mother, just across the street. A small brown dog at her side. Something inside him leaps skyward in a shower of sparks, and he almost cries out in joy.

Then his mother glances down at the dog, which is nosing in a manicured flower bed, and it is not his mother at all. Just a woman. Who doesn't resemble her at all, actually; only in the most superficial ways—an East Asian woman with long black hair, carelessly pulled back in a knot. The face, now that he can see her more clearly, is nothing like his mother's. His mother would never have such a dog, this little amber powder puff like a teddy bear with black-button eyes, a pert velvet nose. Of course it isn't her, he chides himself, how could it be. And yet there is something about the way she holds herself—the alertness of her posture, the quickness of her eyes—that reminds him of her.

The woman notices him across the street, watching her, and smiles. Perhaps he reminds her of someone, too; perhaps at first glance she mistook him for someone she loves and now that love spills over to him, a largesse. And because she is looking at him, because she is smiling at him and perhaps thinking fond thoughts about this little boy who reminds her of someone she loves, she does not see it coming: a fist, smashing into her face.

It happens in seconds but it seems to stretch on forever. Out of nowhere. A tall white man. The woman crumpling, turned to rubble. Bird's own body petrified, his scream cemented in his throat. The man towering over her, kick, kick, kick, soft sickening thumps like a mallet on meat: her belly, her chest, and then—as she curls up like a shelled shrimp, arms over face, trying to protect what she can—the curve of her back. Her cries wordless sounds, hanging in the air like shards of glass. The man himself says nothing, as if he is doing a job, something impersonal but necessary.

No one comes to help. An older couple about-faces, as if they've remembered something urgent elsewhere. A man hurries away, bent over his phone; cars flow by, unperturbed. They must see, Bird thinks, how can they not? The dog, ankle high, barks and barks. A doorman emerges from the building behind and Bird nearly sobs with gratitude. Help, he thinks. Help her. Please. Then the doorman pulls the door shut. Bird can faintly make him out on the other side of the thick plate glass, blurred and ghostly, watching as if it were a scene on a TV screen: the woman's cheek against the sidewalk now, the jolt of her body with each blow. Waiting for it to be done so that he can open the door once more.

The woman has stopped moving and the man looks down at her—with disgust? With satisfaction? Bird can't tell. The dog is still snarling and barking, furious and impotent, its small feet scuffling the pavement. With a swift movement the man brings his boot down, hard, on its back. The way he might crush a soda can, or a cockroach.

Bird screams then, and the man turns and spots Bird watching him, and Bird runs.

Blindly, as fast as he can. Not daring to look behind him. Bookbag hammering against him like a drumbeat. Sweat-soaked shirt hot then cold at the small of his back. Is she dead, he thinks, is the dog dead. Did it matter. The man's eyes still drill at the nape of his neck and his stomach heaves and he retches, but nothing comes out. He darts down an alleyway and huddles behind a dumpster, catching his breath, the back of his throat raw and burning.

He'd forgotten: in fairylands there is evil, too. Monsters and curses. Dangers lurking in disguise. Demons, dragons, rats as big as oxen. Things that could destroy you with a glance. He thinks of the man at the Common. He thinks of his father, his broad shoulders and strong hands, lifting him back to his feet. But his father is far away, cocooned in the soundless library, where the outside world cannot reach. He has no idea where Bird is, and this more than anything makes Bird feel terribly alone.

He stays there for a long while, trying to smooth his breathing, trying to steady his hands, which won't stay still. When he's finally ready, he rises on shaky feet and picks his way back to the corner. He's run backward, several blocks off course. When he reaches Park Avenue, he moves quickly and cautiously, scanning the streets. He feels conspicuous now; he notices people noticing him. He understands, as he hadn't before. Perhaps he'd been invisible once, but the spell has worn off—or maybe it had only ever been in his imagination. People can see him, and at last he understands how small he is, how easily the world could shred him to pieces.

It's late afternoon by the time he finally reaches the address: a big brick building, flowered window boxes, a huge green door. Not an apartment building—a single-family townhouse, a thing he had not known existed here. The Duchess's castle. Cautiously, he studies it from across the street. In stories you might find anything inside a castle: riches, an enchantress, an ogre waiting to devour you. But this is it, the place his mother has sent him. Street name and numbers written in her own hand. A leap of faith, then.

He climbs the marble steps and reaches for the brass knocker and raps it, three times, against the green-painted wood.

It feels an eternity, but it's really only a minute or two before an older white man answers the door. He's a bit stout, in a uniform: shiny brass buttons on navy-blue wool, like the captain on a ship. He eyes Bird coldly, and Bird swallows twice before he can speak.

I am here to see the Duchess, Bird announces, and as if by magic, the captain nods, and steps aside.

A foyer of sunny yellow, a fireplace with a fire lit, even though it's only October. Cream-colored tiles on the floor, studded with squares of ambery brown. A marble-topped table with scrolled legs squats in the middle of the room, its only apparent purpose to hold the biggest vase of flowers Bird has ever seen. All around him the lights are haloed with gold.

I'm here to see the Duchess, Bird repeats, trying to sound surer than he is, and the captain squints down at him.

I'll have to call up, he says. Who may I say is here, please?

And because he is hungry and thirsty and exhausted, because he has walked for miles on an empty stomach, because his head feels uncannily detached from his body, like a balloon floating just over his shoulders, because he feels slightly unreal and he's not sure this place is real, let alone this city, nor the Duchess he's come to see, Bird answers as if he were in a fairy tale, too.

Bird Gardner, he says. Margaret's son.

If you will wait here, the captain says.

Bird hovers uncertainly by one of the chairs near the fireplace. It is covered in sandy velvet and reminds him of a throne. With his fingertips he traces the chiseled grooves on the arms, and words his father has taught him float back: Mahogany. Alabaster. Filigree. He clears his throat. On the mantel is a little gold clock, a little golden woman gesturing decorously toward the time. Almost five. Soon his father will head home and discover that he is gone.

The captain returns. If you'll follow me, he says.

He strides through an archway and down the hall and Bird trails behind him, cautious, peering around corners, waiting for a monster to spring. But all they pass is a palaceworth of luxuries. A paneled silk screen, stitched with cypress trees and cranes and a pagoda in the far-off distance. A sofa of yellow silk with cushions shaped like candy rolls; a huge oval dining room, its floor a dizzying parquet. Everything here seems to be touched with gold: the handles of the urns and vases on the mantelpieces, the twisted tassels on the drapes, even the claws of the lions' feet on which the tables and chairs rest. Then they are at the foot of a grand swooping staircase spiraling up and up and up, a lush tawny carpet spilling down its center. He has never seen such a staircase. A delicate chandelier dangles on a chain swathed in velvet. Bird counts: one story, two, three, four, and far above them a compass-shaped skylight, a blue crystal pool of sky.

This way, please, the captain says. And then Bird sees it: just beside the staircase, a little elevator, wood-paneled and parquet-floored. An elevator in a house, he thinks in awe. The captain gestures with one hand and Bird steps inside, feels as if he's climbing into a polished nutshell.

She's waiting for you upstairs, the captain says. He pulls a brass grate shut, caging Bird inside.

As the elevator shudders upward, Bird's mind whirls. Around him the brass bars of the grate rattle, as if something is trying to get out, or in. He has no idea what he is heading toward. What will the Duchess be like? Will she be kind, or will she be threatening? He pictures the evil queens from storybooks, all malice sheathed in charm. Trust, he thinks to himself: in the stories you had to trust strangers on your quest. Even this elevator is decorated, as befits a palace. Miniature golden frames around sketches of ancient buildings and winged women. A small white telephone. On the back wall, a round mirror bulges and flexes, bending his face back to him in distorted form: an ogre's, or maybe a dwarf's.

At last the elevator opens. A living room, as big as their apartment back home. Another table; another bowl billowing with flowers. In the polished surface he can see his own face peering back up at himself. Underfoot the carpet is gold patterned. The home of nobility, for sure.

And then there she is, gliding through French doors at the end of the room: the Duchess. Younger than he'd expected: regal, tall, blond hair clipped short around her head. Pearls. A blue drapey pantsuit instead of a gown, but it is clear to him she is a woman of power. For a moment Bird's voice deserts him, and he simply stares up at her. She doesn't break the silence, just looks down at him in bemusement.

Are you the Duchess? he finally asks. But he already knows she is.

And who do we have here? she asks. One eyebrow raised. Skeptical.

Bird, he says, trembling. Margaret's son.

For a moment he fears she will say, who? But she doesn't. Instead she says, rather coldly, Why are you here?

My mother, he says, the answer so obvious it feels ridiculous to say it. I came here to find her.

What makes you think she's here? the Duchess asks. The smallest tendril of curiosity curling the edge of her voice.

Because, he says, and pauses. Feeling for the answer inside

himself. *Because I want to know why she left me. Because I want her back. Because I want her to want me back, too.*

She sent me a message, he says.

The Duchess purses her lips, and he can't tell if she is perplexed or pleased or angry. For a moment she's like a teacher, weighing the answer he's given, deciding between praise and punishment.

I see. So your mother—she asked you to come here?

Bird hesitates. Wonders if he should lie, if this is a test. His chest tightens.

I'm not sure, he admits. But she left me this address. A long time ago. I thought—I thought you might know where she is.

From his pocket he pulls the scrap of paper, or what remains of it. Tattered and crumpled, edges smudged with blue dye from his jeans. But there it is, in his mother's handwriting: the very address in which they stand.

I see, the Duchess says again. And you came here alone? Where's your father?

How does she know about his father, Bird thinks with a jolt.

He doesn't know I'm here, he says, and as the words pass his lips, it hits him again how alarmingly true this is. His father has no idea where he is; his father cannot help him or save him.

The Duchess leans closer, scrutinizing him, her eyes needle-sharp. Up close he can see that her face is only just beginning to wrinkle, that her hair is not yet gray. She's maybe the age, he realizes, that his mother would be.

So who does know you're here? she demands. A steel glint of menace in her tone.

Bird's throat swells. No one, he says. I didn't tell him. I didn't tell anyone. I came alone.

You can trust me, is what he wants to say. A sweaty panic slithers over him, that he might have come so far and in the end be turned away. That this dragon of a Duchess and her gilded palace might swallow him and trap him forever.

Interesting, the Duchess says. She turns away, and to Bird it feels like a very bright light being switched off. Wait here, she says, and without another word she sweeps out, leaving him alone.

Bird circles the room, unable to be still. Dusty-gold drapes at the windows, through which he can see the glitter of traffic on the street below. A grand piano in the corner. On the end table, a silver-framed photograph of a woman and a man: the Duchess, much younger and with longer hair, hardly more than a girl, and someone who might be her father. The old Duke, he decides, though the man in the picture is wearing a polo shirt and khakis, and they seem to be on the deck of a sailboat, blue sky and bluer water colliding at the horizon behind them. A stern, almost angry expression on his face. He wonders where the old Duke is. He wonders how the Duchess knows his mother. He wonders what his mother has been doing all these years, away from him. If she will recognize him when she sees him. If she's sorry, if she ever thinks about him. If she regrets.

Outside the sky has darkened, hardening to flat, steely gray. To his amazement, he isn't hungry at all anymore. He imagines his father arriving at home to their tiny cinderblock dorm, finding the apartment dark and deserted. Searching for him. Calling his name. It's okay, Dad, he thinks, I'll be back soon. He feels oddly alert and alive, his veins electrified. He is almost there. After all this time.

Far off in the recesses of the house, a clock strikes, a deep sonorous chime. Five o'clock. And then, as if it is a signal, the Duchess returns.

If you really are who you say, she says, then prove it. What color is your bicycle?

What?

You should be aware, she adds, that if you aren't who you claim, I have no compunction at all about calling the authorities.

I— Bird stops, bewildered. His father has not let him ride a bike since that day he fell off and the neighbor called the police.

I don't have one, he blurts out. The Duchess's face remains calm and impassive and blank.

What kind of milk do you put on your cereal in the morning? she asks.

Again Bird is too baffled to speak. He hesitates, but the only thing to do is tell the truth, however odd it seems.

I eat my cereal dry, he says.

Once more the Duchess makes no reply. Where in the cafeteria do you eat lunch? she says, and Bird pauses, seeing himself as if from above, a solitary dot perched on the steps with a brown paper sack.

I don't eat lunch in the cafeteria, he says. I eat outside. By myself.

The Duchess says nothing, but she smiles, and by this he understands that he has passed.

So you want to see your mother, she says.

It is not a question.

Well then. Come with me.

In the hallway she presses a button on the wall and a panel slides away. Magic? No: an elevator, cunningly camouflaged in the hall. The same elevator, in fact, in which he arrived. At a touch of the Duchess's finger, the button labeled B glows the color of flame. When the doors open again, they are in a dim cave: an underground garage, a sleek black sedan with the engine already running. A mustached man in a suit stands at attention beside the waiting car. The footman, Bird thinks, as they slide into the back seat.

And then they're off.

The car glides up the ramp and out of the garage and injects itself into the crowded streets: smoothly, liquidly, regally. From inside, Bird can hear nothing at all. Not the voices of the throngs that gather at street corners, thinning and bunching with the rhythm of the crossing lights, like a great snake inching its way downtown. Not the growling engines of the cars that surround them in a pack. Not the honking that he knows must pierce the air, those deafening blares of impotent frustration. There is simply no sound, and through the tinted windows the city scrolls by in sepia, like a silent film. To him they seem to be not driving but floating.

Seat belt, please, the Duchess says beside him. It would be a shame to get this far and then crack your skull open.

Bird opens his mouth and the Duchess shuts it with a glance.

I'm not here to answer questions, she says. That's your mother's job, not mine.

After that she says nothing at all, as they weave along the river and down into a long tunnel and then back out again into twilight, the moon just beginning to emerge. Time moves in fits and starts, starting and stopping like the traffic around them, and sometimes Bird dozes and wakes to find they haven't moved at all, and sometimes he is sure he hasn't closed his eyes but they seem to have teleported a great distance, nothing outside familiar, and then around them the traffic congeals and clots once more, slowing them to a crawl, and finally—he doesn't know how much time has passed—the sun has gone down and the streets around them are calm and nearly deserted, lined with brownstones, and the car pulls to the side of the road and stops at last.

Listen carefully, the Duchess says, with new urgency in her voice. As if this is the last time she'll speak to him, as if the real test is about to begin. Follow these instructions precisely, she tells him. I can't be responsible for what happens if you don't.

To Bird, bleary-eyed, half-dizzy with excitement and fatigue, this does not seem strange. In fact, he expects no less: in stories, there are always inscrutable rules to obey. *Ignore the golden sword; use the old and rusty one instead. No matter how thirsty you are, do not drink the wine. Do not speak a word, even if you are pinched and beaten, even if they cut off your head.* After the car drives away, leaving him standing on the sidewalk, he does exactly what the Duchess has commanded. He walks two blocks over and three blocks up, crosses the street, and there it is, just as she'd said: a big brownstone with a red door, every window covered. *It will look deserted, but appearances can be deceiving.* As instructed, he ignores the wide front stoop and skirts around to the side of the house. *No one must see you enter the gate.* Twice a car passes while he's hunting for the latch, the rough wood of the gate snagging at his fingertips, and then he has it, the metal cool and solid and smooth. He glances over his shoulder at the lighted windows in the houses all around him, and when he's sure there's no one watching, he turns the catch and the gate swings open.

At the back of the house is a door. You must be absolutely silent as you approach. With tentative feet, Bird picks his way through the tangle of weeds and grass. This must have been the back garden once, untouched for ages; here and there he stumbles across a sapling, scrappy and saucy, whipping its branches in his face. But in the moonlight he sees the faint glitter of a path, shiny grit embedded in the cement to point the way, and he follows it toward the dark hulk of the house. *Enter these five numbers—eight, nine, six, zero, four—and it will open for you.* He feels his way along the wall of the house, as if stroking a sleeping dragon with his fingers, looking for the soft spot: brick, brick, brick, and then there is the door, a keypad. Too dark to see, but he counts the buttons, presses the passcode. A faint beep. He turns the knob.

Inside: a narrow hallway leading into a darker gloom. *You must shut the door behind you, even though it will be completely dark. You won't be able to see her until you do.*

Slowly he closes it, and the outside world narrows to a wedge, then a sliver, then disappears. The latch clicks, sealing him into darkness.

And then he hears footsteps, hurrying toward him. A small light clicks on, scattering golden sparks across his sight.

His mother, astonished. Holding out her arms. Throwing them around him. Her warmth. Her scent. The shock and wonder and delight on her face.

Bird, she cries. Oh Bird. You found me.

II

So here he is: Bird. Her Bird.

Taller than she'd expected; thinner. The last scrapings of baby fat nearly gone from his face. A lean, cool face, a skeptical face, a hard set to his mouth, a squaring of the jaw she can't quite place. Not Ethan's; certainly not hers.

Bird, she says. You've gotten so tall.

Well, he says, suddenly reserved. It's been kind of a long time.

He doesn't trust her, she can see that already: the way he lingers by the door, not meeting her eyes. Yet, she thinks. He doesn't trust her *yet*. She flicks off the light.

We have to avoid attention, she says.

She can see him thinking, already: *What is this place?*

The hallway is narrow and behind her Bird's footsteps slow as he picks his way between unfamiliar walls. A stutter-step, a pause. The soles of his sneakers scuffing the floor as he drags his feet.

This way, she says. Wait. Be careful, the floor's uneven here. Watch your step.

She is speaking quickly, uncharacteristically chatty, words tripping over each other as they fall from her mouth, but she can't help it.

I knew you'd figure it out, she says, as they make their way down the darkened hall. I knew you were smart enough.

How, he says.

At the entrance to the living room she stops and waits for him to catch up, and his hand brushes the small of her back, reaching for something known, something steady. She wants to take it in hers, to press it to her face, but she knows he's not ready yet.

Someone told me, she says.

After the darkness of the hallway, the living room is blinding. Bird's hand flies to shade his eyes, as if he's stepped into blazing sun. She watches him bring the room into focus, taking it in piecemeal. The wallpaper, peeling off in strips, like old skin. A faded and fraying sofa hunched by the wall, a folding card table covered with tools. A single lamp minus its shade, naked bulb staring. She can see his eyes swiveling to the plywood nailed over the window frames, the blurry bull's-eyes on the ceiling where the rain has seeped in. To herself, shaggy and overgrown, in ragged T-shirt and worn-out jeans. Hiding like a hermit in the murky darkness. It is not where he expected her to be. She is not who he expected, either.

You must be tired, she says. I've got a room ready for you.

She leads him upstairs, the orange-red stair runner muffling their steps. All the way up, square blotches in the wallpaper mark the places where pictures once hung.

Whose house is this?

No one's, anymore. Careful. Watch your step. The banister's broken here.

At the landing, she opens the door at the top of the stairs. A large room that clearly belonged to a small child, once upon a time: when she flips the light switch, the ceiling lamp features a clown's face, a red-nosed screw holding the glass dome in place. In the corner a crib still stands, one side lowered, the mattress bare. She's swept the room clean, but this cannot make it inviting. Part of the ceiling plaster has crumbled, exposing the slender wooden slats beneath, like bones. The windows are sheathed in black.

Garbage bags, she explains. To hide the light. We have to be careful—the neighbors think it's abandoned.

Bird sets his bookbag on the floor, touches one hand to the plastic stretched over the window frame. She's done the same herself many times, feeling the faint tremble as a car thrums by on the street below.

I set this up for you, she says. Just in case you made it. She smooths the sleeping bag laid out on the window seat, fluffs the small throw pillow at its head. I'm sorry I don't have a proper bed. More comfortable than the floor, at least.

Bird shrugs one shoulder and half turns away. From outside, the thin wail of a siren worms its way through the plastic sheeting, growing louder, then fading again. If everything was different, she thinks, if she'd had all those years with him as she should have, perhaps this language would be less foreign. The language of those beginning to shed their childhood: all gestures and subtext, all reserve and disdain. Maybe she would have learned to understand it. She wonders if Ethan does.

Are you hungry? she asks, and though she's quite sure it's a lie, he shakes his head no. Just rest then, she says. We'll talk later.

She pauses, then turns back.

Bird. I'm so glad you're here.

As a toddler, he'd cried when other people cried. Certain songs on the stereo filled him with pins-and-needles tingling and moving even a finger would increase the agony. How unbearable, that Jackie Paper came no more. How tragic, that she was leaving home after living alone for so many years. How terrifying, to be the only living boy in New York. The music peeled his skin away, note by note, and the naked muscles throbbed and stung. Stop, mama, he would sob, make it *stop*, and Margaret, in horror, ran to the stereo and paused the music and folded him in her arms.

It stunned her, how hungry and wondrous he was at it all. He was a quiet child, watching intently, soaking everything in—the good and the bad, the joy and the pain. The pink nipples of the cherry tree swelling into blossoms. The dead sparrow folded up small on the sidewalk. The exuberant rush of loose balloons soaring upward into a wide blue sky. How porous the boundary was between him and the world, as if everything flowed through him like water through a net. She'd worried about him, moving through a rough world as a tender bare heart, beating out in the open where anything could cause a bruise.

This boy standing in front of her looks like Bird and sounds like Bird. She'd know him anywhere, that face. But there's something between them now, through which she can't quite see or hear him clearly, something opaque and hard, a layer of tortoiseshell. As if he's standing, always, just beyond arm's length. Something has scarred over in him. Oh Bird, she thinks.

Upstairs, Bird peeks out into the hallway. No light, only a faint gibbous glow on the wall from the single lamp downstairs. He tiptoes past dark room after dark room. In the bathroom, the toilet and sink are green-streaked and grimy; moss stretches from the rusty bathtub in a lush carpet. Only one other room seems to be occupied. A bare mattress lies in one corner, an old table lamp, shadeless, squats beside it on the floor. His mother's room. The sharp scent of sweat in the air. His mother, who'd planted flowers in the sunshine and whispered stories into his ears at night, has somehow become this strange woman lurking in the shadows. He wishes his father were here, to explain this. To help him understand. To decide what to do.

Back on the landing, the light from downstairs seems dingy, like something reused, and he has to guide himself by his fingertips all the way down the hall and back to his own lonely room.

When Bird wakes, Margaret is sitting on the floor by his bedside. Feet curled under her on the worn carpet, her gaze resting softly on his face. As if she's been studying him in his sleep, patiently waiting for him to wake. Which she has.

What time is it, he croaks. Under the darkened windows it's impossible to tell if it's night or daylight.

Just past midnight, she says.

She's brought him a mug of instant coffee. Which he doesn't like, she can see it in his face, of course he doesn't like it, what kind of mother brought her child coffee, she should have brought something else, though coffee is all she has. She is out of practice at this, at everything. But the mug is warm and cozy in the chill of the room, and he struggles to a seat, sips it. She sips hers, too. Bitter, but comforting. Like strong medicine.

The gas is shut off, she says. So no heat, no real cooking. Just a hot plate. But the water and power are still on. Which is all I need.

What is this place? he asks, but she doesn't answer. There are other things she needs to explain first. Start at the beginning, she reminds herself. This is why you called him here.

Bird, she says, I want to show you something.

She takes him up another flight of stairs, to the third floor, where all the rooms are empty. Through their half-open doors, the bare hardwood looks like deep water: dark receding into darker. She'd gone into them once, when she first arrived. The dust had piled up in drifts, like snow. Old furniture, missing feet and legs, half-kneeling on the floor; an old record player with the record still on it, too scratched to play. Everywhere there were signs of the outside, creeping in, taking over. In the bathroom, one long arm of ivy had twined its way through a broken pane and was groping for the latch; in a bedroom she'd found a forest of mushrooms sprouting from the rain-soaked carpet beneath a crack in the wall.

Now, at the top of the steps, she reaches up into the shadows, feeling for the cord, and when she finds it and pulls, a trapdoor swings down, a ladder unfolds. Her instinct is to take his hand, to guide him, but she fights it. As she knows he would, too.

This way, she says, climbing up into the thick clouded gloom. Without waiting for him.

Behind her, she hears Bird setting a first hesitant foot on the bottom rung. She forces herself to keep on going, to keep walking away. To trust that he will follow. At the far end of the house, she stops and turns back to look at him for the first time. Her eyes are used to the dark, but his are not, and he follows more by sound than by sight, feeling his way with his hands, guiding himself by the beams that run underfoot like railroad tracks. It is dusty and cold, and small slivers of moonlight pierce their way through chinks in the siding, forming bars of light he ducks his head to avoid as he picks his way along the length of the attic. When he reaches her, she sets her shoulder against the hatch on the ceiling.

Here we are, she says, as the latch gives way with a shriek. Watch your step.

They step onto the flat roof into a pool of night. It is chilly, and the wind scrapes across the top of the city like a knife leveling flour from a cup, but as they emerge Margaret feels herself going soft at the corners. At the beauty of it all.

Around them, the city spreads out like a dropped cloth, all peaks and ridges and hidden folds. Even at this quiet hour, here and there bright ribbons of cars weave along the streets; in the distance a forest of steel trees stretches upward, grasping at the moon. She can just make out the starry glitter of far-off windows, reflecting shattered moonlight in their darkened panes.

The roof is bare; all there is up here is the city, and the sky, and them. No railing, just the sharp clean edge giving way to the ground below. Beside her, she hears Bird catch his breath, and for a moment she sees him: her son, as she remembers him. Curious, alert. Eyes aglow. Marveling at how there is so much life, out there.

I didn't—he begins, and then stops. Slowly he takes a step out onto the flat plain of the roof, then another. Cautiously, as if on rocky terrain. I didn't know the city was that big, he says. One hand reaches out, as if a fingertip might brush the tip of a downtown skyscraper.

It's something, Margaret agrees. I only come up at night. Just in case anyone's watching. It's amazing, isn't it, she continues, turning toward the horizon. So much bigger than I imagined, before I got here. The first time I came to the city when I was young, I walked everywhere I could. Just trying to take it all in.

Bird's head swivels the merest bit in her direction, and she knows she has caught his interest. She pretends not to notice.

Of course, she says, I got to see a lot of it from my job. I learned my way around pretty well.

She pauses, waiting. Wondering if Ethan has told him anything. If Bird knows anything at all. But after a moment, Bird bites.

What job, he says, without turning. As if it doesn't matter to him at all.

A messenger. I carried letters, and things. Back during the Crisis. I rode a bicycle, she adds, as if as an afterthought.

Bird says nothing, but for a moment the scrim between them

effaces. She has never told him anything about her time in New York, anything about her life before him; first he was too young, and then she was gone. As far as he knows, her life before him is a clean blank slate. She watches him adjust to it, this new piece of information. This new image of his mother: whizzing through the city, bearing things.

What kind of things, he says.

Deliveries, mostly. Sometimes papers that needed signing. So many things were closing then, there weren't as many trucks. We bikers were cheaper and faster and gas was so expensive, too.

She watches his face. Food, sometimes, she goes on. And medicine, when people got sick and couldn't go out. We'd pick it up at the pharmacy, leave it on their step.

We? Bird says.

There were a lot of us. All trying to scrape by.

She considers whether to say more. Wait, she decides.

Is that how you met my father?

Margaret shakes her head.

He was in a different world. A student. It was an accident that we even met at all.

She pauses.

How is he, she asks. Unsure how to ask what she really wants to know: who is he now, has he changed in all these years apart, after everything that's happened. He must be worried sick about Bird, she thinks, with a pang of regret. She wishes she could call him, to assure him that Bird is all right. But it's too dangerous; nothing's changed. Not yet. He will have to trust—the way she's trusted him, all this time, to keep their child safe.

Bird shrugs, a single shoulder rising and slumping again. So noncommittal, even his shoulders don't agree.

He's fine, he says. I guess.

She waits, holding her breath, but he says nothing more. All this time Bird's gaze hasn't left the city below, the dense milling swarm of it. One hand still rests half raised, as if he's propping himself up on air, or trying to grasp the edge of the skyline. She waits, lets the moment breathe and drift, trusting it to find its own way to land.

Why did you leave, he says at last.

It is easier to ask these things up here, somehow, where everything except them is small and far away.

She spreads her arms wide, as if to dive, tips her head back, closes her eyes. The moonlight catches in her hair, frosting it with silvery glints. For a moment, frozen there, she looks like the figurehead of a ship, sailing boldly forward into strange new waters. Then her hands drop to her sides, and she turns back again.

I'll tell you, she says. I'll tell you everything. If you promise to listen.

S he begins the story while she works: hunched over the folding table, coils of wire and long lengths of pipe laid out before her. Carefully, she selects a pipe and twists a cutter around it, grinding off segments the length of her thumb, smoothing the edges with a file. Around her a halo of silver dust emerges. Bird sits at the edge of the carpet, waiting. Watching. Outside, beyond the blacked-out windows, morning light slowly tints the grayscale world.

Let me tell you first, his mother says, how I came to the city.

Her parents' aspirations carried them across the sea, so for her, an aspirational name: Margaret. A prime minister, a princess, a saint. A name with a pedigree as long as time, a solid trunk growing from rugged roots: in French, la marguerite, the daisy; in Latin, margarita, the pearl. Both of her parents were good Catholics, back in Kowloon, educated by priests and nuns, brought up on Communion wafers and confession and daily Mass. Saint

Margaret, defeater of dragons, often depicted half in, half out of a dragon's mouth.

A thing she wouldn't learn until later: the bomb in their mailbox two months before she was born. Just enough to blow the aluminum door off its hinges and warp it from within, as if a tiny enraged creature had tried to punch its way out. A new mailbox, a new home, her father the new engineer at the factory in their little Rust Belt town. Minimal explosive power, the police said. Just a prank, who could say why. Afterward, Margaret's father dug out the kinked metal pole, hair plastered to his forehead with sweat, Margaret's mother watching from the threshold with one hand resting on her belly, Margaret still growing inside. From their windows, their new neighbors watched, too, silently, and then, as the pole came free and the dented mailbox tipped to the ground with a clang, went back inside.

PACT was decades away, but her parents felt it already: the eyes of the neighborhood scrutinizing their every move. Blending in, they decided, was their best option. So after she was born, they dressed her in pink corduroy overalls and Mary Janes, tied ribbons in her pigtailed hair. When she got older, they would buy her the clothes off the headless mannequin at the department store; anything it wore, she wore. Surreptitiously, they studied the neighborhood children and bought Margaret what they saw: Barbies, a Dream House, a Cabbage Patch Kid named Susanna Marigold. A pink bike with white-streamered handles; a toy oven that baked brownies by the light of a bulb. Suburban camouflage from the Sears catalog. Her father's saying: *The stick hits the bird that holds its head the highest.* Her mother's: *The nail that sticks up gets hammered down.* She never, in her memory, heard her parents say a word in Cantonese. Only later would she realize what she'd missed.

On Fridays they ordered pizza and played board games; on Sundays they went to church, the only black-haired heads at Mass. Her father began to watch football and drink beer with the neighborhood men. Her mother bought a set of CorningWare and learned to make casseroles. Margaret herself was bookish and loved poetry. Like her parents, she strove for *unremarkable*, anchoring herself firmly in the hill of the bell curve. To be noticed was to invite predation; better to blend seamlessly into the foliage. She earned average grades, met expectations but seldom exceeded them, caused no trouble and set no examples. Graduation, a scholarship to school in New York: *the city*, her mother always called it. As if there were only one. It was an intangible promise that lured her: that in the city, there was more than one way to be. Then the grit of the city scoured away the enamel of her to reveal something molten and pulsing inside.

In those first days, she dressed like her idea of a New Yorker: black jeans, high heels, silky blouse. Glamour, sophistication. Mystery. Then, two days after arriving, she got off the N and a bearded figure in an emerald ball gown glided past, gathered their skirts, and squeezed into the seat she'd just left. Not a head turned, and as the doors closed, they extracted a copy of *The New Yorker* from the folds of their dress and began to read, and then the train swept them away and out of sight. In the days to come she would see much more. A man weaving his bike through stalled traffic, making loud siren noises with his mouth. *Baa-DOO baa-DOO baa-DOO.* An elderly woman with a cane thumping her way down Broadway, singing at the top of her lungs in time with her steps: *Our God is an awesome God / He reigns from heaven above.* A man pressing a woman against the side of a stoop, her knees knotted around his waist, the whole narrow passage thrumming with their cries, funneling them like a speaker to the street beyond. No one paused or smirked or looked around; everyone hurried away, intent upon their own business, their own lives. It began to rain, sheets of water blanketing the city, and Margaret stepped into a nearby bookstore, rattailed and drenched, and no one batted an eye. Here no one noticed you, she realized. Which meant you could do anything, be anything. In the bathroom she peeled the sodden socks from her feet and dried them under the hand dryer and no one said a word. When they were dry, she put them back on and felt the warmth curl between each toe. She'd never felt so free.

She cut her hair, then added a purple streak. Seeing how far she could take it before a head turned, before anyone gave her a second glance. She changed her clothes, piece by piece: higher heels, shorter skirts, jeans ripped to more hole than denim. She pierced things. No one ever gave her a second glance. Not like home, where people always gave her a second glance, and sometimes a third. Where she had to be on best behavior, always, to give no one a reason to notice her: a bird keeping her head down, a nail nestling into soft, safe wood. Staying unnoticed was how you survived.

Things were already starting to fray, even then. Cut hours, lower wages. Prices beginning to climb. But it wasn't everywhere yet: you still saw people buying new clothes, eating in restaurants. At night certain parts of town still shimmered and hummed with the collected energy of people who gathered just to be young and alive in the dark. It was still possible to enjoy things. To waste time. It was still possible to sit on a park bench or out on the stoop and watch other people go by, smiling and laughing, and smile back.

Margaret plunged herself into the city. She got a job waitressing. She skipped class and walked around and around the city, exploring its corners and crannies, devouring it. She made friends. In Chinatown you could still hear people speaking Cantonese then, and she bought Chinese newspapers and a dictionary, pored over the characters at night, learning their parts and their sounds the way she might learn a lover's body. For the first time, she realized that her old life had chafed like a too-tight coat. She learned to drink, and to flirt. She learned to give pleasure, and to take it. She was writing by then, lines scribbled on scraps of paper, on grocery receipts, on the white backs of minty gum wrappers, each word a chip of diamond, flint edged and biting. They felt like the work of a different person, someone she hadn't known she was carrying within her. The Crisis was coming, would be there soon, but there were still magazines and time for poetry and people to read it, and editors liked her tempestuous rhythm, the marvelous wild suppleness of her lines. Images that sank their teeth into your heart and refused to shake free. They never paid, but it didn't matter. At night she and her friends would pool their handfuls of bills and change for bottles of wine, drinking it from plastic cups in someone's dorm room, a ring of them sitting with mouths stained red.

In those days, the city was at fever pitch, as if everyone could feel the storm coming, the air electric, crackling with potential. Her parents thought it demented, but to her it seemed the sanest and most logical course: if the world was on fire, you might as well burn bright. Late nights that turned into early mornings; just enough money to buy coffee wherever she happened to end up. Walking home in the dawn hours to save cab fare, watching the city shift from gray to gold as the sun rose. She went to parties, danced, kissed strangers just to see what would happen. Often they'd end up in someone's bed—hers, theirs, someone else's. Beautiful men. Beautiful women. The world, at that time, was full of them, all of them furiously incandescent like dying stars.

Later, when she thought of that time she would picture a nightclub, the air thick and black and steaming around her. Bodies jostling, slick with sweat. Flecks of light circling the room, fragments of illumination: an eye, a lip, a hand, a breast. The feeling of dissolving into a crowd, a shapeless sweaty pulsating thing, all of them moving separately to the same beat, bound together by the moment. Above their heads: bright lights that would flick on when the night was done, if they hadn't fled yet. Below their dancing feet: the floor grown sticky with spilled liquor. There was no curfew yet.

It started slowly at first, the way most things did. She'd been a junior. Shops began to shutter, windows soaped over from within. Here and there at first, like cavities in teeth, and suddenly whole blocks were empty, all over the country. The rents too high, the customers too few. More panhandlers, rattling coins in paper cups plucked from trash cans, more signs markered on scraps of cardboard. FAMILY OF 5. LOST MY JOB. ANYTHING HELPS. Everything cost more and everyone had less to spend. Clothing stores marked down their sweaters—ten percent off, twenty, forty-five, and still they dangled on the racks. No one even tried them on. No one had the money, or the time, anymore. One in ten unemployed, the statistics ran. Then: one in five. People began to lose their cars, then their homes. People began to lose their patience.

The restaurant where Margaret worked shut down: forty-five years in business, but no one came in anymore except the men who ordered coffee and lingered in the corner booths, sipping it long after it grew cold. Her boss wept as he pulled the grate across the door; he'd played behind the counter as a boy. When she asked other restaurants if they were hiring, some of them laughed. Some of them simply shook their heads. One manager told her, gently, to go home. It's going to get worse, he said, before it gets better. *If* it gets better. He had a daughter about her age who had just lost her job, too.

They would never fully agree, the economists, on what had caused it: some would say it was just an unfortunate cycle, that these things happened periodically—like cicadas, or plagues. Some would blame speculation, or inflation, or a lack of consumer confidence—though what might have caused *those* would never be clear. In time, many would dredge up old lists of rivalries, searching for someone to blame; they would settle, in a few years, on China, that perilous, perpetual yellow menace. Seeing its sabotage behind every stumble and fracture of the Crisis. But at first all they agreed on was this: it was the worst crisis since the 1980s, then since the Depression, and then they stopped making comparisons.

Those who'd been at the top locked their doors, hunkered down to wait it out. As stores closed, they ordered from afar, paying the rising prices. Those who'd been *comfortable* tightened their belts, began cutting coupons, cutting back, cutting down on everything they could—no more travel, no more leisure, only less, less, less. Those who'd just barely stretched a paycheck from one Friday to the next stumbled down a steep staircase of losses: first their jobs, then their leases, then their pride. All across the country, people couldn't make rent; by then evictions were happening daily. The pictures were everywhere: furniture dumped unceremoniously on the sidewalk, families huddling curbside on their couches, passersby gawking as the landlords changed the locks. Foreclosures rippled block to block until swaths of neighborhoods were deserted.

A *correction*, the news called it at first, as if all that time when people had mostly gotten by, had mostly been fed and housed, had been a mistake; as if things were getting better, instead of the opposite. In Houston, the lines at food banks stretched for blocks; in Sacramento, you'd wait for hours and come away with a can of beans, a few boxes of crackers. In Boston, people dozed in the pews of churches, waiting out the night, and in the morning there were more outside.

Soon there were protests in the streets. Strikes. Marches that were peaceful. Marches with guns. Windows smashed, things seized or set aflame: anger and need made manifest and tangible. Police in full battle gear. All across the country, the same story repeating, just at different scales. In New York, Margaret watched the city begin to empty around her. The ones with houses and families elsewhere sought shelter with them, sharing expenses, making do. The ones who didn't disappeared in other ways: hiding, or holed up, or dead. You could hear birdsong, suddenly, between the pillars of buildings. The *economic crisis*, the newspapers began to call it, and then, as it became more than economic, as people began to lose their confidence, their sense of purpose, the willingness to wake up in the morning, their ability to keep trying, their optimism that something could be different, their memory that anything had ever been differ-ent, their hope that anything would ever improve—other phrases took hold. *Our ongoing national crisis*, the headlines kept saying, and soon, economizing even in words: the Crisis. The capital *C* the only extravagance still allowed.

At the college, classes were postponed, then cancelled. The dorm grew quieter and quieter as parents called children back to the safety of their homes. From Margaret's parents, somber updates: furloughs at the factory, shortages at the stores. I'm okay, Margaret told her parents, I'm staying, everything's fine, don't worry about me. Be careful. I love you. Then, after hanging up the phone, she scoured the hallways, gleaning what she could from bags of trash abandoned on the way out. Clothing and too-big shoes, which she took anyway. Blankets and books, half-eaten packages of cookies. Most of the rooms were shut, their message boards wiped bare, except for one, a scrawl of black: SEE YOU ON THE OTHER SIDE. She touched her finger to the letters. Permanent.

Three weeks later, she ran into another person in the halls for the first time: Domi. They'd had a class together, back when there still were classes: Marxism and 20th-Century Literature. Chic and worldly Domi, perfect streaks of eyeliner winging their way toward the sky. Rhymes with *show me*, she'd said, one brow arched. Now, without makeup, her eyes looked bigger, younger. More rabbit than hawk.

Didn't think anyone else was crazy enough to still be here, Domi said. Come on. Time to go.

Domi had an ex who had a girlfriend who had a sister with a two-bed in Dumbo. Six of them squeezed into it now: the sister and her boyfriend in one room, the ex and his new girl in another, Domi on the couch and Margaret in a sleeping bag on the living room floor. The room so small that, when they held out their arms in the dark, their fingers intertwined.

In the darkened brownstone, she tells Bird these things as she unwinds wire from the spool, strips the red plastic away to reveal gleaming copper marrow. There is a deftness to her work, a precision, like watching a clockmaker set each gear into place. Bird sits, knees hugged to chest, mesmerized: by her story, by her hands. Outside the blackened windows, it is midmorning, the Crisis is long over, the city pulses and churns, but inside it is eerily quiet in the glow of the single lamp. The two of them together in the soundless bubble, listening.

The sister with the apartment still had a job, one of the few that did. She worked for the mayor, taking calls, trying to match people with the services they needed. What people needed was rent, meals, medicine. Reassurance and calm. What she had to offer was sympathy, a promise to pass their concerns along.

Another number they could try. Sometimes broken bricks came through the office windows; other days, bullets. Soon the desks huddled at the centers of the rooms. Her boyfriend was a security guard in an empty skyscraper in Midtown, once so busy there were three banks of elevators: one for the lower half, one for the upper, one an express straight to the top. Now everyone had been sent home—furloughed or fired outright—and he circled the lobby beneath eighty-one floors of abandoned rooms. There were computers up there, ergonomic desk chairs, couches of tobacco-hued leather. Those who had sat in them no longer had access to the building, and those who owned them were in their houses on Long Island, in Connecticut, in Key West, waiting for the Crisis to abate. One day, when no one had any money and they were all hungry, the boyfriend snuck upstairs, filched a laptop, sold it, and brought home nine overstuffed plastic bags of groceries so heavy they cut rings into his hands. They'd eaten for two weeks off that.

Domi's ex and his new girlfriend took odd jobs where they could: boarding up the windows of businesses gone bust, loading crates onto trucks for those leaving the city. He was a stocky, burly guy, bald by choice; his new girl was sandy haired and wiry and quick, both of them alert to opportunities. A warehouse in Queens closed down and they'd celebrated: nearly a month of pay loading pallet after pallet onto a cargo ship, until it sailed away—back to Taiwan or possibly Korea, none of them knew where, just *away*—and the warehouse stood empty and echoing, shafts of sunlight slicing down through dusty air. When they couldn't find work they scavenged, combing the streets, collecting cans to sell for scrap, anything useful they could repurpose.

They visited the rich neighborhoods where the garbage held treasures, the owners watching them from behind double-paned windows above as if they were crows picking carrion. Once they'd spotted a man in Park Slope being carted out on a stretcher, draped with a white sheet. His brownstone, for the moment, left unguarded. After dark, they'd come back and crept in. The furniture and clothes were all gone already, but they'd stripped yards of copper pipe and wires from the walls, and the girlfriend found a watch—a small silver bangle of a thing, still ticking, engraved *To A from C*—which she'd buckled onto her wrist before they vanished into the night with their haul. None of them felt guilt, at least not then. Things could sit unused and wasted or they could be turned into heat, a full belly, a night spent tipsy and giddy as they all waited for either the Crisis or the world to end. An easy choice to make.

As for Domi and Margaret: they became messengers. Cycling through the city, down half-empty streets, in the unnerving quiet of a half-deserted Manhattan. It was cheaper than mailing things, and the post office was struggling—fewer funds, carriers laid off, gas exorbitant, packages stolen right off the truck—and for three dollars a biker would get it there in an hour. Margaret went first: one morning she'd spotted a bike propped against a stoop, and when it was still there that evening, unchained, she took it without regret. A fleet of messengers crisscrossed the city, and she recognized their faces, learned their names as their paths overlapped. A few weeks later, when they found another bike, Domi joined them, too.

At night, parts of town turned rough. Men out of work sat in the park, burning their last few dollars on a fifth of whiskey, and by evening they grew resentful and belligerent. Women learned the hard way to avoid them. Since childhood, Margaret had mastered how to check over her shoulder, to gauge risk from a gesture, to fight if she could not flee. Domi, who'd grown up in Westport with her father—summer house, riding lessons, in-ground pool—was less prepared. Sometimes she cried out in her sleep, hands flying to shield her face, as if someone were trying to gouge out her eyes. Margaret climbed up beside her, held her tight, stroked her hair, and Domi stilled and quieted. In the mornings, the few stores stubbornly clinging to life might find their windows smashed, shelves stripped bare, alarm bell ringing ferociously, though no one had answered the call. Some people tried not to go out at all, and soon Margaret was running errands and delivering messages, too. Five dollars a run, then ten, though for those in need, she would do it for one. Medicine from the drugstore, a bag of groceries. Tampons, batteries. Candles. Liquor. All the things people needed to survive another day. She folded the dollar bills they gave her and tucked them into the cups of her bra; at the end of the night, back in the apartment, she counted them, soft as damp felt with her sweat, and smoothed them out again. By then she wasn't thinking about poetry at all.

You got used to it, after a while: all the new rules the city and the governor imposed, trying to keep order—when you could go out, when you had to stay in, how many people could gather at one time: few, then fewer. Sometimes waves of sickness rippled over the city, then the state: not enough people at work to pay hospital bills, not enough doctors or medicine anyway, just referrals for Advil from the drugstore on the corner, or something stiffer from the liquor store next door. Lines everywhere, everything in short supply except anger, and fear, and grief. Tents clustered like toadstools at the feet of overpasses and bridges. Based on the news, it was the same everywhere. You got used to waiting, to the men who squatted on sidewalks, holding signs scrawled on cardboard: ANYTHING HELPS. You learned to keep watch on them without meeting their eyes, to skirt them at a distance. Your ears pricked for the sounds of shouting, the high jangle of breaking glass; even before you recognized it, your feet would already be turning you down another street, steering you safely around. You got used to sandwiches of whatever you had—ketchup, mayonnaise, salt, whatever made bread palatable enough to choke down—to rebrewing coffee grounds, once, twice, sometimes for a whole week if you needed; even mostly water, it was something to keep you warm. You got used to not speaking to people on the street, to edging past them, both of you on your way to somewhere else, and to the sirens that flared and then quieted like an infant's stifled cry. After a while you stopped wondering where they were headed, stopped thinking about whose need they were going off to serve. Somewhere out there, you knew, wealthy people were barricaded in their fortresses, fed and warm, if not happy, but soon you stopped thinking of them. You stopped thinking about other people at all. You got used to that, too, eventually, just as you got used to people disappearing: gone back home, gone elsewhere hoping for better, sometimes simply gone.

What you couldn't get used to—what she never got used to—was the quiet. In Times Square the lights changed red to green and back again and sometimes not a car went by. Overhead the gulls screamed and dove toward the empty harbor. When she spoke to her parents it was brief, a few minutes at a time; service was spotty and minutes were expensive and all they needed to know, really, was that the other was still alive. Sometimes she would ride through Central Park and see not a single person, not on the footpaths, not on the lake, no sign of a single other human except the tents that dotted the Sheep Meadow, springing up overnight, disappearing just as quickly when word of police sweeps came. In the silence between things there was too much time to dwell and no matter how fast she pedaled, she couldn't leave her thoughts behind.

In the honeyed glow of the lamplight her hands tremble.

The Crisis. The Crisis. Bird has grown up hearing about it: We must never forget the turmoil of the Crisis, everyone has said, his whole life; we must never again go back to that. But it is impossible to explain what it felt like.

Evictions and protests daily, then nightly, people clamoring for assistance, for any kind of aid. The police fired rubber bullets and sprayed tear gas; cars plowed into the crowds. Each night sirens whirred to life and wailed away across the city; the only question was which way. Fires began to spring up all over the country—Kansas City one night, Milwaukee and New Orleans the next—frantic signal fires from those deserted and desperate. In Chicago, tanks rolled past department stores on Michigan Avenue, protecting their glossy wares. No one agreed on who to blame—not yet—and with no focus, outrage and panic and fear swelled over everything, hot and thick, rasping your lungs. It was there in the silent darkened streets after curfew, in the slate-gray shadows of the buildings and the echoing footsteps of your shoes on the deserted sidewalk. It flashed sharp and bright in the lights of the police cars as they went by, always on their way to somewhere else more urgent, which was everywhere.

How to explain this to someone who has never seen it? How to explain fear to someone who has never been afraid?

Imagine, Margaret wants to tell him. Imagine if everything you think is solid turns out to be smoke. Imagine that all the rules no longer apply.

I'm hungry, Bird ventures, and Margaret returns with a jolt, glances at her watch. It's past noon, and he's had no breakfast, either. She curses herself mentally. It's been so long since she's taken care of anyone.

She sets down the wire cutters and wipes her palms on the thighs of her jeans.

I know I've got something, she says, rummaging in a plastic bag beside the sofa. After a moment, she emerges with a single granola bar.

I get caught up in working, she says, almost embarrassed. I forget to keep food around. Here, you take it.

Bird peels the foil from the bar, then hesitates. It's starting to make sense to him: his mother's whittled features, the dark rings beneath her eyes. Whatever it is she's doing, it is consuming her. She is barely eating, maybe barely sleeping, too. All day, all night, she is working—or whatever this is.

Eat, his mother says gently. Get some food into you. I'll get more tonight.

From under the table she pulls another plastic bag: inside, bottle caps, the kind you'd unscrew from a two-liter bottle. Red, white, orange, sickly highlighter green—sticky, still smelling faintly of cola and caffeine and acid fizz. She sets a handful on the table, picks one up, inspects it. Tallies them two by two. For weeks she has been gathering them, these small bright rounds plucked from the sidewalks and the dark mouths of garbage cans.

But what are you doing, Bird says, between mouthfuls of granola, what are they *for*?

Margaret takes one cap and sweeps the rest to the side, plucks a transistor from the pile: red and yellow striped, like a sprinkle from a child's birthday cake. She touches the soldering iron to one of its spindly wire legs and the hot biting scent of rosin fills the air.

Let me tell you, she says instead, about meeting your father.

She'd been a wild thing, when they met.

Two years into the Crisis: *Fuck everything* was her motto by then. People came and went, sometimes on purpose, sometimes without warning, and you'd never know where they'd gone, if it was part of their plan or an accident, or worse. Sometimes on her deliveries, people spat in her face, told her this was China's fault, accused her of wringing America dry; she'd begun wearing a bandanna, pulled high to the bridge of her nose. Fuck this, fuck everything, she and Domi agreed, by which they meant: don't get attached to anything, or anyone. Just survive. They said it to each other almost fondly, like a greeting, or a good-night kiss. Fuck everything, Domi would murmur as they fell asleep in the living room, and Margaret, rolled in a blanket on the floor, would squeeze her hand and whisper it back, the day's sweat drying on their skin to a fine crystal grit.

And then came Ethan. Domi's birthday: still celebrated, celebrated with vengeance in the face of it all. Liquor enough to make a party; the apartment full of people, gathering limits be damned; the air hot and sticky, like someone's breath. Domi was drunk already and didn't notice him, but Margaret felt a tingle zigzag between her shoulder blades. A friend of a friend of a friend, out of place in a charcoal-gray suit. A suit! She felt an irresistible urge to dishevel him. The room was dizzy and humid and loud and she drifted away from Domi and crossed the room and put her hand to his throat and caught the knot of his tie in her fist.

They ended up outside, on the fire escape that was little more than a ledge, so small that when they both squeezed onto it they were close enough to kiss. Between their feet: Domi's broken flowerpot, full of cigarette butts and ash. Ethan, he said. Just finished at Columbia when the Crisis put everything on hold. All night, people came and went in the room behind them, laughing, drinking, forgetting—for the moment—everything else. Neither of them noticed. The night air gathered close like a blanket drawn over their heads. They talked and talked until they found themselves squinting into the peach-colored sunrise spiking its way between the buildings. Inside, the party had burned down like a banked fire. A handful of people curled up on the rug and the sofa, a tangle of lonely puppies. Domi had gone off to bed, not alone.

I should go, Ethan said, and Margaret took his jacket from her shoulders, where he'd placed it in the late-night chill, and handed it back. It was the only time they'd touched all night.

She wanted to kiss him. No: she wanted to bite him, hard enough to draw blood.

It was nice meeting you, she said, and went inside.

The next evening, after curfew, she walked across the bridge and uptown, ducking into the shadows when the few cars still out flashed by. She left her bike in the apartment: outside, even locked-up bikes would be stripped of parts by morning, and Ethan, he'd said, lived on the fourth floor. Now and then she passed someone else and they exchanged a brief glance before moving on, each of them on their own mysterious errands. A hundred and twenty blocks uptown to Ethan's building, where his window glowed like a wide-awake eye. She climbed the fire escape and set her fingers in the half-open window, and at the noise he looked up, startled, put his book down. Lifted the sash and let her in.

In the morning, a ring of her tooth marks blossomed on his bare shoulder.

Domi didn't like it.

You've changed, she said, all you think about now is *him*. She said it like that—*him*—a fragment of pit she needed to spit out.

Your fancy boyfriend, she said. With his fancy apartment. So much *nicer* than here.

The truth was that it was a studio, three flights up, just one big room with a futon for both couch and bed and an old claw-foot bathtub in the kitchenette—but it was safe and warm. Ethan's family wasn't particularly fancy or rich—his mother was a nursing-home aide, his father an engineer—but they did have connections: his landlord was an old friend of his mother's from high school and had rented to him at a steep discount; Ethan could afford to wait out the Crisis a long time. The truth was that Domi could have been in her own apartment, too—a much nicer one—if she'd chosen: her father's electronics company made the innards of half the cell phones and computers in the country; he owned two yachts, a small private plane, houses in London and L.A. and the south of France. One on Park Avenue, too, where Domi had grown up: she'd pointed it out to Margaret one afternoon, and they spat on the sidewalk and fled before her father's driver could chase them away. Her mother had died when she was eleven, and a month later her father married the Danish au pair and Domi swore that once she left home she'd never speak to him again, and she hadn't. In college, she'd ripped up his checks and mailed back the pieces.

So that's it, Domi said, you're just going to hide out with your rich boyfriend and ignore all this, while the rest of us scrounge?

Margaret's hands were chapped and raw; a week ago someone had grabbed at her coat, tearing it, hungry for more than she was offering, but she'd gotten away. She had mended the rip with yarn—red, the only color she'd had—and the stitches traced a jagged gash along her collarbone.

Fuck both of you, Domi said, but Margaret didn't answer. She was already on her way out the door.

He spoke half a dozen languages fluently, could get by in even more. Not bad for a white boy from Evanston, he'd joke. His parents had both loved traveling, had chosen a different country for each vacation; he'd been to four continents before he was ten years old. He was an only child like Margaret, and this was one of the things that drew them together: the feeling that they were the last twigs on the family tree, grafting themselves together for strength, to forge something new.

How about Cantonese, she'd asked, and he shook his head.

Only a little Mandarin. And not very good Mandarin at that.

And then: We could learn it together. The two of us.

He specialized in etymology: the meanings of things. As a boy he'd played Scrabble and done crosswords with his father; his mother had coached him for the spelling bee. For his birthdays and Christmas, he'd always asked for books. These days, with libraries and stores shuttering, he had nothing to read but the row of dictionaries lined up on the windowsill. The first morning, after they woke, she rose from his bed and crossed the room to look at them. Fat yellow ones for different languages: French, German, Spanish, Arabic, some she didn't even recognize. Dead languages: Latin, Sanskrit. A sprawling English one the size of a phone book, pages thin as Bible leaves. Slowly she'd traced her fingers along the spines and then turned back to him—both of them still undressed from the night before, their skin burnished to gold in the midmorning sun—in wonder. As if she suddenly recognized him as someone she already knew.

For Ethan, words carried secrets, the stories of how they came to be, all their past selves. He would find the mysterious ways they connected, tracing their family tree back to pinpoint the unlikeliest cousins. It was proof that despite the chaos around them, there was logic and order to the world; there was a system, and that system could be deciphered. She loved this about him, this unshakable belief that the world was a knowable place. That by studying its branches and byways, the tracks it had rutted in the dust, you could understand it. For her the magic was not what words had been, but what they were capable of: their ability to sketch, with one sweeping brushstroke, the contours of an experience, the form of a feeling. How they could make the ineffable effable, how they could hover a shape before you for an eyeblink, before it dissolved into the air. And this, in turn, was what he loved about her—her insatiable curiosity about the world, how for her it could never be fully unraveled, it held infinite mysteries and wonders and sometimes all you could do was stand agape, rubbing your eyes, trying to see properly.

Holed up in the apartment, they read, pulling one dictionary or another from the shelf and poring over it, stretched across the futon, one's head pillowed on the other's thigh. Reading passages aloud, dissecting meanings, each of them digging: she mining words like precious gems, arranging them around the outlines of the world; he excavating the layers fossilized within. All the traces of people trying to explain the world to themselves, trying to explain themselves to each other. *Testify* had its roots in the word for three: two sides and a third person, standing by, witnessing. *Author* originally meant *one who grows*: someone who nurtured an idea to fruition, harvesting poems, stories, books. *Poet*, if you traced back far enough, came from the word for *to pile up*—the earliest, most basic, form of making.

Margaret had laughed at this. That's me, she said, a piler-up of words.

Krei, she read, meant *to separate*. To judge. Like a sieve, Ethan said, separating the good from the bad. And thus, *krisis*: the moment at which a decision is made, for better or for worse.

With one finger she'd traced the delicate line of his sternum, circled the soft hollow at the base of his throat.

So a moment, she said, in which we decide who we are.

Outside there were sirens and shouting, and sometimes gunshots—or were they firecrackers? Waves of unrest rippled state to state like a wildfire, the whole country tinder-dry and eager to burn. In Atlanta, unemployed protesters had set the mayor's office ablaze; they'd called in the National Guard. Bombs kept going off at statehouses, in subway stations, on the lawns of governors' mansions. There were emergency meetings and votes and marches and rallies and nothing seemed to change. It can't go on, people kept saying, in the few spaces where they still dared meet: in the aisle of the grocery store, picking what they could from sparse shelves; in apartment building hallways as neighbors passed and over fences as people raked fallen leaves— any attempt to maintain order and neatness and normalcy in an era that was anything but. It can't go on, everyone said, but it kept going on.

Inside: Margaret and Ethan drank tea and ate crackers from the cupboard. After her shower, she put on one of his old shirts, washed her dress in the bathtub, hung it over the rod to dry. They closed the windows, then the curtains. They read. They made soup. They made love.

The way he handled her, like butter to be licked off a finger. In bed afterward, her cheek pressed to his back, she had never felt so calm. It felt good: a stretch after weeks spent coiled. One morning, she simply stayed.

She'd sent Domi a letter when she left: a faltering attempt to say goodbye after their last, worst fight, which had ended with Domi stripping off the jacket Margaret had handed down to her—*Take it, I'd rather be naked*—and storming out. It was a whole precious sheet, front and back, and afterward she couldn't remember which things she'd written and which she'd held back, trying to avoid Domi's wrath, trying to spare Domi pain. All she knew for sure was that Domi never called, never came by, and eventually Margaret stopped waiting.

In the quiet of Ethan's apartment, poems came to her like timid animals emerging after a storm.

She wrote about the hush of the city, how the pulse of it had changed with so many people gone. About love, and pleasure, and comfort. The smell of his neck in the early morning. The warm soft den of their bed at night. About finding stillness in the whirr that had been there for so long, a quiet place in the grinding, never-ending shriek of the Crisis. There was nowhere to publish these poems; only the big newspapers could afford to keep running, and that with government support; no one had time for poetry, for words, but she wrote phrases on scraps of paper, in the wide margins of Ethan's dictionaries, and someday they would form the first grasping branches of her own book.

No one saw it yet, but by then, almost imperceptibly, the story of the Crisis had begun to solidify. Soon enough it would harden, like silt from turbid water, settling in a thick band of mud.

We know who caused all this, people were beginning to say.

Ask yourself: who's doing well because we're on the decline? Fingers pointed firmly east. Look how China's GDP was rising, their standard of living climbing. Over there you got Chinese rice farmers with smartphones, one congressman ranted on the House floor. Over here in the U.S. of A. you got Americans using bucket toilets because their water's shut off for nonpayment. Tell me how that's not backwards. Just you tell me.

The Crisis was China's doing, some started to insist: all their manipulations, their tariffs and devaluations. Maybe they'd even had help, dismantling us from within. They want to take us down. They want to own our country.

Suspicious eyes swiveled to those with *foreign* faces, *foreign* names.

The question, people kept saying, is what are we going to do about it?

A frantic phone call from her mother, her voice nearly unintelligible: someone had pushed Margaret's father down the stairs at the park. He'd passed by them, the man who'd done it—they were heading down, he coming up—but they hadn't even glanced at him, and then he had turned and shoved her father with both hands, right between the shoulder blades. Margaret's father was sixty-four and had grown thinner, slighter, his body still compact but no longer as strong as it was, touches of arthritis gumming his hips and shoulders, and he had tumbled down, not even trying to catch himself, just down, like something already dead, the edge of the bottom step shattering his skull just above his ear, all of it so sudden neither of them even had time to scream. By the time Margaret's mother understood what had happened and turned to see who'd pushed him, the man was gone. Her father never regained consciousness, and two and a half hours after her mother's phone call, he was dead. The next morning, reeling from grief, her mother had a heart attack in the kitchen of their empty house—now too big for her alone—and this time Margaret, still trying to book a plane ticket, got the news from a police officer who'd managed to find her, as next of kin.

It was already happening then, though she didn't know it yet: already happening not just in the push down the stairs but in the people who watched the elderly man fall and shrank away from the man who'd pushed him, letting him pass—whether out of shock or fear or approval, none of them would ever dare to ask themselves. It was already happening, in the three people—a middle-aged woman, a young man in his twenties, a mother pushing a stroller—who passed by before the fourth called an ambulance, in the moment they saw the elderly woman crouching over her husband's tangled body, not screaming but murmuring to him unintelligibly, in a language neither of them had spoken in decades, even in private, pulled out of her now in a desperate hope that these words would be rooted deeply enough inside him that he might still hear.

I didn't realize he was hurt, the woman would say to her husband later, when they saw a report about the *unfortunate incident* on the news. I thought maybe he slipped and fell or something, I didn't want to embarrass anyone.

I heard her speaking Chinese or whatever, the young man would say, I just knew it wasn't English, and you know, what they're saying about China these days—it seemed better not to get involved.

The mother with the stroller would say nothing. She would never even see the news; her baby had a new molar coming in, and neither of them was sleeping through the night.

An isolated incident, the police report would say a few weeks later. No leads on the man who'd done the pushing. No evidence of why he might have done such a thing.

It was happening in other cities, in infinite variations: a kick or a punch on the sidewalk, a spray of spit in the face. It would happen everywhere, here and there at first, then all over, and eventually the news would stop reporting the stories, because they weren't new anymore.

We can fly home, Ethan said. Plane tickets were scarce and expensive, but they had some money saved. We can fly home and take care of whatever needs doing.

She didn't know how to explain there was nothing left to go home for anymore. That it wasn't home any longer. Instead she focused on a different word: we.

I want to leave New York, she told Ethan. Please, let's just leave. Anywhere else.

It didn't make sense, exactly; her parents had never been to New York; she'd left their house years ago; why this need to flee? But on another level it did make sense, this urgent need she felt to start over. To begin again somewhere in her new orphaned state, in a new place where she could cushion herself from the hard corners of the world. She wanted to be a bird keeping her head low. She wanted to not stick up. Ethan emailed his father, who reached out to his network: neighbors, colleagues, old roommates, friends of friends, all the dividends of goodwill he'd collected over the course of his gregarious life. Someone always knew someone; it was how things happened in his world, and neither of them thought much of it then, except to be grateful: as it turned out, Ethan's godfather's brother was golf buddies with a Harvard dean, who said the university was hiring, or would be soon. A few phone calls, a résumé slipped over the transom, and soon Ethan found himself newly employed as an adjunct in the linguistics department.

Within two weeks it was settled. They said goodbye to no one; they'd lost touch with everyone they'd known in the city by then. They took little with them because they had little to take: a suitcase of clothes between them, a stack of dictionaries. They would start again from scratch.

He can't imagine it. She can see it on his face: the puzzled look of someone trying to feel what they've never felt. To see what they've never seen. Her father had told her a parable once, blind men trying to describe an elephant, able to grasp it only in parts—a wall, a snake, a fan, a spear. A cautionary tale: how futile to believe you could ever share your experience with another. Details pour out of her now like sharp grains of sand, but it's still just a nightmare someone else had. Nothing can make him understand it but living through it, and she would give her life to make sure that never happens.

But how *did* it end, Bird asks, and she thinks: yes. So much more to tell.

She sank into her new life like it was a thick down comforter. In their little house in Cambridge, purchased with every penny they'd saved—the only upside to the Crisis, Ethan joked grimly, so many houses for sale, cheap—she painted the walls a warm orange-gold. The color she wanted their lives to be. They repaired the windows, sanded the floors, planted a garden: squash and tomatoes, lettuce of a shocking green. Inside the tall fence that hemmed in their postage-stamp of a yard, it was easy to imagine the rest of the world was like this, too. It was easy to forget the Crisis still raging outside, because with money and luck and connections they had simply stepped out of it, the way you'd step out of a blizzard, into warm dry shelter.

For everyone else, it came to an end with a snowy video clip from a security camera. The footage showed a grainy gray figure, shrouded in a hoodie, skulking outside an office building on a DC street. It all happens quickly: a dark-suited man emerges from the lobby, the hooded figure raises a gun. A flash of light. The dark-suited figure crumples. And then, just before fleeing off-screen, the man in the hoodie glances up at the security camera, as if just noticing it for the first time, his sunglassed face centered in the still frame.

The dark-suited figure, news reports explained as they ran the clip on a loop, was a senator from Texas, one of the most hawkish on what he called *the Chinese Crisis*. He'd made a name for himself with fiery calls for sanctions, polemics on the creeping menace of Chinese industry, thinly veiled insinuations about loyalty. But with the assassination attempt, public opinion made a swift U-turn: though the face of the man in the hoodie was too blurry to identify him, it was clear enough to show that he was East Asian—*based on the context*, analysts concluded, *likely Chinese.* Police departments were flooded with calls pointing fingers at neighbors, coworkers, the barista at the corner café. On social media, dozens of photos—pulled from online records, dating profiles, work portraits, vacation snapshots—were posted side by side with the still frame from the security tape by those sure they'd cracked the case. All in all, amateur sleuths would positively identify the culprit as thirty-four different men, aged nineteen to fifty-six and none resembling another, and because of this the shooter would never be apprehended, no one would ever be charged, and every Asian face would always remain a suspect—of the shooting, or of secretly sympathizing with it. From his hospital bed, bandaged shoulder prominently featured, the senator beat his drum. *You see? They'll stop at nothing, even cold-blooded murder. And who might be next?* Editorials weighed in: *not just an attack on the physical person of one senator, but an outright attack on our government, on our very way of life.*

A few tried to defend the shooter: *Look at the hate this man's been spewing; violence is never right, but can you blame him, really?* Chinese American organizations quickly condemned the unknown shooter as a lone wolf, an outlier, an aberration. He does not speak for us, their statements seemed to plead. But it was too late. Suspicion spread like ink on wet cloth, bleeding outward until everyone was tinged. It was the same dirty tint that would be used, for years to come, to justify the sidelong glances at anyone who might seem Chinese, to excuse the refusals of service and shouted slurs and spat-in faces, and later on, the baseball bats, the booted feet.

It was the catalyst needed to pass PACT. Everyone was tired of the Crisis; it had dragged on for nearly three years, long enough to ratchet everyone into submission. To most people, PACT seemed temperate, sensible even: patriotism, public vigilance. Why *wouldn't* you support it? Margaret watched a video of the president signing it, a group of lawmakers clustered around his desk. Just over his right shoulder, the injured senator, arm still in a sling, nodded grimly.

PACT will protect us from the very real threat of those who undermine us from within, the president said. All loyal Americans—including loyal persons of Asian origin—need fear nothing from this law.

He paused for a moment, then signed his name with a flourish at the bottom of the page. Cameras flashed. Then he turned and presented the pen to the sling-armed senator, who accepted it daintily with his uninjured hand.

PACT: Preserving American Culture and Traditions. A solemn promise to root out any anti-American elements undermining the nation. Funding for neighborhood-protection groups to break up protests and guard businesses and stores, for make-work projects churning out flags and pins and posters encouraging watchfulness, and *reinvesting in America.* Funding for new initiatives to monitor China—and new watchdog groups to sniff out those whose loyalties might be divided. Rewards for citizen vigilance, *information leading to potential troublemakers.* And finally, most crucially: preventing the spread of un-American views by quietly removing children from un-American environments—the definition of which was ever expanding: Appearing sympathetic to China. Appearing insufficiently anti-China. Having any doubts about anything American; having any ties to China at all—no matter how many generations past. Questioning whether China was really the problem; questioning whether PACT was being applied fairly; eventually, questioning PACT itself.

In the days after PACT's passage, things calmed slowly, imperceptible at first as stars moving across the sky. Quiet in the streets stretched for one, two, ten nights in a row. People began to find work again. The noises of the city ground back to life, like the clearing of the throat after a long period of silence. Here and there, as buy-American orders resuscitated the idled factories, stores began to reopen, grocery shelves became fuller. People staggered back out into daylight like survivors from a fallout shelter. Blinking and bewildered and groggy. Timid and cautious and shell-shocked. Anxious, above all, to move on.

PACT, its proponents insisted, would strengthen and unify the nation. Left unsaid was that unity required a common enemy. One box in which to collect all their anger; one straw man to wear the hats of everything they feared.

Reports began to trickle in. A Chinese American man, punched in the face in DC; two middle-aged aunties, pelted with garbage in Seattle. A Chinese American woman in Oakland, dragged into an alley and groped, while back on the sidewalk, her baby screamed in its stroller. Margaret's father, it turned out, had been one of the first but far from the last.

Soon it became clear that anyone who might remotely be mistaken for Chinese was at risk. In Miami, a Thai man heading to his office was stabbed; in Pittsburgh, a Filipino teen walking home from swim practice was beaten with a hockey stick;

in Minneapolis, a Hmong woman was pushed into traffic, nearly hit by a bus. The perpetrators were seldom caught and even more rarely charged: it was hard to prove they'd acted because the victim was—or was thought to be—Chinese. *The average American*, one judge ruled, *cannot reasonably be expected to visually distinguish between various varieties of persons of Asian origin.* As if they were types of apples, or breeds of dogs; as if those *persons of Asian origin* did not count as average Americans themselves. As if any of this might be justified by careful distinguishing on the part of the one wielding the bat.

The persons of Asian origin, conversely, were scrutinized thoroughly. A vigil for the Thai man in Miami was dispersed by police for unruliness. A rally for the young mother in Oakland refused to disband, ending in two arrests. The Chinese American man punched in DC was discovered to have an outstanding speeding ticket and was jailed for thirty days. The Filipino teen had fought back, giving his attacker a concussion, and was charged with assault. Soon, when the protests and vigils and demonstrations refused to abate, the first of the PACT child re-placements would begin.

The simple truth was that like most people, Margaret did not think much about any of this. The new act focused on those who held un-American views—but she was doing nothing of the sort. She was buying a table runner, warm slippers, a new bedspread. Magazines were printing again, showing beautiful people and beautiful lives to ogle and emulate; it was possible once more to dine at a restaurant, to have a white-shirted waiter pour you wine. Like everyone, she was trying to build a new, shiny, beautiful life. What could be more American?

A house, a husband. A yard ringed by a fence. Two kinds of boots, rubber for puddles, fur-lined for snow. Scented candles and trivets, a recycling bin, an electric toothbrush, all the paraphernalia of domestic life. All the things she thought she'd been happy to escape. If someone had told her at twenty where she'd be five years later, she would have laughed in their faces, to hear that she not only had these things again, but that she wanted them. Craved them. The only part she would have believed was Bird: she'd always wanted a child. Back in Ethan's tiny apartment they'd daydreamed, the two of them, imagining what their child would be like. Soon, to their delight, they would find out.

Inside her, Bird began to grow. The size of a lentil. The size of a pea. The size of a walnut, then a lemon. Each morning Ethan kissed her belly, just above the navel, before heading to work. A year ago, she and Domi would have been standing face-to-face, gripping their handlebars, steeling themselves for the gauntlet of the day. Armor check, they called it, and that was all they would say. Not goodbye, not see you later, though it meant all those things. Margaret might straighten the collar of Domi's scuffed leather jacket; Domi might tug Margaret's scarf higher over her throat, hiding her face. Armor check, each of them would say, before riding away. Packed into those two words: take care, come back safe, I love you.

Now, in the quiet house, southern sun and sparrow song pooling through the windows, she wore a long soft dress, under which Bird was just beginning to swell. Woolly slippers in which she could not run. Earrings. There was no need for armor here, yet she missed Domi most in these moments, when she remembered there was no more need for toughness.

Ethan's parents came for a visit, and Margaret made up the second bedroom—soon to be the nursery—with clean white sheets. In the kitchen, his mother taught her how to make shepherd's pie, Ethan's childhood favorite. Through the doorway, Ethan watched them, aproned and haloed in the afternoon light, Margaret holding a wooden spoon in one hand as she jotted notes on an index card with the other, his mother setting her free hand on the growing round of Margaret's stomach, so tenderly it might have been a baby's head.

Bird grew: the size of a peach, a mango, a melon. How to understand it, these mystifying sensations, the baffling new phenomenon that was her body? Margaret headed for the public library—now reopened, thanks to private donations—down streets softly humming once more. Stores had reopened, too, one by one, selling fancy notebooks and candy and jewelry; there were people strolling the sidewalks again. It was like the first days of spring after a long and snowy winter, everyone hungry to not be alone. For a brief glorious moment, strangers smiled at each other in passing, so happy to see one another: *You're still here? Me, too!* Still relieved, back then, not yet afraid. Glints of red, white, and blue on everyone's collars and coats.

In the library, nothing had been removed yet; everyone was simply happy to have books again. The young librarian at the counter pointed her to shelf after shelf: Margaret wanted to know much more than *what to expect*, and at night, as they lay in bed, she read tidbits to Ethan. Mother pandas crawled into a den alone; for the first months of the cub's life there was no other world but the dark snug den, no other creature but its mother. Cuckoos crept into other birds' nests, laid their eggs among strangers, and flew away, trusting the other mothers to raise their young as their own. The octopus laid its eggs in strings, like long garlands of pearls, guarded them until her death, starving as she blew air across them to keep them alive.

She grew larger. From within, Bird thrummed against her: his heels the mallets, her belly the drum. She could feel his hiccups, a microscopic ping. When he turned over, she felt the movement inside her stillness. What's it feel like, Ethan asked, wondrous, and she tried to explain: what the ocean floor felt as the waves rolled out, then in. The librarian slid another book across the counter toward her as she ventured farther and farther from shore. Some fish needed no mate, laid eggs and hatched them alone, every fishling a perfect copy of its mother. Some single-celled creatures simply divided, neatly unzipping themselves in two. Each week, another book, another marvel. Another piece of the eternal mystery, life's need to make more life. From the animal world to the plant: Milkweed trees sent their seeds aloft on the wind, to grow far from home; pinecones flared open at their mother's feet, a skirt of stubby seedlings scrabbling for space and light. Succulents would grow anew from a broken-off leaf, pushing roots out into the air, then down into the soil: a piece of its own body, transformed into its child. She thought of the Bible verse her own mother had once made her recite, for Sunday school: *bone of my bones and flesh of my flesh.*

She found mothers everywhere, even in the garden, tending

her plants. When the frost is coming, she learned, the way to ripen tomatoes on the vine is to twist their roots. Pull until the earth cracks, until the spider-hairs below snap like cut strings. This tells the plant: Your end is near—save what you can. Give up on growing taller; give up on leafing wide. Think only of the fruit, dangling in hard green fists. Exhaust yourself. Let your leaves shrivel and yellow. Nothing else matters. Push until there is nothing left of you but a dry stalk holding a round red globe aloft. Wither, pushing that one sweet fruit into ripeness, hoping that in summer something of you will sprout again.

Wakened at night by Bird's restless somersaults, she wrote: tender things that clung to one another, tentatively, like fish eggs. One poem, two. Then a dozen. Then enough for a book. One of those nights, Bird eight and a half months in her belly, she'd had a craving. That morning Ethan had bought her a pomegranate, and she tore it in bloody halves with her hands. They'd finally come available again, after the Crisis, and it felt like the luxury it was, heavy with tiny gemstones. Glistening seeds showered onto the floor, red droplets splashed on the tile. How many trees might spring from that one hard globe? This was its job, she understood suddenly: to create all these seeds, and then to explode. From within, Bird kicked at her, gently this time. As if playing a game. Did the pomegranate know, she thought, did it ever wonder where they went, how they turned out. If they'd ever managed to grow. All those bits of its missing heart. Scattered, to sprout elsewhere.

When the book was finished, this would be the poem on the last page.

. . .

It is painful to admit: back then, she had believed that PACT was progress, that they had moved past something. That they were on their way to something better. That if she behaved, none of it would apply to her. Now and then, on the news, there were still reports of unrest: neighborhood patrols discovering *radicals* who threatened public order; investigations of *suspicious activities*. But that was elsewhere, abstract and nebulous. Isolated incidents. What was concrete was here: the private roiling of Bird inside her, like a ship rolling on the sea; her husband, warm and solid in their bed. The long nights they spent reading side by side on the couch, her feet in his lap, sharing favorite passages so often that afterward, she felt she'd read his book, and he hers. She knitted small socks. Ethan painted the nursery. When Bird tapped his feet within her, she tapped back. She bought an apron. She roasted a chicken. She arranged dishes on a shelf.

She had never been so happy.

As she tells him this, she coils the wires neatly round her fingertip and tucks the bundle into the bottle cap. A twiddle of the screwdriver and the little capsule is sealed, a fat plastic pill.

Bird can't stop himself. What is it, he asks.

Resistance, his mother says, and sets the bottle cap on the tabletop with all the others.

Rumors started. Of nighttime knocks at the door, of children ushered into black sedans and whisked away. A clause buried in the folds of the new law, allowing federal agencies to remove children from homes deemed un-American. A few journalists had pointed it out, before PACT had been passed; one congress-woman had questioned whether it might lead to misuse, whether it was truly necessary. But the consensus—on Capitol Hill and among the public—was that the perfect was the enemy of the good, that too much was better than nothing at all. That all tools should be used to safeguard national security, that nothing should be off the table. Of course no one had an interest in split-ting up families. Only for the most dire cases.

A few of these cases made the news. In Orange County, a march protesting anti-Chinese bias spiraled into a clash with bystanders hurling epithets, ending with riot police, tasers, a Chinese American three-year-old struck by a tear-gas canister. For the officer, paid leave; for the protester, a full investigation into the family. Cable-news anchors pointed out this was not the first march the child had been taken to; on social media, photos showed her as a toddler perched on her father's shoulders, an infant strapped to her mother's chest like a bomber's pack. Never mind that the parents were second- and third-generation Amer-icans, that their grandparents had been Angelenos before Union Station erased Chinatown. Instead, the parents' booking photos flashed on-screen, their faces dark-haired and glaring and so obviously *foreign*. Not one of us. From the hospital, the child was whisked away. The best possible outcome, headlines agreed. Pro-tecting a child from learning such harmful views.

Margaret, reading the news on her phone, a milk-stoned Bird dozing at her breast, thought: *awful.* And: *How could those people endanger their child.* She tried to imagine carrying Bird into the crush of a mob, flash bombs bursting at their feet, the bite of tear gas setting her nostrils aflame. Her mind slammed its door on the thought. There he was, safe here in her arms: her Bird. Long lashes resting on cheeks softer than anything she'd ever touched. A small furrow rumpling his eyebrows. What troubling dreams could a baby already have? She smoothed the creases with the pad of her thumb until his face went calm again. Beside her, Ethan's hand squeezed her shoulder, then cupped Bird's head. She would never do such a thing, she promised Bird silently. None of this would ever apply to them.

The next march protesting anti-Chinese hate, in Queens, was sparsely attended; after that, there was a long stretch with none.

What she thought was about her poems, her garden, her husband. Bird. She pushed seeds into the soil and watered them until threads of green shoots emerged. She set cutoff milk jugs over seedlings to shield them from the night chill. She knit a blanket for Bird from cream-colored wool. Late at night, she made love to Ethan. In the morning, content, she baked banana scones, licked honey from the spoon.

Ethan's parents came to visit when they could: for Bird's birthday, for Halloween bearing candy he could not yet chew, for Christmas laden with gifts heavier than their small recipient. His mother shared feeding tips with Margaret; one afternoon, when Margaret dozed on the sofa, exhausted, with a tantrum-drained Bird on her chest, Ethan's father spread a blanket over them and then clicked off the light. Margaret and Ethan had said only that her parents had passed, and it warmed both of them to see the eagerness and openness with which Ethan's parents enfolded Margaret into their lives.

He looks just like her, Ethan's parents kept saying, and they'd thought this was a compliment at first—and maybe it was, though later both would wonder if it was also a twitch of discomfort, someone else's face so clearly stamped on a child they felt should have been *theirs*. Privately, Margaret and Ethan thought Bird simply looked like Bird. Looking down on him late at night, they could pick out small features and trace them to their source—Margaret's cheekbones, Ethan's eyelashes—but where they saw resemblance was in the expressions: the two parallel wrinkles that appeared on Bird's forehead when he was thinking, the dimple in his cheek, like a fingerprint, when he laughed. That was Ethan's wrinkle on Margaret's brow, Margaret's dimple just southeast of Ethan's mouth. It was a strange and unsettling experience, watching expressions that they knew flit over the face of this small person, part them and part the person they loved most, and they sensed that this would be only the first of many strange and unsettling experiences that parenthood would bring.

Margaret wrote more poems. Publishers were printing again, and when Bird was three, a small, plucky press agreed to publish her book. A split pomegranate on the cover, so close up it resembled an organ, or a wound: you had to look twice to see it for what it was. *Our Missing Hearts* was praised by a few poetry critics and read by almost no one. Tens of copies sold, she'd said to Ethan drily, who reads poetry anymore? and he'd joked, Who ever read it before?

It didn't matter. The world was full of poems to her then.

She taught Bird to catch fireflies: hands cupped, lemon-lime light flashing in the cracks of his fingers. And then to let them go, spiraling into the night like a dying spark. She taught him to lie still in the grass and watch the neighborhood rabbits nose in the clover, so close his breath stirred the fine white fluff of their tails. She taught him the names of flowers and bugs and birds, to identify the low *coo-coo-coo* of the mourning dove and the brash scream of the blue jay and the singsong *phoebe* of the chickadee, clear and fresh as cold water on a summer day. She taught him to pluck honeysuckle blossoms from the vine and touch the end to his tongue: such sticky sweetness. She pulled the shell of a cicada from a pine tree's trunk, turned it over to show the neat slit down the belly where, having grown, it had wriggled out of its old self into something new.

And she told him stories. Stories about warriors and princesses, poor brave girls and boys, monsters and magicians. The brother and sister who outwitted the witch and found their way home. The girl who saved her swan-brothers from enchantment. Ancient myths that made sense of the world: why sunflowers nod, why echoes linger, why spiders spin. Stories her mother had told her in childhood, before she stopped speaking of such things: how once there had been nine suns, baking the earth to dust, until a brave archer shot them one by one out of the sky. How the monkey king tricked his way into the heavenly garden to steal the peaches of immortality. How once a year, two lovers, forever separated, crossed a river of stars to meet in midair.

Did that really happen? he asked each time, and she smiled and shrugged.

Maybe.

She filled his head with nonsense, with mystery and magic, carving out space for wonder. A haven in their long-ago Eden.

Enough for today, she says, setting down the pliers.

In part this is selfish. She is drawing out this moment of calm, lingering in the sweet times, before the bitter things she has to confess. But there are things she needs to do before dark, and they will take time.

She lines up the bottle caps she's completed, tallying them two by two. Fifty-five. Much fewer than on a usual day, but that's to be expected: wading through the bog of the past slows her hands. Slows everything. Fifty-five little round capsules, brimful with transistors, a watch battery, a small metal disc. And wires, so many wires. Packed down tight into a cap the size of a coin and sealed up tight, simple and primitive and dangerous as a stone. She bundles them all into a plastic shopping bag emblazoned with a yellow smiley face: *Thank you for your patronage.*

Bird waits while she disappears upstairs into her room, and when she comes back, she has donned a baggy sweatshirt, a folding straw hat with a wide brim. She looks just like the trash-picking women who roam the streets, looking for bottles and cans to salvage.

Stay here, Margaret says. She hesitates, then says: You'll be fine and I won't be long.

She says it firmly, trying to convince herself more than him.

Stay inside, she adds, and keep quiet. She loops the bag of bottle caps around her wrist, then lifts a trash bag from the corner. Inside, cans and soda bottles clink as it settles over her shoulder. There's a sour smell in the air and he can't tell if it's the bag, or her clothes, or her.

I'll be back soon, she says, and heads into the hall.

After his mother has gone, Bird lifts one of the still-empty caps and twists it between his fingers, his thumbnail tick-ticking along the ridged sides. His mind tick-ticking over what he's just heard.

It's difficult to imagine, the world his mother has described. The world of the Crisis, and the world before that. In school, when they've studied the Crisis, it has always seemed like a story in a book: something made up to impart a lesson. A cautionary tale. It is different, to hear his mother tell it. To hear how it felt and sounded and smelled, to imagine her in the midst of it. To see the scars etched in her hands from those jagged days.

The mother he remembers coaxed frilly green leaves from the earth and bright globes of vegetables from their vines. She let bees land on her fingers, spread butter on his toast, spun shimmering fairy tales in the darkness. This mother is a different creature entirely, lean and wiry, almost feral, a ravenous look in her eyes. Her hair uncombed and greasy, a harsh animal musk on her skin. It makes it easier to believe the things she's telling him: the Crisis, her wildness. How she survived. It fills him with apprehension, too, at what she might be doing now. He thinks of his mother, bent over the table, whispering stories to him, the point of the cut wire glinting in her hand. Her mouth set firm and tense in a straight grim line. He thinks of the bottle caps: little time bombs, ready to be detonated at a moment's notice. Candy-colored bits of shrapnel to perforate the city. She wouldn't do that, he thinks, but the truth is, he's not sure. He's seen the look in his mother's eyes, a hardness he does not remember from childhood, a razor-edged glint that would slice you if you looked too long.

When Margaret returns, nothing seems to have changed: the trash bag of cans is still over her shoulder, the plastic bag still dangles from her wrist. She peels off her hat.

Are you all right? she asks. You weren't scared, while I was gone?

You've been gone for three years, Bird thinks, a few hours is nothing. He bites back the words.

I'm fine, he says.

His mother reaches into the plastic bag.

I didn't know what you liked, she says, so I got some of everything.

Granola bars, nuts, candy, cans of soup, packages of salted almonds, a carton of Minute rice. As if she'd gone aisle by aisle, plucking an item from every shelf. It saddens him and touches him all at once, that she had no idea what he wanted, and that despite not knowing she had still tried so hard to please him.

It's been such a long time, she says, since—

She stops, looking down at the bounty between them.

I should have brought you real food, she says, embarrassed, and Bird can see the meal she wishes she'd procured: hot and nourishing, balanced and wholesome. Green vegetables, mashed potatoes, corn glossy with butter. Meat sliced thin and fanned out on the white china plate. He understands: it's been a long time since she's taken care of anyone, and she's nearly forgotten how. It's been so long she'd forgotten such a meal could exist, let alone the world in which someone might eat it.

It's okay, he says, this is fine. And he means it.

They settle on cups of instant noodles, something to warm their hands. The bottle caps, he sees, are all gone.

When the noodles are ready, she slides a steaming cup toward him along with a plastic fork. They are lemon-yellow and intensely salty, and Bird wolfs them down. On the other side of the coffee table, Margaret pauses, forkless, then slurps hers straight from the cup.

How long have you been living here, Bird asks. He fishes up the last dregs of his noodles.

Almost four weeks. Though *living* isn't the right word. This is just temporary, while I get things ready.

This only raises more questions for Bird. Ready, he says, ready for what? What are you doing?

Have some milk, she says, filling a mug and nudging it toward him. It builds strong bones.

She fills one for herself and takes a gulp.

Besides, she adds, it won't keep. No fridge. So drink up.

From the bag she pulls a can, pries up the ring with a fingernail, pops the lid off. Inside, jewels of fruit glisten.

Dessert, she says, setting the can between them, and this gesture, small as it is, warms him: he has always loved canned peaches and she still remembers this. He spears a golden wedge with his fork.

Do you like school, she asks suddenly. Is your teacher nice? Are the other kids kind to you?

Bird shrugs, a one-shoulder twitch, and scoops up a sliver of peach. It is her fault if they're not, but he does not want to tell her this. They call me Noah, he says instead. Dad told them to.

His mother pauses. She's barely eaten any of her noodles, and now she sets her cup aside.

Is he happy, she asks.

Her voice is calm and even, as if she's asked about the weather. Only her hands give her away: her thumbs press so hard against her fingers that the nails have turned white.

Like most children, Bird has seldom considered whether his father is happy or not. Each morning he gets up and goes to work; he tends to Bird's needs. Yet as Bird thinks about it, there is a melancholy around him, that hush he'd ascribed to the library but maybe—he realizes—is rooted much deeper.

I don't know, he says. But he takes good care of me.

It feels important to say this, though whether he's defending his father or reassuring his mother, he isn't sure.

His mother smiles, a small sad smile. That was one thing I never worried about, she says. Then: Does he still read the dictionary?

Bird laughs. He does, he says. Every night.

She does remember, he thinks, even that tiny thing. It makes her a little less of a stranger.

He doesn't like to talk about you, Bird admits. He said—he said to pretend you don't exist.

He expects this to sadden her even more, but instead she nods.

We agreed that was best.

But why, Bird insists, and his mother sighs.

I'm trying to tell you, Bird. I really am. But you need to hear everything, the whole story, to understand. Tomorrow, okay? The rest of it, tomorrow.

As he heads up the stairs, she calls after him.

Do you want me to call you Noah, now? If that's what everyone else calls you?

One hand on the creaking bannister, he pauses.

No, he says, cheeks suddenly aglow. You can still call me Bird. If you want to.

The next morning, back at the table, she works faster, hands moving quickly, aware time is running out. She begins without preamble. Like plunging into the ocean before she has time to be afraid.

Two weeks after Bird's ninth birthday. Over breakfast, Ethan had suddenly paused, stunned, and set his phone before her. Heads bent over the screen, they'd read the headline together: CONFLICT ERUPTS AT PROTEST; 6 INJURED, 1 DEAD. Below, a photo of a young Black woman—long braids pulled back in a ponytail, glasses, yellow hat. Still standing, eyes still clear and open, mouth still parted in a cry, a millisecond before her mind knows what her body already feels: a red rose of blood just starting to bloom on her chest. Clutched in her hands, a poster: *ALL OUR MISSING HEARTS*. And a caption: *Protester Marie Johnson, 19, a first-year student at NYU from Philadelphia, was killed by a stray bullet in police response to anti-PACT riots Monday.*

The first of many such articles, but they would all use the same photo.

This young woman—Marie—had read Margaret's book in her dorm room. She was studying developmental psychology, planning to become a pediatrician, and with each news report of a child taken, the last lines of the last poem had come back to her, insistent as an infant's cry. Nine years after PACT's passage, there were more and more of them: the few that made the news here and there, framed as stories of negligence and endangerment, the parents portrayed as reckless and careless and callous; but others, too, shrouded in rumor and secrecy and shame.

Just rumors, some people scoffed; re-placements happened only in a few isolated cases. Others insisted PACT removals were a necessary evil: a rescue, for the child's good, and society's. *Can't rock the boat*, one commenter wrote online, *and be surprised when your kid gets washed overboard*. But for every child you heard was taken, how many families said nothing, stopped protesting, stopped everything, hoping their good behavior would earn their children back?

The night before the march, Marie bought sheets of posterboard at the drugstore. With fat-tipped scented markers, she jigsawed words onto the sign, sketched the solemn face of a child below. After the march, they'd found the markers and the rest of the posterboard on the floor of her dorm room, blank and unused, beside a spread-eagled copy of Margaret's book.

After that: vigils. Campaigns to remember Marie. Online, thousands of people changed their profile photos: Marie after Marie after Marie, a sea of them crying out, flushed with youth and fury and pulsing lost life, every one of them brandishing the poster with Margaret's words. People googled those words, and up popped the name Margaret Miu, the title of her book. The poems she'd written while pregnant, in a sleep-deprived haze nursing Bird late at night, watching the sky turn from black to navy to bruised grayish-blue.

Not even her best line, she'd always thought, not even one of her best poems, and yet here it was. Clutched in this dying child's hands.

Those lines began appearing online, the adopted slogan of those opposed to PACT. At the protests that sprang up here and there, quick flares of grief and rage. On pins, as graffiti, on hand-lettered T-shirts. They're all over campus, Ethan said, wide-eyed. Margaret, seeing one for the first time, stopped dead in the street, jolting back to life only when someone behind bumped into her, cursed, and elbowed his way past. She felt as if she'd come around the corner and run into some uncanny version of herself. She had never been to a protest. She had never, in all honesty, thought much about PACT at all.

Someone painted the lines on the wall of the New York Department of Family Services, on the sidewalk outside the Justice Department. All over the country, anti-PACT marches began to spring up like brush fires. Anti-PACT protesters hurled eggs—then rocks—at the cars of pro-PACT senators and officials. Always, always carrying posters bearing Margaret's lines. The protests were short and sporadic—but they were long enough for passersby to take photos, and soon those photos were everywhere, and so were Margaret's words.

Who would ever, she said to Ethan, have expected a poem to go viral. Neither of them laughed. It was the least unbelievable thing of all the unbelievable things that had happened in the past few years.

Then a talk-radio show did an investigation into the sign, the poem. Margaret.

Who's inspiring these lunatic protesters? he asked. Well, I'll tell you: a radical female poet named Margaret Miu, lives in Cambridge, that liberal bubble. And—surprise surprise—she's a kung-PAO.

A cable-news host who'd defended PACT from the beginning— Chinese *American*? he'd said, there's no such thing; you know where their loyalties *really* lie—picked up the story. He scanned the photo from the back of Margaret's book and flashed it on-screen. Letting her foreign face say it all.

People like this, he said, are the reason we *need* PACT. You know who her main audience is, who's buying her books? I'll tell you. I've looked up the figures. Young people. College kids, high school kids. Could be even middle schoolers, who knows. Kids at that age are so impressionable. And this woman's influence is *skyrocketing*. You know what her sales figures show? Four thousand copies of her book sold last week alone. Six thousand this week. Next week it'll be ten. I tell you, we'd better take a lot closer look at what's in those poems. There's a very real danger of our kids being corrupted. This is what PACT is *for.*

On message boards—and soon, in the authorities' offices— people combed through Margaret's lines. *Scattered, to sprout elsewhere*—might that not be an encouragement for spreading harmful ideas? This poem about a spider, clutching its empty egg sac—*hollow and dry with only air inside*—well, it wasn't hard to interpret that as a metaphor for America, clinging to *hollow* ideals until it died. And this one, about tomatoes, disturbing their *sturdy roots*: how could you read these lines as anything other than urging others to strike at the roots of American stability?

The anti-American ideology was clear, which made it all the more dangerous that people were reading these poems—nearly fifty thousand copies sold so far, an unheard-of number for a book of poetry, especially from a minuscule press. That, in and of itself, was suspicious; of course the Pentagon should take a look; one could not rule out the possibility that messages were coded in the lines. Regardless, these poems weren't just un-American, they were inciting rebellion. Endorsing and espousing terrorist activity. Persuading others to support insurrection. Look how many anti-PACT protests were happening.

It just goes to show, one official thought, as he branded Margaret's file with a crisp red stamp. Born here, but clearly American in name only. Probably learned it from *her* parents. That foreign mindset rooted deep, he mused; maybe it twined all the way down in the DNA. Maybe it wasn't ever possible to straighten their loyalties out.

Margaret got a call a week later from her publisher: they'd been ordered to cease publication of her book, to destroy any warehoused copies. Can they really do that, Margaret asked, and her editor sighed. He was a reedy, bespectacled white man who could recite Rilke from memory; the press operated out of a rented two-room office in Milwaukee. For weeks he'd been getting threatening emails and phone calls, the most recent one with detailed suggestions about what should be done to his seven-year-old daughter. That's not all, he said. They've also sent a subpoena to look into our finances and our other authors. Not even just the Asian ones—everyone. To see if we've funded anyone else *un-American.* It was strongly implied that if we didn't comply, they'd find ways to shut us down. I'm sorry, Margaret. I really am.

Within a month the publisher would shutter anyway, all its stock pulped, all its files deleted. Libraries, flooded with angry calls about the book, began to pull it from their shelves. PACT supporters held a rally in downtown Boston, collecting copies and burning them in an oilcan on City Hall Plaza. The post office began to monitor Margaret and Ethan's mail.

It got worse. Someone dug online, posted their address and Margaret's phone number on social media. *Dont like this PAO CUNT & the poison she's feedign our kids?* he wrote. *Call her up & tell her.*

What are we going to do, she said to Ethan, as she silenced her phone. It had been ringing for the past twenty minutes and for a while she'd answered and hung up immediately, but every time it just began to ring again.

Ethan put his arms around her. He had already spoken to the police; there was nothing illegal, they informed him, about posting publicly available information. He'd sworn at them and hung up. It was Saturday morning, and on a normal day, they'd have been at the kitchen table eating waffles, sunlight streaming onto their plates. Instead, all morning Ethan had been pacing around the house, pulling the curtains shut, nudging Margaret and Bird away from windows.

It will stop, she assured him. It has to stop. They'll get tired of it. I didn't even do anything. I've never been to a protest. All I did was write a poem.

It didn't stop. No one seemed to be getting tired except for Margaret and Ethan—and Bird. What's wrong with your phone, Bird kept asking, who keeps calling? Rotten fish and bags of dog shit and broken glass began to appear on their front step, and one day, a single bullet, still in its casing. After that, Bird was no longer allowed to go outside alone, even into the backyard.

People are crazy, Ethan told him. Don't worry. You're safe.

Did you know, the talk-show host said a few days later, that this Margaret Miu—she has a kid? Nine years old. Yeah. Can you believe it? And his name—get this—his name is *Bird*.

The comments online:

That's child abuse, right there. Enough said.

People like that shouldn't be allowed to reproduce.

Can you imagine what kind of shit she's teaching him at home? Imagine having her as your mother.

Poor kid. Let's pray Family Services checks them out soon.

That night, after they'd put Bird to bed, Ethan's mother emailed him. *My friend Betsy forwarded me this article about Margaret.* It was the first of many articles, some of which she would forward and many of which she would simply read as they dinged, one by one and sometimes two or three at a time, into her inbox, forwarded by ostensibly well-wishing acquaintances: *I remember you mentioned your son's new wife (?). Is this the same Margaret Miu?!*

As articles and news reports and headlines accumulated, Ethan's parents read and discussed, measuring the woman they'd met and loved, the woman their son adored, the woman who'd borne their grandson, against the woman the news portrayed. The person they knew—or had they?—against the person everyone else seemed to see. How many times had they met her? How well could you know someone in that time? On their weekly phone calls, Ethan ranted to his parents about the latest developments—the anonymous emails filling Margaret's inbox, the notes duct-taped to their front door. It was not until Ethan stopped speaking, exhausted by rage and fear, that he noticed his mother's uncharacteristic silence.

She always seemed so *kind*, his mother said, in tones of profound sadness and betrayal, and Ethan understood then: a story had settled in his mother's mind, and there was nothing he could do to rewrite it. In the weeks to come, Ethan's parents did not call him, and when he and Bird moved to the dorm, he would not send them his forwarding address.

Then came the note. A scrap of paper from Bird's teacher, Ms. Hernández, slipped surreptitiously into his bag. *Dear Mr. and Mrs. Gardner,* it read in her neat, looped cursive. Tall proud *S*s. Upright and rigid-backed *P*s. *The school has received a call from Family Services. I have been summoned to speak with them Monday morning and they will likely wish to speak with you soon thereafter.* And then: *It seemed only fair to let you know.*

A warning. A kindness, really.

She packed that night, a single bag. One she could carry on her back, small enough that she could walk as long as needed; a bedroll and all the cash they could gather. The bedroll had been Ethan's originally. It's warm, he said softly, pulling it from the back of the closet, and she could hear his voice snagging as they imagined all the nights to come when they would no longer be lying beside each other. She'd taken it and turned away quickly, bending over to buckle it to her bag, but in truth she couldn't face the pain in his eyes, and wasn't sure he could face the pain in hers. They'd agreed: she wouldn't write, she wouldn't call. Nothing that could be traced. She'd leave her phone behind. Any ties unsevered could unravel, so they would cut her, the traitorous PAO mother, out of their lives. They would give not even the slightest pretext to take Bird away. Whatever it takes, they agreed. Whatever needed to be done or said to keep him safe.

The next morning, she had tried to say goodbye. A Saturday, late October. The leaves just loosening from the trees. We'll be fine, Ethan told her. Both of them understood he was reassuring himself as much as her. He buried his face in her hair, and Margaret burrowed against his chest, breathing him in, all the words she was not brave enough to speak trying desperately to escape her mouth. When they finally let each other go, neither could look at the other. Ethan hurriedly shut himself in the bedroom, because really, what else was there to say, and he couldn't bear to watch her leave. Bird, oblivious, was kneeling on the living-room carpet, piecing together plastic brick after plastic brick. It was a house, and the roof kept falling in, the arch of it too high for his child's hands.

Birdie, she said. Her voice splintering. Bird, I have to go.

She expected questions, as soon as he saw her backpack: a thing she never carried, which he certainly would notice. Why're you carrying that? Where are you going? Can I come, too? But he didn't turn. He hadn't heard her at first, he was so absorbed in what he was doing, and she loved that about him, loved the way his attention focused, intense as summer heat, on the thing he wanted to understand.

Bird, she said again, louder this time. Birdie, my darling. I'm going now.

He did not turn around, and she was grateful for this: grateful not to see his eyes in this last moment, grateful that he did not run to her and press his face into her belly as he usually did, because how then could she ever hope to peel herself away.

Okay, he said, and she ached at his trust, how confident he was that she would be right back, as she always had. It was she who turned then, turned and hoisted her backpack on her shoulder and went straight out the door, before her heart could change her mind.

Two days later, when Family Services arrived, her things would already be piled on the curb. When they questioned him, Ethan would shake his head and his son's heart would crack. No, he didn't know where she'd gone. No, he didn't share her views, not at all. Quite the opposite, to tell the truth. No, he couldn't honestly say he was sorry. He'd tried to make things work for the sake of their son, but a man could only stand so much, right? Well—let's just say he was relieved that she'd no longer be an influence. Yes, exactly. Much better off without.

Her books? Absolutely not. Seditious trash. He'd burned them all.

A bus to Philly, scarf pulled up, shielded by sunglasses. Eleven hundred dollars cash in her pocket, most of their savings. She did not have a plan just yet, only a hope: someone she thought might help, who might give her a place to pause and decide what to do next. But first, before she could pause, she needed to pay respects, to apologize. To atone. Slouched in her seat, she tugged her knit hat down nearly to the bridge of her nose, dug her chin into the collar of her coat. She refused to cry. Instead she watched the highway whir by in a blur of gray and white. Beside her, a man with a mustache snored, the roll of fat on his neck trembling with each breath.

The small suburb where Marie Johnson had grown up had neat green lawns dotted with flowering shrubs and old oak trees, tidy wooden houses with crisp coats of paint over edges softened by age. Marie's house could have been any one of them: from the outside, it did not look like a house in mourning. But she knew it at once, from the news reports that had flashed it over and over on-screen, always with curtains shut tight against the cameras sizzling outside. Now, months later, the neighborhood had returned to some semblance of normalcy: a few yards down, a man yanked the chain of his leaf blower and it ground to life with a throaty growl; across the street an older woman in flowered gardening gloves deadheaded a chrysanthemum with schoolmarmish rigor. At Marie's house, the only signs of life were the car in the driveway and the thin gap between the curtains, letting the afternoon sunlight slice inside.

As a girl, Marie must have played here. Maybe she turned floppy cartwheels on this patch of grass and chalked hopscotch grids on the sidewalk squares. Maybe she ran through the sprinkler on hot summer days, fleeing—then chasing—the curtain of spray. Margaret could see it, could hear her squeal, like Bird's, rising like the peal of a bell. On her back, the rucksack chafed wide red welts into her shoulders. She rang the bell.

The woman who answered might have been ten years older than Margaret, but Margaret had the feeling she had lived life-times more. Her face was still young, but there was something worn and heavy about the way she carried herself, as if she had been stretched past what she should hold. Behind her a man, broad shoulders rounded and hunched, reading glasses perched on the tip of his nose, a newspaper folded in his hand.

Mrs. Johnson, Margaret said. Mr. Johnson. I'm here about Marie.

It came pouring out of her then, in a confused torrent: apologies and confession, explanation and regret and self-recrimination. Her poems, her intent, her horror and sadness at Marie's death. I didn't mean, she kept saying. I never imagined. I didn't expect. Even as the words slithered from her mouth back to her own ears she realized her mistake. What she desperately wanted— reassurance, comfort, absolution—she had no right to ask of them, and they had no reason to give to her.

They're after me, she found herself saying. Pleading, half begging, her own fear shrill in her ears. They blame me for all this. And they're right.

Before her, Marie's parents stood in the entryway, impassive. Down the street, the man with the leaf blower cut the motor and the air went quiet. She was still on the front step; she hadn't even waited, she thought, before laying all this at the feet of this man and this woman who had lost their child. It was hopeless, she was hopeless; how could you ever apologize for this.

I am so very sorry, she said finally, and turned to go.

What did you come here for, Marie's father asked. He folded the newspaper in half, not angrily, but calmly. As if he had read enough news to last a lifetime, as if this were the last newspaper he would ever read again. He looked at her directly, without flinching: he was past fear, now. You think we have anything to say to you? he said. Our baby's dead and you come here, looking for what. Wanting us to feel sorry for what *you* went through?

His voice was quiet, the kind of voice you'd use to talk in the library, and somehow this froze Margaret more than if he was shouting.

You think you know her? he went on. They all think they know her. Everybody thinks they know her, now. You got people wearing my little girl's face on their chests, who don't care about her or who she was. Just using her name to justify doing what they want. She's nothing but a slogan to them. They don't know the first thing about her. You don't know the first thing about her either.

Around them, the ever-present noises of the suburbs—cars ambling by as if they had nowhere urgent to be, a sky-bound crow's squawk, the inevitable dog bark from some indeterminable distance. Continuing on, as if nothing were amiss.

What is there to say, he finished.

He turned and retreated into the dark interior of the house.

For a moment, Margaret and Marie's mother stood there on opposite sides of the doorway: Margaret frozen on the front step, the breeze chilly on the back of her neck, where sweat dampened her hair. Marie's mother with one hand braced against the jamb, as if she were keeping the house from collapse. Eyes half squinted against the sun, her back cast in shadow. Studying Margaret. Margaret wondered what she saw. She thought, belatedly, of the Asian and Black worlds, orbiting each other warily, frozen at a distance in a precarious push-pull. In her childhood: a young Black girl shot, Los Angeles on fire, Korean stores aflame. Her parents had fumed, reading the news, indignant at the damage, the *delinquency*. And then, years later, a young Black man dead in a stairwell, a Chinese American cop's finger on the trigger. There'd been outcry on all sides—an accident, police brutality, scapegoating—until the circles separated again into an uneasy truce. More than once, her mother had been shoved on the street by a Black teen, taunting her with ching-chong chants. Yet also: soon after she'd moved to New York, she'd been in Chinatown picking fruit from a cart when a Black man drove by in an SUV, rap blasting from the rolled-down windows so loud the pear in her hand shivered, and the shop owner, a wiry older Chinese man, gritted his teeth. Those thugs, he said, as if it were something they already agreed on, and spat, and she'd been so stunned that—to her shame—she'd simply nodded, paid, and darted away without a word. It weights her, this history, heavy as the pack on her back.

I'm sorry, Margaret said, again. I should go.

You have children? Marie's mother asked suddenly.

One, Margaret said. I had a son. The past tense, unintended, shocks her. How easily her mind has accepted what her heart cannot. Have, she corrects herself. I have a son. But I won't ever see him again.

A long pause between them, stretching and swelling until it wrapped around both of them, thick and plush. Then, to Margaret's surprise, Marie's mother reached out, touched Margaret's wrist.

Welcome to the worst club in the world, she said.

The Johnsons' house was cozy and tidy but everywhere there were signs of their daughter. Mr. Johnson, lips clamped shut, shook his head at his wife and disappeared up the stairs, but Mrs. Johnson led Margaret into the living room. On the mantel, a framed photograph of Marie in cap and gown, paper scroll in the crook of her arm like a sheaf of flowers. High school graduation, Mrs. Johnson said. Salutatorian. In the corner, a music stand, a flute case, sheet music covered in flurries of impossibly high notes.

She did marching band. But what she really loved was the classical stuff.

Her hand brushed the leatherette, wiping a fleck of dust from the latch.

I wanted her to keep it up in college. But she said she wouldn't have time. She had so many plans.

Margaret still had not taken off her backpack; she was not sure if she was invited to stay. In this crowded living room she felt like a large and lumbering animal, every movement threatening to knock some part of the past to the floor. She held her breath, as if that might make her smaller and stiller, as if that might help anything.

Mrs. Johnson took a small china elephant from the mantel,

turning it over. After a moment she found what she was looking for, held it up so Margaret could see: a thin seam of glue circling the uplifted trunk.

You see this? she said. My friend went on vacation, to India, and brought me back this. Marie was maybe seven, or eight? She loved it. She'd play with it, put it in her pocket, carry it around. One day I came home from work and she'd broken off the trunk. Did I give her hell. I told her she had no respect for other people's things, didn't I tell her to be careful, why didn't she listen to me. No, Mama, she said to me, I wanted to see what was inside. She did it on purpose. I told her she was on punishment for a month. The next day I found it like this.

She tipped her palm where the little elephant stood, letting the light catch its curves.

She'd patched it back together. You can barely see where the break was. Only if you know where to look.

Gently she set the elephant back on the mantel.

That was Marie, she said. No one out there will remember those things. Just me.

The two women stood there in silence. In the shaft of light that sliced through the crack in the curtains, dust motes hovered.

Will you tell me, Margaret asked. She took the older woman's hands between hers, and Mrs. Johnson did not pull back. A kindness that humbled Margaret, because it was one she had not earned. Will you tell me about her? she said. Who she was. What she was like.

I'll tell you. But only if you promise to remember. That she was a real person, not a poster. That she was a child. My child.

. . .

She stayed for two days, listening. Letting Marie's mother tell her anything and everything that came to mind. Mr. Johnson avoided her, eyeing her with brittle wariness, tucking his glasses into the breast pocket of his shirt before leaving the room.

He doesn't trust you, Mrs. Johnson said, as her husband passed by in the hall. Not an apology; a simple statement of fact.

But Mrs. Johnson led her into Marie's bedroom, where they sat together from sunup until darkness fell. Mrs. Johnson roamed the room, speaking softly, touching this and that, reminiscing. Picking up Marie's hairbrush, her rings, the ocean-smoothed stones she'd kept on the windowsill, each awaking a memory like a talisman. None of the stories were important. A visit to an aunt in North Carolina, a day at Six Flags, Marie's first trip to New York as a skinny, gawky adolescent: Mama, I want to live *here*. All the stories were unbearably important. The time, as a toddler, she'd farted in church, right after the minister had said *Let us pray*. The red shoes she'd loved so much she squashed her feet into them for months, refusing to give them up, insisting they still fit until they split at the seams. How, as a teenager, she'd clipped words she liked out of her magazines, saving them like confetti in a blue envelope—*nebulous, muscovado, smithereens*. I just like the way they sound, she'd said.

I don't know what she wanted to do with them, Mrs. Johnson said.

She talked and talked, picking her way from memory to memory, crossing a wide ocean on stepping-stones. Remember this, Marie's mother said, again and again. Hold on to it. As if

memory were a bead that might spring from her fingers, clatter
to the floor, roll into a crack and disappear. Which it was. At
night, swaddled in her bedroll in the Johnsons' living room,
Margaret jotted down what Marie's mother had said, each word
echoing like a chime. But while Mrs. Johnson talked, Margaret
simply listened and listened and listened.

The second night, Marie's father stepped in from the hallway.
He looked at his wife, sitting on their daughter's flowery bed; at
Margaret, cross-legged on the floor.

You know the last thing I said to her, he said.

No greeting, no introduction. As if he'd been waiting a long
time to say just this.

She told me, on the phone. How there was this protest planned,
protesting PACT, how she planned to go and hold up a sign. I
said, Marie, that ain't about you. You think those PAOs would
stick their necks out for you? You think any of them care when
we get followed in stores, or shot in traffic stops? Just let it be.

He paused.

She'd been doing research, he went on. Trying to trace our
family tree. In high school, she got curious. She was at the library all the time, looking at databases and census records, trying to find her roots. Our roots. What she found was a big blank
spot. No records, before Emancipation—except for one. A bill of
sale, for my maybe-ancestor. Age eleven. To a Mr. Johnson in
Albemarle County, Virginia.

Another pause. He looked down at Margaret, and she looked
up at him. Listening.

I didn't want her to go. But she was set on it. She just said:
It's wrong to take children from their families, Daddy. You know

that. And she didn't want to argue so we just hung up and the next day she went to that march.

He stood there, framed by the doorway, a strong man made fragile by grief. Margaret's mother had crossed the street when she saw men like him approaching. Out of disdain? Out of fear? She didn't know and wasn't sure it mattered. At the factory where her father worked, there were only a handful of Black men, and her father hadn't socialized with any of them. Not my kind of people, he'd said, and she hadn't bothered to ask what he meant.

You weren't wrong, Margaret said at last. You weren't wrong. But neither was Marie.

A small tug at a complicated knot that would take generations to unpick.

Mr. Johnson settled himself down on the bed next to his wife, who put her arm around him and turned her face to his shoulder, and they sat there quietly, the three of them, in Marie's room, Margaret a witness to what they'd lost.

After a long, long while, he said: You know what keeps coming back to me? This one night, I came home from work.

The memory seeping out of him, like water filtered through stone.

I don't even remember how old she was. She might've been five, she might've been fifteen.

Margaret did not question; she understood this, how slippery and elastic time was in the fact of your child, how it seemed to move not in a line but in endless loops, circling back again and again, overwriting itself.

She was laughing, Marie's father said. Laughing and laughing and laughing. Laughing so hard she couldn't stand up. Laughing so hard tears were running down her face. I came in and I saw her there, rolling on the carpet. Just laughing. Marie, I said, what's so funny? She just kept on laughing. Until I started laughing, too. I couldn't help it.

He was half laughing again, as the memory of it swirled around him, pulling him back into the past.

Finally she calmed down and she just lay there. Catching her breath, looking at the ceiling, big smile still on her face. Marie, I said again, what's so funny? She let out a big sigh. She looked so happy. Everything, she said. Everything.

She left Marie's family with a request, and a name.

Put her in a poem, Mr. Johnson said, she'd like that. You put her in a poem, okay? Make other people remember her.

I'll try, Margaret said, though she knew, already, that no poem could encapsulate Marie, just as no poem could encapsulate Bird. There would always be too much left unsaid.

Mrs. Johnson said nothing, just hugged Margaret, even tighter than Margaret hugged her. They would never speak again, but they were linked now, as those who've been through something terrible together are forever fused, in ways they don't always understand.

The name was the librarian's, though the Johnsons only knew her last: Mrs. Adelman this, Mrs. Adelman that, that's all that came out of Marie's mouth all of high school, her mother said, she spent all her free time over there. Across town; catch the bus on the corner. Margaret walked instead, following the trail of bus stop signs, the bus itself lumbering past her at encouraging intervals, reassuring her she was still on the path. By the time she reached the library, six buses had passed her, and perhaps it was because of this that she had the feeling, ascending the steps of the library, that she had been here before, that some previous version or versions of herself had already arrived, were already within, had already discovered what she herself was only now entering to find.

The library was not the vast marble hall she'd expected, but warm and cozy, the carpet and walls and shelves all the honeyed tan of an old leather armchair, like a great-aunt's living room, and at the desk in the back corner sat only one librarian, an older woman with a streak of white slicing through her graying hair right at the temple—a lightning bolt emanating from her brain—and penetrating eyes, and the most regally upright posture Margaret had ever seen, and she had let her instinct guide her.

Mrs. Adelman? she said. I'm here about Marie.

The librarian said nothing at first, just studied Margaret in silence for a long time. As if they'd met in a past life and she was trying to place her. Then a change came across her face, like clouds in a strong breeze shifting across the sky.

Oh yes, she said. I know *you.*

Then, after a moment of quiet: I gave her your book, you know.

It was one of many books the librarian had given Marie over the years. They'd first struck up a friendship, the two of them, when Marie came in trying to trace her roots. Mrs. Adelman had helped her find the right archives and historical societies to contact, and she had been there, too, when Marie had reached the hole in the records where the rest of her lineage had been erased. Her own grandparents had fled Munich in the 1930s, but the rest of the family had stayed, and though it wasn't the same, she knew the pain of fault lines in family history that you could not see across. Then, as Marie grew older and her interests broadened, Mrs. Adelman had loved following her mind, feeding this girl whose appetite to *know* was omnivorous and insatiable. *Notes of a Native Son.* Biographies of Gandhi and Grace Lee Boggs. Books on ecology, on tarot, on space exploration and climate change. And poetry, too: Marie had started with the poems from school, Keats and Wordsworth and Yeats, and had come looking for more, and the librarian had helped her find it: Lucille Clifton, Adrienne Rich, Ada Limón, Ross Gay. All of these books the librarian had given to Marie and Marie had dutifully returned each two weeks later, never once overdue. The week Marie headed off to college, she'd come to the library one last time and Mrs. Adelman had slipped a slim parcel in blue wrapping paper across the counter. Written inside the flyleaf: *You never need to give this one back.* On the cover, a close-up photo of a split pomegranate, seeds glistening like jewels.

We've removed it, Mrs. Adelman said. Not my decision. After Marie, people started calling in. Some of them wanted to borrow it. But then, once the talk-radio shows and those cable guys went after you, people got scared. How could we keep such a book, they wanted to know. If you were really a subversive, how could we risk letting young minds see it? In the end the higher-ups decided it was easier to just remove it. The mayor was nervous.

Same thing's been happening other places, according to my friends. Not just your book; anything with the remotest ties to China. Anything Asian. Anything that might be a risk.

It's cowardly, Margaret said, and Mrs. Adelman said, Well, they've got children, too, you know.

There was a long silence.

Your son, Mrs. Adelman said. The news said you had a son. How old?

Nine, Margaret said. Ten in the summer.

In silence she tried to imagine Bird's birthday. Would there be a cake? Candles? What would they celebrate? Would he miss her? All she can picture is a dark room.

So before they removed him, you removed yourself.

Margaret nodded dumbly.

It devastated Marie, Mrs. Adelman said. Those children taken to silence their parents, and the news not even mentioning it. Everyone staying quiet, pretending it didn't happen, saying they deserved it. All those families, split apart.

On the news they showed only a few, the cases where it seemed clear-cut, the right answer obvious and uncomplicated.

How many? Margaret asked.

Too many, Mrs. Adelman said. Not just protesters, either. Anyone opposed to PACT. And more every day.

Margaret had the sudden feeling of picking up on a frequency she had not previously been able to hear. It had grown dark; by then the library had closed. No one had come in.

Hardly anyone comes in these days, Mrs. Adelman said. People are nervous. If they come in, they get what they want and go.

Where can I find them, Margaret asked. The families. How can I reach them.

I've *heard*, Mrs. Adelman said slowly. There are people starting to try to track down the children who've been taken. In hopes of reuniting them with their families.

Is that still possible, Margaret asked, if there are so many of them.

Nine years into PACT, it felt like fighting gravity, or the tide. These protests, people said, shaking their heads, on the news, in the streets. Exercises in futility. All it does is bother the rest of us.

The librarian shrugged. You tell me, she said. If the protests are nothing, then why are you here?

Where can I find these families, Margaret asked, and Mrs. Adelman said, I know of one.

She followed a trail of whispers. The name Mrs. Adelman provided led to more: a friend, a neighbor's sister. I heard of someone. I know someone. No email, no cell phones, nothing that could be traced. One by one she found them, bearing the name of the one who'd sent her as a token of trust. Listening.

Gradually she began to understand how it happened. You said something and someone didn't like it. You did something and someone didn't like it, or perhaps you didn't do something and someone didn't like it. Maybe you were a journalist and you wrote an article that talked about re-placed children, or mentioned the attacks on Asian faces, or dared to question their demonization. Maybe you posted something on social media that criticized PACT, or the authorities, or America. Maybe you got promoted and your coworker got jealous. Maybe you did nothing at all. Someone would appear on your doorstep. Someone called, they'd say, though they would never say who, citing privacy, the sanctity of the system. It only works, they said, if people know they won't be named.

Don't worry, one of the officers would usually say. I'm sure it's nothing. Just our duty to check.

Sometimes it did turn out to be nothing. If you were well connected, if you showed the proper deference, or if perhaps you had a friend in the mayor's office or the statehouse or, even better, the federal government, if in their background investigation it turned out you'd donated money to the right groups, or perhaps if you were willing to donate money now—well, then, perhaps you could make clear that you would never instill dangerous ideologies in your child. But so often it was not nothing. Most often, by the time the officers came: there was something. You had done something, you had said something, you had not done something, you had not said something. If you didn't have the resources to buy your way out with money or influence, at the end of it, they took your child and put them into the back seat of a car already waiting at the curb, and then they were gone.

She'd believed it was just a handful of extreme cases, the ones that made the news—high-profile, cautionary tales. But mostly, she learned—as she found one family, then another—it happened quietly. Nothing reported at all, their removals and re-placements unannounced. The families reported nothing themselves: speaking about PACT was complaining about PACT, which would only prove their disloyalty. Most of them stayed silent, hoping that in their silence, what had been taken would be returned. People began to hold their children closer, began to bite their tongues. They shied away from discussing PACT at all, afraid they might be next. Editors and producers wielded their red pens more freely: Let's not say that, best not to ruffle feathers. It happened so slowly that you might not even notice it at all, like the sky turning from dusk to dark. The calculation everyone made before parting their lips, before setting fingers to keys: how important was it to say? You glanced at the crib in the corner, at your child sprawled on the rug with their toys.

By the time she'd spoken with five families, she understood: it was more people than she'd realized, more people than she'd ever thought of. It had been happening all along, and she'd never known. No, she admitted to herself: she'd never chosen to know.

By the seventh family, she had run out of money. She had to be careful, too: passersby might not recognize her offhand, but if the police stopped her, even on the slightest of pretexts, they would demand ID, and everything would unravel. She had an unconvincing fake license, purchased in an alley for a hundred dollars—another name, a photo of another Chinese woman who looked nothing like her except the part of her hair and the wary expression on her face. But the police would run it through the system and discover the fraud immediately. After that it would happen quickly: they would arrest her for using false ID, they'd investigate further, they'd check their files for persons of interest, and it would only be a matter of time before they figured out who she really was. Margaret Miu: dozens of counts of incitement to her name, one for every anti-PACT poster and protester bearing her words. And now, liable for Marie's death, as well.

So she moved with caution: keeping to quiet streets, careful not to attract attention. She thought of her parents, the mantra of her entire childhood: *Don't stick out.* So little had changed in all that time; it was just a little more obvious now. In her head she heard her mother's stunned voice on that last phone call, pictured her father's face in the moment before he was pushed. Unaware of what more was to come. *Hide*, they would have said to her. *Head down, out of sight.* But she did not want to hide. Now she understood that there were so many more stories than she'd imagined. Each person she spoke to knew another, sometimes two more, or three. In her head she did the math. Too many to ignore. How could everyone not know?

The bus dropped her in Chinatown, and she walked up, up, up, following Third as the street numbers climbed higher. The same route that her son would take years later. As she walked, she remembered the long treks uptown, after curfew, from that crowded apartment with Domi and her ex and his sister, up to the quiet golden bubble she and Ethan shared. She remembered, still, how to avoid the corners where policemen stood, the areas where she might be conspicuous, and she skirted these, taking the long way around, looping down side streets and around corners until she was sure she was in the clear. Working her way over to Park, she found it: the red brick townhouse with huge apple-green doors. The round window set in the white arch above, like a Cyclops's watchful eye.

Hello, she said, as the door opened. A middle-aged white man wearing a decorous navy suit and a deferential expression. Is this still the Duchess residence?

When Margaret was at last ushered through the marble-floored entryway and up the sweeping staircase, there she was. A little plumper, a little older. New wrinkles creasing from nose to chin, bracketing her mouth. Eyes tired, faintly ringed. But still the same.

Well, well, Domi said. Look who it is.

She had never expected to see Domi again. After the way they'd parted, after the last thing Domi had said to her: *Sellout. Whore. Fuck you.* She'd put Domi out of her mind, packed their time together in the smallest box she could, taped it firmly shut. Then, years later, scrolling the news while Bird napped, she'd spotted a headline: the largest gift ever given to the New York Public Library. The name beneath leaping out like a ghost from the shadows. *Electronics heiress Dominique Duchess.* Duchess Technologies. And a photo. Last time she'd seen her, Domi had been in a man's leather jacket and lug-soled boots, both hand-me-downs from Margaret. The blond of her ponytail streaked dark with sweat and grime. In the photo she was impeccable in a tailored Chanel suit. Her hair was blown to pale gold, clipped short in the businesslike bob Domi had always mocked: rich man's wife, she'd called it, after her stepmother.

Margaret scrolled through the article. New head of Duchess Technologies. Founded by her late father—inherited after his death. Groundbreaking audio components—smallest and lightest—revolutionized cell-phone technology. And the caption: *Ms. Duchess, at home in her Park Avenue residence.*

She remembered that house, that rare single-family, the golden numbers gleaming against the brick, the lantern above the entrance, patinaed to green, held aloft by twin swirls of iron. *Snakes,* Domi had said, looking up at them, *I thought they were snakes, as a kid.* They'd been hungry that day; she remembered her stomach growling. Her feet throbbing. The sound their spit made as it hit the sidewalk. *Fuck you,* Domi had screamed up at the windows, and then, as her father's face appeared behind the glass, she'd grabbed Margaret's hand and they'd jumped on their bikes and fled, laughing, pedaling and pedaling until their thighs ached.

So Domi called Daddy after all. Margaret clicked the browser window shut. Well, fuck *you,* Domi, she thought.

But in the following years Domi appeared again and again, in small sharp flashes. Donations to women's shelters, to food banks, to union groups. Donations for health-care assistance. Donations to libraries, a string of them, all over New York, here and there all over the country. Margaret watched, holding these acts up to the Domi she'd once known, as if holding a sealed letter to the light. The night before she left, she'd scribbled down that address on Park Avenue—the one person who might help, the only person left besides Ethan who'd ever cared about her—and hidden it in the safest place she could think of, because it was too painful to go without leaving even one bread crumb behind.

And here she was. Life had a strange symmetry, she thought: years ago she'd left Domi to take refuge with Ethan; now it was the other way around. Domi touched Margaret's arm, and her hands, once red and chapped from the cold as she clutched Margaret's in the night, were soft and pale, like just-risen dough. Margaret kissed her on the cheek and it, too, was tender, so tender she expected to see the imprint of her lips on Domi's skin.

It's good to see you, Domi said.

In the end Domi had decided to hide, too. At the depth of the Crisis, around the time Margaret had left New York, Domi had called her father. Help me, she said, and he'd sent a car within the hour. He'd whisked her out of New York to the safety of the countryside, a summer cabin in Connecticut she hadn't seen since she was a child, which her father had built when the land had been cheap, before his company took off, before they'd had any real money. When he'd still just been Claude Duchess, a young upstart businessman; when her mother had still been alive. Over the years, as his company had grown, he'd acquired the parcels of land around it, chipping out a larger and larger pocket of wilderness around them; he'd added a powerful generator, a fresh coat of paint—but it still bore the traces of what it had been, just a simple house set away from everything, beside a rocky little ocean inlet. So when he wanted to escape the unrest in the city, what better place than here, in the past, a time when everything was still in the future for him, when the world was nothing but possibility? Here alone, out of all his houses, they did not have to hear protests in the streets or the eerie silences in between; here, there was nothing but the constant whoosh of the ocean's waves. Here, they could pretend they were not eating cake while everyone else had no bread.

Domi had stepped inside, steel-toed boots clumping against the polished wooden floors, flecks of city grit still ground into her roughened palms. There was her stepmother on the leather sofa, reading a magazine, but her bedroom was exactly as she remembered: the way her own mother had decorated it in her childhood, all pink and lace and pearls. Welcome home, her father had said awkwardly. Elsa had grudgingly left her alone, and that was how they'd weathered the Crisis, the three of them: circling each other at a distance, trapped like flies in the amber of the past. Their fortune vast as a mammoth ship, unswayed by the currents and waves that buffeted smaller, lesser boats. They could order what they needed, afford whatever it took, for as long as it took. All they had to do was wait.

A few months after PACT passed, Domi's father and Elsa were headed to the Maldives—a weekend vacation, to celebrate the return to *normal*—when their private plane crashed into the Pacific. Everything had gone to Domi: the houses in Malibu and Provence; the apartment in the 16th arrondissement and the townhouse here on Park; the electronics empire, smaller than before the Crisis, but still ticking out crucial parts for phones and smartwatches, still more than enough to support all this. And all the secrets too: accusations from her father's factories in Hanoi and Shenzhen, complaints about long hours, hazardous materials, years of ignored reports. The donations to senators who'd passed tax cuts and exemptions for men like him, who'd go on to champion PACT and everything that came after. All hers now, to tabulate and reckon and repay.

I'm finding out, says Domi, some of things he did. For me, or so he thought.

She and Margaret were sitting in the glass-roofed courtyard— the winter garden, Domi called it—glasses of iced tea sweating in their hands. A square pocket of green lined with potted arborvitae, carved into the belly of this vault of a house. Rooms of sturdy furniture and solid brick fortressed them on four sides, filled with all the fine trinkets Domi's father had collected and kept. Above, thick glass sheltered them from possible rain. They could not be seen or heard from outside; for the first time in weeks, Margaret found she could catch her breath. And yet she felt like an insect sealed in a jar.

So now what, Domi said. What are you going to do? Hole up here, forever, with me? Get a fake passport and flee the country?

There was the faintest whiff of mockery in her voice, and Margaret couldn't tell if it was aimed at her, or at Domi herself. Of course there were places where a person could hide: Margaret could take a new name, lie low. Keep her head down; start again. She thought again of her parents, how they'd lived their whole lives trying to avoid trouble, and in the end it had ferreted them out anyway. Maybe sometimes, she thought, the bird with its head held high took flight. Maybe sometimes, the nail that stuck up pierced the foot that stomped down.

Not hiding, she said. Something else.

The idea was not fully formed in her mind yet, only a need:

the need to make up for years of choosing to look away, of remaining deliberately incurious. For thinking that it didn't matter as long as it was somebody else's child. It was just starting to come to her, the seeds of it barely beginning to root: what she would do with these stories, the messages of hope and love and care and longing. She would go out and gather them, like grains of rice gleaned from threshed-out fields. She would find as many as she could.

To Domi, she said: I need your help.

All over the country, zigging and zagging, she traced the flow of information. Emails could be hacked, calls intercepted. But libraries shared books all the time; pooling information was part of their work. Crates of books shuttled between them, crammed with loaned bounty: rare texts on obscure painters, guidebooks on esoteric hobbies. It was the librarians' job to sort these books, to label each with a slip bearing the requester's name, to set them on the shelf behind the counter in neat rows, ready to be claimed.

Now and then, though, an extra book would find its way into a crate and arrive in some faraway city, unannounced. A clerical mistake; a simple human error. With no one to meet them at the gates, these stowaways would simply be set aside, to be shipped back home in the next crate. No one would notice, of course, if a librarian idly riffled through it, nor think anything amiss if they found a slip of paper inside. People left things in books all the time, and most libraries had a bulletin board where these mislaid items were thumbtacked: bookmarks, of course, but also sales receipts, travel brochures, business cards, shopping lists, cancelled checks, toothpicks, popsicle sticks, plastic knives, once even a strip of bacon sealed in a plastic sandwich bag. No one paid much attention to these things, and no one would notice if a librarian happened to pluck a note from a stowaway book, or from the bulletin board, and pocket it.

The messages were short. To a casual observer they resembled a list of call numbers, an arbitrary jumble of letters and digits and decimal points. But to those who knew to pull out the stray books, who collected these missives from their far-off colleagues, they said volumes. Encoded in them: the names of children who'd been taken, a brief description. The names and locations of their families. All over the country, a scattered network of librarians would note this information, collating it with the Rolodex in their minds, cross-referencing it with the re-placed children they might have learned about. Some kept a running written list, but most, wary, simply trusted to memory. An imperfect system, but the brain of a librarian was a capacious place. Each of them had reasons of their own for taking this risk, and though most of them would never share these reasons with the others, would never even meet them face-to-face, all of them shared the same desperate hope of making a match, of sending a note back, sandwiched between pages, with a child's new location. A message to reassure the family that their child still existed, even if far away, to place a bottom on the deep hole of their loss. Librarians, of all people, understood the value of knowing, even if that information could not yet be used.

Such messages were rare, though a handful of children had been found. More often, the notes were memorized or jotted down, then tucked into a new book to be passed forward in the next crate to the next city, the lists of the missing and the re-placed growing like twin prongs of a long sharp fork. There were so many names, and the network was few and patchwork, dependent on memory and luck, two dots aligning just long enough for someone to make the connection and join them with a stroke. Meanwhile, all that could be done was to remember, and to pass the information along: to the next librarian, the next city, and—when she could persuade them—to Margaret.

One by one she searched out the families whose children had been taken, the ones waiting in vain for the holes in their lives to scar closed. She met them on lunch breaks, on park benches, walked round and round the block with them, holding their cigarettes, waiting for them to be ready. If they wanted, sometimes she talked to them about Bird, telling them about him, about what she missed, which was everything. Other times she simply waited with them, as long as it took. Days of visits that passed in silence; three hours sitting wordless in the park. Ten blocks, fifteen, fifty. Until they trusted her. Until they wanted to speak. Until they wanted their stories to be told.

Tell me, she said. What you want to say to them. What you want them to hear. What you still remember. She wrote it all down, just as the words came out.

They are not just Asian American families, she finds: there are white journalists who'd researched the re-placements, Latina activists who'd organized protests. Not all of them want to speak to her. Some don't trust her, with her Chinese face: You all caused the Crisis and you want us to feel sorry for you? Some Asian Americans don't trust her either, sure she's only making things worse. They've seen what happened when they spoke up; now, twice shy, they shake their heads and close the door in her face without a word.

Other people are angry: if you hadn't written that poem, they insist, this would never have happened. Some believe she has deliberately egged on the protests, that she is behind it all. She does not argue or try to explain as their voices chase her down the hallway, out onto the street. Some are afraid: families who have no papers, who live in terror of raids, or worse. And some people chide her for coming too late. One older woman—a Choctaw woman, whose granddaughter had been taken—looked at Margaret for a long time with weary eyes, then clicked her teeth.

You think this is something new? She shook her head.

Margaret listened. She began to learn: there was no new thing under the sun. About the schools where Indigenous children were shorn and stripped, renamed, reeducated, and returned home broken and scarred—or never at all. About children borne across borders in their parents' arms only to be caged in warehouses, alone and afraid. About foster children pinballed from home to home, their own families sometimes unable to track their path. Things she'd been able to not know, until now. There was a long history of children taken, the pretexts different but the reasons the same. A most precious ransom, a cudgel over a parent's head. It was whatever the opposite of an anchor was: an attempt to uproot some otherness, something hated and feared. Some foreignness seen as an invasive weed, something to be eradicated.

But most of the families are hungry to speak, ravenous with story. She wrote down how their children had been taken, what they wanted to say to those children, the most precious things they would never forget, the things they needed said but did not dare to say themselves. Trying to save every one, all the stories hushed and hidden, all the faces and names too precious to be forgotten. She scribbled them down, in a notepad she carried in the left cup of her bra, the writing so small you'd almost need a magnifier to read it. When that notebook was full, she got another, then another, tucking the old ones into the pocket of her jeans, the side of her sock. Bearing them on her body. At night, she leafed through the pages, engraving the names and stories on her heart, Bird and Ethan haunting every word.

In the early days, it was the librarians who took her in. Some had lounges and sofas; a few even had shower stalls for the staff who'd once biked to work but were long gone. At the others, once the librarian had headed home, she wandered until she found a quiet corner, away from windows. In the shelter of a high shelf she would spread out her bedroll, and then, as she tried to settle her mind for sleep, she would allow herself the luxurious pain of thinking about Ethan and Bird. In the day, she sealed them out, but paused here in the night, the rags she'd stuffed into the gaps of her mind worked loose, and they seeped back in, like fog.

She longed for the broad firm comfort of Ethan curled against her back, the calm that enveloped her whenever he was near. So many things she wished she could tell him: the stories she'd heard, the families she'd met, all the things that would be easier to hold, together. Small joys, too: the silver-green dragonfly that had landed on her forearm, stilled its wings, then vanished again; the improbable red of the maple leaves just beginning to fall—things that felt only half real when she could not share them with him. And Bird: he was the hollow to which her mind, like water, inevitably ran. How tall was he—up to her nose? Her brows? Would he be able to look her straight in the eye? Did he still clip his hair short or had he let it grow shaggy, did it hang in his eyes, was it still the same brown as Ethan's or had it darkened with age to coffee-colored, or even black like her own? Had he lost the last of his baby teeth, and if so, had Ethan plucked them from beneath his pillow and saved them, did Bird even put them beneath his pillow anymore or did he no longer believe in such childish things? What had happened at school today, did he smirk at an inside joke with a friend, was someone unkind to him, was it raining where he was, and if it was, had he remembered his rain jacket or was he soaked to the skin? What was he dreaming, far away, did he still sleep with one arm thrown across his face like a blindfold, were they happy dreams or sad, did she ever appear in them, did he remember her at all, and if he did, was it with love or with hate? She hated herself in these moments, when she tried to picture Bird's face and knew that what she remembered was growing further and further from the truth, that she had missed so much that could never be retrieved.

Most nights, she got up and roamed the library, not daring to turn on the lights but guiding herself by the maze of shelves, fingertips walking the spines of the books. Eventually she would pull one down, something about its feel catching her attention, and take it to bed, burying herself in whatever it had to say. Programming languages; basic electronics; French cuisine. The evolution of the panda's paw. One night, she found she had selected a biography of a poet: Anna Akhmatova. Akhmatova was so beloved in Russia, it said, that you could buy a porcelain figurine of her, wearing a gray flowered dress and a red shawl. It was said that in 1924 most homes had one, though this was impossible to verify, because many of the figurines were later smashed during the Terror. Akhmatova was forbidden to write, Margaret read, but she did so anyway. She wrote about her friends, arrested and dying in prison camps. She wrote about her former husband, shot for treason. Most of all she wrote about her son, locked in a prison that she visited daily but was never allowed to enter. Finally, agonizingly, she wrote about Stalin—effusive, flowery, goose-stepping praise—hoping that her compliments would persuade him to pardon her son, but they did not. Years later, when her son was released at last, he believed that his mother had not tried to free him, that she cared more for her poetry than for him, and their relationship was never the same.

Margaret told this story to herself over and over, so that she would not forget it.

Once upon a time in Russia, a poet was forbidden from writing her verse. Instead of silence, she chose fire. Each night she wrote her lines on scraps of paper, working them over and over, committing them to memory. At dawn she touched a match to the paper and reduced her words to ash. Over the years her words repeated this cycle—resurrection in the darkness, death at first light—until eventually their lives were inscribed in flame. The poet murmured her poems into the ears of her friends, who memorized them and carried them away tucked under their tongues. Mouth to ear, they passed them on to others, until the whole world whispered with the poet's lost lines.

The next morning, the librarian found her with head pressed to the page, mirrored letters tattooed on her cheek.

As she gathered more and more stories, a curious thing began to happen: some of the families invited her into their homes, asking her to join them at the table, offering a spare bed if they had it, a sofa if they didn't, a folded blanket on the floor when that was the best they could do. The gentle nighttime noises of a home comforted her: the soft padding of slippered feet shuffling through the dark from bedroom to bathroom and back again; the tangled murmur of adult voices speaking softly, even though the children were not there to wake; the quiet creaks and ticks of a house settling, as if, its occupants sleeping, it could finally loosen its girdle and breathe. But they punished her, too: late at night, the only one awake, nestled in the core of someone else's life, she missed Bird and Ethan even more, the hurt of it so vicious the room blurred.

One night, curled in her bedroll on the floor of a family's kitchen, she awoke to a man's hands on her. She'd startled, every muscle in her body iron-tense, coiled to fight. But no: it was the father, carefully spreading a cover over her. Mohamad, his name was. Earlier that evening, she'd sat beside him and his wife and eaten maqluba and listened to them tell the story of their son. *I was a child when the Twin Towers fell*, he had said toward the end. Someone spray-painted filthy things on our garage door. Someone broke our front window with a brick. My father hung a huge American flag on our house, for a while.

He'd paused, and his wife took his hand.

None of our neighbors did or said anything to help us, he said.

Now, the night had grown cold, and here he was tucking a blanket around her with such tenderness she might have been his lost child.

When he had gone, Margaret touched it with her hands and felt unimaginable softness, plush and warm, like the shaggy pelt of some luxurious beast, and she fell into a deep sleep. In the morning, she awoke to find it was just a blanket, of course—a large, soft, fluffy one, printed with the bold striped face of a tiger. For the next three nights she slept under the tiger skin, as she thought of it, and when she left that apartment she had embraced the couple and carried the warmth of that tiger blanket inside her like a benediction.

Miles and months passed. A year, then two. She marked the time by Bird's age: now he was ten, now he was eleven, now eleven and a half. The list of things she knew she had missed grew and grew. Learning to swim, learning to dance; new interests and obsessions she could only begin to imagine. A birthday, then another. The days were a blur of buses and trains, of tired tramping across cities, and at night she dreamed of hovering high in in the clouds and seeing herself from above, a small speck crossing the landscape. A fly crawling over an endless map.

What kept her going was this: every few weeks, a news story caught her eye. She'd abandoned her phone when she left home, of course, but she heard snippets of radio as she passed a store, or scavenged newspapers discarded on the sidewalk. Over and over they came, her own words echoing back to her, not on signs or in marches this time but woven into strange happenings, things so odd—half protest, half art—that they caught people's attention, forcing them to take note; things that unsettled them days and weeks later, knotting a tangle in the chest. Bursts punctuating the static of those endless days, pushing her onward.

In Nashville, statues appeared in the early morning mist, a hundred ghostly children cast from ice. ALL OUR MISSING HEARTS, read a sign chained around one's neck. The police arrived with handcuffs at the ready, but whoever had placed them was gone. Just a prank, one officer radioed back to the station, it's just ice, but— Around them, commuters paused, shaken for once out of their routines. Some snapped photos, but most simply stood mesmerized, even just for a moment, watching in silence as the small faces slowly, slowly dissolved and blurred. One of them reached out and touched what had once been the face of a little girl, melting a thumb-shaped indent in her cheek. The police shooed them away, cordoned off the area, set up a perimeter in case the perpetrators returned. It took most of the morning for the statues to melt, and for hours the officers on duty would glance up at the skyscrapers and see the silhouettes of people in the windows above, staring down at the fading blocks of ice, and later, at the dark damp patches where children had once stood.

In Des Moines one morning, the main street was painted red, block after block after block. From the news helicopters above, it looked like a stream of blood slicing straight through the city. Stenciled on the sidewalk where the source of the river would lie: BRING BACK OUR MISSING HEARTS. Those who discovered it first found that the paint was still wet, and as they walked away they left trails of footprints that grew indistinct, then disappeared. That night, and in the days and weeks to come, people would find streaks of red on the soles of their shoes and the cuffs of their pants and the sleeves of their jackets and pause, thinking *blood*, their chests seizing, patting themselves for the hurt.

In Austin, outside the governor's mansion: a giant concrete cube with a crack running down the center, a crowbar by its side. Etched into the cube, four chiseled letters: P A C T. Etched into the crowbar: OUR MISSING HEARTS. One by one, passersby picked up the bar and hefted it, but no one dared swing, and when the police arrived they'd confiscated it as a dangerous weapon. The cube they loaded onto a flatbed and hauled away.

The authorities made no official statements, hoping to avoid publicity, but these happenings were so bizarre, so eye-catching, that they attracted attention. In the days after each happened, photos of them splashed across social media, going viral each time; eyewitness accounts and videos circulated from those who'd been there and seen it. Newspapers who might have ignored a march or a protest sent photographers and reporters to the scene. Pranks, some authorities insisted, when pressed. Just meaningless pranks. Others took a harsher tone: Subversion. A threat to civil society. Des Moines had spent a hundred thousand dollars painting the streets black again.

But they kept happening, and Margaret, on the road, watched. She noticed that people complained about marches blocking traffic, about the futility and inconvenience, but something about these strange happenings caught their attention and held it. She spotted passersby pausing on the sidewalk to zoom in on the photos on their phones or linger over articles about them before tossing their papers into the trash. She overheard people talking about these happenings on street corners, on subway platforms, over coffee on café patios. Not irritated or dismissive, but filled with curiosity and sometimes even delight at the unexpected weirdness of them. *Did you see? Did you hear about? Isn't it crazy? What do you think—?*

By the time Bird was eleven, these happenings were nearly monthly. Each time she saw her words in one, she felt a peculiar and not unwelcome glow—even as she knew that with every mention of *missing hearts*, another line appeared in her file. One more thing she would be held responsible for, though she knew no more about them than anyone else. It was as if those words were their own independent creatures, off leading their own life—which, in truth, they were. What did you call it—surely not pride, because you could take no credit for these accomplishments, you could only marvel like a stranger at the things this *being* had gone on to do without you. It kept her moving, the thought that others out there were thinking about the children who had been taken, too. Each happening she heard about jump-started her again when the journey and the weight of the stories had nearly drained her dry. We haven't forgotten, they seemed to say, have you?

Who's doing it? she asked one of the librarians. Who's behind them all?

Those art pranks? the librarian sniffed. Margaret had noticed this, a certain disdain for the protests from the librarians—and it was understandable, that when they were painstakingly gathering grains of information, listing and tracking and trying to keep records, these happenings felt trivial and frivolous and showy.

What makes you think it's even the same people, the librarian said, sliding the name of another family across the counter, and Margaret thanked her, and departed.

For there were always more children, more stories. It was like picking up seashells on the beach: one more, one more, one more. Each wave depositing another on the wet and gleaming sand. Each shell a relic of a creature once there, now gone. Bird was nearly twelve, and still there were more; she could continue this forever, traveling round and round. Counting the next and the next in an endlessly increasing line.

One day, overcome, she sent a postcard: no message, just a small line drawing. A cat beside a little door. A clue, if they would accept it; an invitation to find the note she'd left for them. To find her. As she dropped it into the mailbox, she imagined it winging its way from truck to sack to the porch of their house. She waited and waited, but no reply came.

Now and then she tried again, each postcard gaining another cat, or two, or five, smaller and smaller, until the entire card was full, the cabinet shrunk to the size of a stamp, then the size of a penny, then the size of a fingernail. There was never any reply. On Bird's twelfth birthday, she took a risk, hunted down one of the few remaining pay phones, and dialed their old number.

Disconnected. By this time Bird had lived a quarter of his life without her; perhaps he didn't even remember she existed. Perhaps it was better that way.

It was then that she decided on a date: October 23. Three years to the day since she'd gone away. She would do it then. In September she sent a note to Domi. It's time, she said. Can you find me a place to stay. Domi, of course, had offered her house, but Margaret had refused.

Somewhere faraway, she said, somewhere no one will look. Somewhere I won't take you down, if I'm caught.

A week later she'd arrived in New York, made her way to Brooklyn and the darkened brownstone. The next day she went out into the city, cap pulled low over her face, in search of bottle caps.

I have someone, the librarian said.

Astoria: a small branch library. Margaret had been in New York for two weeks already, camped out in the darkened brownstone, making final preparations, filling her bottle caps. Two weeks left to go. She should stop collecting stories; already she had more than she could use. But she did not want to stop. What she wanted was to find every one of them, though she knew this was impossible, because there would always be more.

The librarian lowered her voice, even though there was no one else in the room, no one else in the building, nothing around them but half-empty shelves. Not a family, she went on. A child.

Margaret sat up straighter. In all these years she hadn't spoken to a single re-placed child. They were well concealed: new

cities, new families, new names. All that was left was the trail
of grief in their absence, the snagged holes they'd left behind.
The few they'd tracked down were inaccessible, fortressed in
their new homes and new lives. Those who were taken young
enough sometimes didn't remember their old lives, their old families, at all.

She wandered into the main branch a couple months ago, the
librarian said. A runaway. From Baltimore, originally. Bold little
thing, she added, half chuckling. Marched in there like a policeman. Said: I need you to help me find my parents. Hands on her
hips, like she was giving them a dressing-down. Said she ran
away from a foster family in Cambridge, up near Harvard.

A tingle cinched the back of Margaret's neck. Cambridge, she
said. How old is she?

Thirteen. We're trying to find out more. They moved her
around a lot at first, and no one's at the address she remembers
anymore.

Can I talk to her? Margaret said, pulse thumping. Where is she?

The librarian studied her warily. The moment Margaret
knew so well: when they decided if she could be trusted, and if
so, how far. How much rope she was to be given, how far the door
was to be pushed ajar.

The scale tipped.

She's at one of the branches, the librarian said. I can get you
the address. We've been moving her around, trying to find a long-
term place for her.

And there she was: a girl, cross-legged on a makeshift pallet.
Big brown eyes like two blazing stars.

Margaret, she repeated, when Margaret introduced herself, are you Margaret Miu?

And in the stunned silence that followed, Sadie smiled.

I know your poems, she said. And then: I know Bird, too.

The government had commissioned a study: Children under the age of twelve, once removed from their parents, could not be expected to find their way back home unassisted. Those above twelve were usually sent to a state-run center; younger children could be placed in foster care. Sadie had been eleven when they'd taken her.

They'd moved her from place to place in quick succession— first West Virginia, then Erie, then Boston—farther and farther, as if trying to pull her from orbit. From her first foster home, she called her old number: disconnected. She wrote letter after letter, zip code neatly printed in ink, plastered with stamps stolen from the second. No response, but she'd remained hopeful: maybe when she'd been transferred she'd missed it; maybe behind her, letters from her parents were trailing like the tail of a kite, always a step too late. Then, at her third foster home in Cambridge, a letter came back: UNKNOWN.

Come with me, she'd said to Bird, but in the end she'd gone alone.

Two buses and a train ride back to Baltimore, with money filched from her foster father's wallet, the address still etched in her memory even though her mother's face had begun to blur. Everything dreamily familiar: the neighbor's tulips, pink against the green lawn. The ambient buzz of a mower on the summer air. The same picture she'd clung to so staunchly for the last two years.

But when she ran up the steps, the door was locked. The woman who answered was a white woman, a stranger. A kind face, mousy hair pulled back in a bun. Honey, no one like that lives here, she said.

She'd moved in six months ago. No, she didn't know who lived here before that. Did Sadie need help? Was there someone she could call?

Sadie ran.

She'd slipped onto the first train out of the station, burrowed into a corner seat, awoke in the bustle of Penn Station. Overwhelmed and alone. She struggled out of the low, rat-colored hallways of the terminal, past the one-footed pigeons scrabbling for crumbs, past the homeless men with cardboard signs and jingling cups, past the scum of litter on the curb. Above her rose a canopy of scaffolding, net nearly obscuring the REBUILDING THE NYC YOU ❤ stenciled across it. Above that, needles of glass and concrete jabbed at the clouds.

And then, out of the gloom, she'd spotted the big gray arches, on the far side of a patch of green.

Back in Cambridge, she had loved the peace of the library. Loitering among the shelves, opening and closing the books still left standing there. Many were gone, she knew, but these were survivors; she took them down from the shelves and flipped through them, breathed them in. Imagined how many others had read and handled these books before her.

One day the librarian caught her. Sadie looked up, her nose to the page, to see the librarian at the end of the aisle, bemused. They'd seen each other often, of course—in and out, each day she came in—but they never spoke. Sadie had no library card, never asked for assistance, never caused any trouble. The librarian said nothing, and Sadie slammed the book shut and pushed it back onto the shelf and fled. But a few days later, when she'd dared creep into the library again, the librarian had waved her over to the desk. I'm Carina, she said, what's your name?

It took Sadie a while to notice: she wasn't the only one who came in but borrowed nothing. Once or twice people came to the counter, held murmured, intense conversations with the librarian, and left, looking anxious or anguished or hopeful, or all three. Now and then wayward books came down the book return, shuddering their way into the collection bin: tattered paperbacks, old textbooks, sometimes just a magazine. As if someone had made a mistake, dropping the wrong thing down the chute. One day she'd wedged herself through the book return, fished one out. A note between the pages with a name, an age, and a description: a child taken, like her. A family's plea that the network would encode, and remember, and pass on.

We are filling in the cracks, the librarian admitted, wherever we can.

So when Sadie had ended up in New York, no trace of her parents anymore, she knew where to go. When she spotted the library, it had felt like something out of a fairy tale: a palace guarded by two mighty lions, pale gray, impassive. She climbed the steps and stretched to set her hand on one massive paw, fingers curving between the broad claws, and it came back to her like a scent on the breeze: a story her mother had read her once. A little girl lost and alone, aided by a lion, the king of that land. She looked around. There was the street lamp. And here in front of her was the magical doorway that might take her home.

The library was almost empty; it was nearly closing time, and Sadie wandered until she found a quiet corner, an old armchair in the children's section, where posters that said READ still hung over half-emptied bookshelves. She curled up and fell asleep and awoke to a young woman patting her shoulder.

Hello there, she said to Sadie. It looks like you're lost.

You're Bird's mom, aren't you? Sadie said.

Margaret touched her hips, her heart, checking for the notebooks that she'd carried so long they felt like part of her flesh.

I was, she said.

He told me about you, Sadie said, and to Margaret it had felt like a sign.

Sadie, young and motherless and fearless. After three months on her own, half wary adult, half child.

I know somewhere she can stay, Margaret said to the librarian.

It took some time, convincing Domi.

You've got to be fucking kidding, M., she'd protested. What do I know about kids.

They were speaking in fierce whispers, while Sadie waited, cross armed and skeptical, at the far end of the living room. Out of the corner of her eye, Domi studied her, and imperiously, unabashedly, Sadie studied her back.

You know as well as I do, Margaret said, that the brownstone isn't a place for a child. And I can't keep an eye on her myself anyway. I've got too much to do.

What is it exactly, Domi said, that you want me to do?

Keep her safe. Just while I'm finishing up. And after it's done, we'll find somewhere better. Maybe we can find her parents. But she needs somewhere now. She's been shuttled from library to library for weeks and they won't be able to hide her forever. It's a miracle they've been able to this long.

She paused. Or are you too cramped for space? she added dryly. A glance around the enormous living room, at the ceiling where, overhead, a half dozen bedrooms sat unused.

Domi let out a long slow breath through her nostrils. Still the sign, after all these years, that Margaret had won.

Fine. But she'll have to take care of herself. I don't have time to be babysitting.

I only need my diaper changed twice a day, Sadie called from across the room.

Domi laughed.

Hmm, she said. She's got a sense of humor, at least.

The two of them sized each other up—the tall blond woman in her suit and high heels, the little brown girl in her hoodie and fading jeans—and Margaret had felt it between them then, the crackle of kindred spirits, of like meeting like.

It was Sadie who'd finally told Margaret, some days later: But Bird doesn't live at that house anymore. Didn't you know? They live in a dorm now. I can tell you where.

Why didn't you tell me, Bird says. Why didn't she come down when I was there?

We'd told her to stay out of sight, Margaret says. So no one would spot her and start asking questions. You'll see her soon, I promise. But I needed this time with you. I needed—

She stops, clippers poised.

Someone's here, she murmurs.

Bird hears it, too: the sound of someone at the back door. It is raining, he realizes; though he can't see it through the boarded-up windows, in the sudden silence he can hear it tapping against the plywood, like small, insistent fingers. Over the rain they hear the rattle of the knob being tested. Then the faint low beeps of the keypad: One number. Another. Another.

Bird turns to his mother, waiting for a cue. To fight or to flee. To brace or to take cover. Margaret doesn't move. A thousand scenarios flicker through her head, each worse than the last. Where Bird will be taken. Where they'll take her. Stay calm, she tells herself. Think. But there is nowhere for them to hide, and even if she takes him by the hand and flees through the front, out into the street, where would they go, in the rain, in this city of strangers? Into whose hands?

Footsteps thud out in the darkened hallway. Someone trying to move quietly, and failing. And then the door to the living room creaks open. It's the Duchess, in a black raincoat. Shaking the wet from her feet.

Fuck, Domi, Margaret says. You scared me.

She lets out her breath, and Bird finds this more unsettling than her profanity, even more than their unexpected guest: that his mother, too, could be frightened.

I couldn't exactly ring the bell, could I, the Duchess says. Or call ahead.

She and Margaret exchange a shrug, and Bird understands: cell phones, of course, can be traced.

What time is it? Margaret asks.

Almost four.

I thought we said tomorrow morning.

The Duchess unzips the raincoat and peels it from one arm, then the other. With a glance she takes in the table, the litter of wire snippings and bottle caps and the shiny coins of the batteries.

So you're still going through with it, she says.

Margaret stiffens. Of course, she says.

The Duchess's gaze sweeps around the room like a searchlight, illuminating things Bird himself has barely even noticed. The garbage can in the corner, overflowing. The foam cup from yesterday's noodles, still slick with oil, on the floor at Bird's feet. Bird himself in three-day-old clothes, his hair unbrushed and untidy, half-obscuring his eyes.

I thought things might have changed, she says. Now that— Her eyes pause on Bird.

Nothing's changed, Margaret says sharply.

The Duchess drapes her raincoat over the back of the armchair. As always she moves like a ship in full sail: puffed with purpose. She settles herself on the arm of the sofa, beside Margaret.

You can still change your mind, she says.

Margaret fiddles with the knob on the soldering iron, lifts it from its wire sheath, touches its tip to the damp sponge. It gives off a faint, resentful hiss.

It's not just about *me*, she says. You know that.

Under the tip of the soldering iron a drop of molten metal shines silver, then dulls to gray. His mother's eyes are shimmering, like sunlight speckles on wind-rippled water. They tighten and twitch, as if she can't quite make them focus.

I have to, she goes on. I promised them. I owe it to— She hesitates. I owe this, she says.

The Duchess places a hand on top of hers, and Bird sees the tenderness there. The affection.

Margaret looks up, her eyes meeting the Duchess's, and the Duchess sighs—not convinced, but resigned. I'll come tomorrow morning and take Bird, then, she says.

Bird's head jerks up. Take me, he demands. Take me *where*?

To see Sadie, Margaret says brightly. Domi will take the two of you out of the city. Just for one day. While I get this—she waves a hand at the table—this project under way.

Somewhere nice, Domi says. I think you'll like it.

Why, Bird says. Unconvinced and wary.

His mother sets the soldering iron down, leans across the table, takes his hand in both of hers.

There are some things I have to do, she says. Which I can't do with you here. Domi'll take you, and bring you to Sadie, and then we'll both come and fetch you back. Do you trust me?

Bird hesitates. On the table, the soldering iron lets off a thin curl of smoke. A hot scent, singed metal and pine. He looks at his mother, her hands calloused and rough. But still they are strong and warm and gentle on his. The same hands he remembers lifting a seedling from the soil, plucking an inchworm from his T-shirt and setting it in the grass. Almost by instinct, they align their hands together, finger to finger, palm to palm, the way they used to when making promises. Now his hands are nearly the size of hers. He looks at the deep brown pools of her eyes, and finally he sees her. His mother. She's still there.

Okay, he says, and his mother closes her eyes, lets out a breath.

Tomorrow morning, she says, in Domi's direction. Say ten o'clock. Come for him then.

She opens her eyes and peels her hand away, then picks up the dangling ends of the wires and crimps them savagely.

We don't have much time left, she says. Still a lot to do.

By the time the Duchess leaves, the rain has slowed to a drizzle. As the afternoon begins to fade, Margaret snaps a lid onto the last cap. It is Wednesday. Tomorrow will be three years since she left home.

Enough, she says, softly, and though Bird can hear it, it's clear she's speaking to herself. As if she's telling herself to let go. Giving herself permission to stop, or to move on, neither of them will ever be quite sure which.

With one hand she sweeps the pile of bottle caps from the table and into a plastic bag. Then she hesitates.

Do you want to come with me, she asks. Just this one last time.

For almost four weeks she's been making and planting them, over a hundred a day, in plain sight. No one paid any attention to the old women who wandered the streets, gathering bottles and cans to sell; if anything, people edged back or turned away, embarrassed or disgusted or both. She'd seen them for years: of all things the Crisis had not changed, of all things that had survived, somehow these women were one of them. Dogged, unproud, patiently sifting the trash for what could be salvaged— and many of them, even before the Crisis, Asian. Their faces reminded her of her grandmother's, her mother's, her own, and she thought of them each time she pulled her straw hat lower over her eyes and shuffled down the sidewalk, bending over garbage bins or at the roots of trees. Dressed like one of them, she could go anywhere, if she was careful.

Still, there were close calls. Sometimes the police came: she never saw those who'd called, only looked up to see them peeking from behind the curtains as the patrol car pulled up beside her. When the officer approached, she would tuck a twenty into his back pocket, but once that wasn't enough. He'd clutched her elbow with tight fingers, his breath hot on the side of her neck, until she followed him into an alley and undid his zipper, slipped her hand beneath his waistband. As he writhed and groaned, she'd fixed her gaze on the badge on his chest until he'd arched backward and scrabbled at her hair and let out one last strangled yelp, and at last she was free to go on her way. When she'd straightened herself and emerged back onto the street, the patrol car was pulling away, and in the windows above she saw the lights on, the people behind it going about their delicate lives, the ragged woman below already forgotten.

Today, she must be extra careful. With Bird in tow, she can't afford a mistake. They will be quick. The last few places she hasn't been.

Stay a few steps behind and pretend you don't know me, she says, pulling on her hat. And wear your sunglasses.

They emerge from the subway at West Seventy-Second Street: the territory of wealthy women with rhinestoned phone cases, of small white dogs on taut leashes. Everywhere the sidewalks are a damp silvery gray, the car windows streaked with rain. On the corners, the bodegas still have umbrellas hooked over their door handles, ready for sale.

Margaret slips the first of the bottle caps from the bag on her wrist, palms it in one curled fist. After a few minutes of searching, they find a spot: a trash can, half overflowing. Crushed beer cans and plastic wrappers spilling onto the wet pavement.

Stand there, Margaret murmurs. Behind the screen of Bird's body, she stoops as if to rummage in the bin, then sticks the bottle cap under the can's lip, against a handy wad of gum. There, she says. That ought to hold it.

Bird takes a step back from the trash can and eyes it warily. To anyone else it would still look innocuous and ordinary; your eyes would glide right past it. Just another of the city's uglinesses you'd do your best to ignore. But to him, now, the place is marked—with menace or promise, he isn't sure which—and he can't seem to turn away.

What will it do, he asks, though Margaret can see what he's already imagining: flash, flames, a mushroom of smoke. She doesn't answer. Already she's pulled the next cap from her pocket.

Come on, she says. We've got to hustle.

For weeks Margaret has done this daily, and her eyes zero in on likely spots: wedged into a sewer grate, buried in a finger-wide crack in a building's foundation. She pokes one cap neatly into the belly of a squirrel half crushed by a truck.

I don't know, she says, wiping blood from her fingertips as she rises from the curb. They might come sweep it away.

She surveys the purpling mash of fur and flesh, the crust of flies beginning to gather.

But probably not, she says. I don't think they'll bother. Not by tomorrow, anyway.

They tuck them everywhere, these little capsules, and soon Bird begins to help, eyes adjusting to see hiding places everywhere, the way your sight adjusts to the dark. Some of the spots Margaret dismisses as too obvious, too neat. Somewhere messy, she says. Somewhere no one will want to touch. Bird runs a half step ahead, then two, then three, finding places for them all. Inside dumpsters reeking sweetly of rotting fruit; in corners where homeless men took their morning piss. At the feet of trees, nestled between bullets of dog shit. He forgets to question, for a moment, what they are for. It is a reverse treasure hunt, a game he and his mother are playing. Bottle cap by bottle cap, the bag on Margaret's arm lightens, and Bird feels a swirl of glee at the clever places they've found, a sense of power and awe when he thinks how many of these caps are hiding out there. He calculates: a hundred a day, for a whole month.

Is that all of them? Bird asks, when she's placed the last one. In a rusted crevice in a lamppost, just outside the entrance to the park.

That's everything, Margaret says shortly, and lets out a sigh—of satisfaction? Of sadness? It isn't clear.

With the last bottle cap planted, she abandons the trash bag she's carried as camouflage all these weeks, adding it to a nearby heap. It is garbage day in this neighborhood and everywhere lopsided piles dot the curb, threatening to tip. Here and there, something has gnawed through the plastic, spilling a plume of trash across the sidewalk. She wipes her hands on the thighs of her pants, looks at him. Her Bird: wide-eyed and impressionable, trusting, eager for the future though he has no idea what it will hold. Half grown, but only half.

What can she teach him, what can she do for him, what can she give him to make up for what's been lost? She wants to buy him pretzels and ice cream and lemonade from a cart, to let him dance through the park, licking the salt and drips from his fingers. To watch him play silly games, rules changing as he goes: leapfrogging broken squares on the sidewalk, jumping high to slap stop signs as they pass. No: she wants to play those games with him. She wants to be just his mother for one day. As if she can correct all these years without her, with one golden afternoon.

A police car approaches slowly, on the prowl. The silhouettes of the officers inside: foggy blurs through the tinted glass.

In an instant Margaret catches Bird by the elbow, yanking him behind a nearby stoop. Crouched behind a pyramid of garbage bags, her arms cinch him tight, so close they can feel each other's hearts beating.

The car glides closer, suspicious. Scans the area. Then moves on.

Something thick and bitter coats the roof of Margaret's mouth. In her grip, Bird's shoulders are still a boy's: unmuscled and bony, terrifyingly breakable. She can't give him the beautiful afternoon he deserves, not yet. It isn't fair, she thinks. The reek of the garbage rises around them in a fug, curdled and clinging. The police car is long gone, but still she cradles him, eyes shut, face pressed into the impossible warmth of his hair. When she finally loosens her arms and looks down at him, his gaze is startled, but trusting. Searching her face for a cue.

It's okay, she whispers. Don't be scared.

I'm not scared, he says. I knew we'd be okay.

With a shaky smile Margaret gives him a final squeeze, rises to her feet.

Let's get home, she says.

They ride the subway back to Brooklyn, Bird at one end of the car, Margaret at the other, so no one will suspect they're together. From afar she studies him: a small fidgety dark-haired figure, crossing one leg over the other, picking at the tape-mended tears in the seat. Behind his sunglasses she can't quite see his eyes, but when she looks closely she spots his furtive glances in her direction, the nearly imperceptible relaxing of his shoulders each time he finds her, leaning against a pole, keeping surreptitious watch from afar. This is the past three years, she thinks, condensed into an instant: orbiting at a distance, guessing but never sure what he is seeing, hoping that the idea of her is reassuring. No, she corrects herself. Not the past three years. This is simply having a child.

Planting the bottle caps, returning home—usually this is a well-rehearsed dance she can do without flinching. But today is different. Today she cannot stay still; every time the train stops, she jumps, warily scanning the other passengers as they doze or idly scroll on their phones. Her gaze darts again and again to the boy at the end of the car, now settled calmly, breaking from his daydream only to catch her eye once and give her the faintest conspiratorial smile. She tries and fails to smile back. Another train rushes by, headed elsewhere, and in the blurred shapes through the window she remembers the shadows of the officers in their cruiser, Bird's face against her shoulder, Bird's body thin and warm and vulnerable even in the cage of her arms. She hates herself for putting him there. When she holds her breath she can still smell the garbage, sour and suffocating all around. The train pulses beneath them, palpitating, the thumps of the wheels and roar of the engine and the sway of the car coalescing into a single word that throbs faster and faster inside her. By the time they reach the brownstone—walking a ways apart, slipping one at a time through the gate into the back garden—it churns in the base of her throat, and the moment they are safely back inside, it erupts out of her, leaving her breathless.

No, she says. No. I'm not doing it.

Bird turns back to look at her, frozen with her back against the door, as if barring the way out. For a moment she looks older, drawn; in the darkened hallway, lit only by the single bare bulb in the living room, her hair silvers, her face turns gray. A woman turned to stone.

It's not worth the risk, she says. In her own ears her voice is leathery, coarse and cracked.

But the bottle caps, Bird says. All the ones we just hid. And those ones you already hid.

It doesn't matter. We'll leave them.

But it's important. Bird shakes his head, as if she is trying to fool him. Isn't it? Whatever you're doing, I know it's going to help.

It doesn't matter, Margaret says again. Forget it. Forget the whole thing,

She rushes to him, clutching him close, cradling his face in her palms, because it is unbearable to remember him in danger, to imagine him ever being in danger again, let alone putting him there herself. Whatever it takes, she and Ethan had promised each other all those years ago, and she still means it. She will do whatever it takes to keep their child safe.

Except. In her arms, Bird stiffens, then pulls away.

But—he says.

His brow furrows, a look she knows because she's felt it on her own face her whole life: trying to unknot what people do and what they say and what they mean. She'd inherited it from her mother, who had probably inherited it from her mother, and here it was on her child's face, too, staring back at her. An unintended legacy.

Birdie, she says. You're all that matters. I don't want to do it anymore. I just don't want to take any chances.

But you said—he begins, then stops again, and she hears everything he isn't saying aloud. But all those kids. Like Sadie. And their families. Isn't that why you left?

We'll find another way to help, she says. Something else. I don't know what. But something less risky.

Her mind is full of hazy, incoherent plans.

We'll figure something out, she says. Some way to stay together, somewhere to hide. Maybe Daddy can find a way to join us. Domi could help. Wouldn't that be wonderful? Bird.

She is babbling now; she can hear it. She grabs at his hands with both of hers, as if he is sinking, or she is, and this might keep them afloat. They are still jammed together in the hallway, the tiny space thick and hot with their breath, still speaking in whispers, but it feels to both of them as if they're shouting. All she wants is to not let him go.

None of this matters anymore, she says.

But even as she says it, she can see his face hardening, small embers in his gaze. How, she reads in his eyes, can you look away now that you know?

So it doesn't matter, he says, as long as it's happening to somebody else.

And she knows: it is too late to convince him, because she has already told him the truth.

Bird, she says, but the sheer disappointment on his face crumbles her voice into sand.

You're a hypocrite, he says.

He hesitates for only an instant, then plunges ahead anyway.

You're a terrible mother.

Margaret flinches, but Bird seems to feel it, too, recoiling as if she's struck him. In his face she sees a mirror of what must be happening on her own: nostrils tense and trembling, eye rims suddenly hot and red. With a sudden jerk, he pushes her away. Then he is running up the stairs, and she doesn't follow. She feels as wrung out and emptied as if she has vomited and vomited until nothing is left inside.

In the dark, Bird falls into a stormy sleep.

He dreams a sharp and jagged tangle. Machines broken and rusted, gears inextricably meshed. Bottles of ink shattering in his hands, dying his fingers a watery blue. Someone has given him a building to hold up, and if he walks away it will collapse. He has caught a snake in a pillowcase, and he stands, bearing the writhing sack, nowhere safe to release it. In the last dream, just before he wakes, he is surrounded by other children, crammed so close he can feel their warmth, hear their breath, smell the sweat on their skin. But none of them speak to him or even look at him. Each time he reaches out they drift away soundlessly, a silent sea parting. Their eyes turning everywhere he is not: down at their dirty palms, over their shoulders, up at the clear and cloudless sky.

He wakes in a panic, burrows into the sleeping bag, tugs it up to his chin. Now he remembers: the bottle caps, the police cruiser, the argument. Everything his mother had told him over the past two days, all the reasons she'd had to leave, and how quickly she'd thrown all that aside. He thinks about the years without her, he and his father all alone, missing her. Once he'd have traded anything, everyone, to have her back.

He can't see anything, not even a crack of light from the hall. He listens for his mother, but hears nothing. Even the noises from outside—though there must be some—are muffled and muted to nothing more than whispers and faint hums. Somewhere she must be here, but he doesn't remember the way to her room, and in the unrelenting dark he isn't even sure he can find his way out. It is as if no one is there at all.

The wail of a siren slices through the window plastic: rising, here, gone. The only sign of life in the world. With a finger he drills into the corner of the plastic, stretching it, until a pinprick hole spreads. He bends down, puts his eye to it.

Outside he expects only more blackness, but instead what he sees is a dizzying array of light. Lights glimmer from window after window in a glittering mosaic. A sea of lights. A tidal wave of lights. Washing down over him in sparkling droplets. Each of those lights is a person, washing dishes or working or reading, completely oblivious to his existence. The thought of so many people dazzles and terrifies him. All those people out there, millions of them, billions, and not one of them knows or cares about him. He claps his hand over the hole, but still he can feel the lights sizzling against his skin like a sunburn. Even curling up inside the sleeping bag, the covers pulled over his head, brings no relief.

Out of him pours a cry so long buried the sound of it is like an earthquake in his throat. A name he hasn't uttered in years.

Mama, he cries, stumbling out of bed, and the darkness reaches up and tangles around his ankles, tugging him to the ground.

When he opens his eyes again he is curled up tight in a ball and a hand rests warm and heavy on the tender V between his shoulder blades. His mother.

Shh, she says, as he tries to turn over. It's all right.

She is sitting on the floor beside him. A less-dark shape against the dark.

You know, I felt the same way, she says, the first night I spent on my own.

Her palm warm and soft on the nape of his neck. Smoothing the hairs that bristle there.

Why did you bring me here, he says at last.

I wanted——she begins, and stops.

How to finish? I wanted to make sure you were all right. I wanted to make sure you would be all right. I wanted to see who you were. I wanted to see who you had become. I wanted to see if you were still you. I wanted to see you.

I wanted you, she says simply, and this is the only explanation she can give, but it is what he needs to hear. She had wanted him. She still wanted him. She hadn't left because she hadn't cared.

The understanding seeps into him like a sedative. Limpening his muscles, scooping smooth the hard edges of his thoughts. He leans against her, trusting her to bear his weight. Letting her arms twine around him like a vine round a tree. Through the tiny hole he's poked in the window covering, a thin strand of light pierces the black plastic, casting a single starry splotch on the wall.

She strokes his back, feels the nubs of his spine under the skin like a string of pearls. Gently she sets their hands together, finger to finger, palm to palm. Nearly as big as hers, his feet perhaps even bigger. Like a puppy, all paws, the rest of him still childlike but eagerly lolloping behind.

Birdie, she says, I'm just so afraid of losing you again.

He looks up at her with the fathomless trust of a sleepy child.

But you'll come back, he says.

It is not a question, but a statement. A reassurance.

She nods.

I'll come back, she agrees. I promise I'll come back.

And she means it.

Okay, he murmurs. He isn't sure if he is speaking to her, or to himself. About what is to come, or what happened long ago.

All of it, he decides. Everything. It's okay, he says again, and he knows, by the gentle tightening of her arms, that she has heard.

I'm here, she says, and Bird lets the darkness absorb him.

When Bird wakes again his mother is gone and it is morning. He is curled in the crib, legs folded nearly to chest, the sleeping bag left behind on the window seat, twisted like a shed skin. He has a dim memory of wanting to be small, of finding this safe place to hide. Of retreating. Draped over him is a blanket he doesn't recognize, heavy and too small and oddly shaped, and then he realizes it is not a blanket but his mother's coat.

III

In the morning, at ten o'clock precisely, the Duchess arrives in her long sleek car, driving herself this time. Just inside the back door, Margaret hesitates. But Bird doesn't. He is eager to go.

Good luck, he says. Confidence beaming from his eyes.

Okay, she says at last. I'll see you soon.

She pulls him close, kisses him on the temple, just where the pulse beats under the skin.

Then Bird, backpack slung over his shoulder, darts through the back garden and out the fence and slips into the car at the curb. There, at the other end of the seat, is a figure silhouetted against a tinted window, turning as he enters. Taller—half a head taller than him now, maybe—longer haired, but the same quick eyes, the same skeptical grin.

Bird, Sadie says. Oh my god, Bird.

She throws her arms around him. Her skin smells of cedar and soap. Bird, she says, I've got *so* much to tell you—

If you're going to gossip about me, please wait until we're out of the city, the Duchess says drily. I don't want to miss anything while I'm concentrating on traffic.

Sadie gives an exaggerated eye roll toward the front seat.

Fine, she says.

In the rearview mirror Bird sees the Duchess's eyes twinkle back at them, and this more than anything reassures him. Sadie is at ease here, in a way he's never seen. As the car shifts back into gear, she settles into her seat and turns her gaze to the window, letting out a soft sigh. It's been months since they saw each other, but somehow Sadie seems younger rather than older, less wary and watchful, as if she's finally able to breathe after a long time without air. As if she no longer has to fight her way through the world alone. He knows this feeling, or something like it: it is what he felt last night, when he'd called his mother and she came to him; it is what he felt this morning, waking under the comforting weight of her coat. He settles back into his seat, too, happy to be just a child for the moment, not in charge, simply along for the ride. There is so much he wants to ask Sadie—he cannot imagine living with the Duchess, for one thing—but he can wait.

Where are we going? he asks, as the Duchess nudges the car back into traffic again.

To the cabin, she says, and then they're off.

She drives fast, the Duchess, Bird and Sadie belted firmly in back and pinned in place by unrelenting acceleration, and as they burst out of the tangled gray nest of the city and onto the open road, it feels like a rocket launch into the stars.

I hope neither of you gets carsick, the Duchess says suddenly, with a glance into the rearview mirror.

Neither of them does. Bird is seldom in a car and the sheer speed of it exhilarates him. The tinted windows deepen the colors outside, turning the sky turquoise, the grass emerald. Even the road, which he knows is ordinary flat asphalt, gleams with a silver sheen. In the Duchess's proximity everything seems richer and more expansive, and this makes such inherent sense to him that he does not question it, simply settles against the soft leather and absorbs it. Beside him, Sadie draws in her breath quickly as a cloud of birds rises from a tree and scatters like a handful of confetti. For the first time he understands why dogs hang their heads out of windows: after so long inside, he, too, feels eager to lap up all he can, the very air tingling with life.

They drive for an hour and a half in companionable silence, the only noise being the occasional whoosh as they whip past another car or truck. The Duchess does not use signals, merely plants her foot firmly on the gas pedal and speeds past as the engine lets out a throaty growl. Bird wonders where the other half of the highway is, the side returning to the city—on the far side of the trees, perhaps. Though he can't see it, it must be there. It is an exercise in faith. His mother has promised him she will come back. Another exercise in faith. He will remember everything and when he returns he will tell her what he's seen.

The Duchess has referred to it as the *cabin* and in the strictest sense this is true: a little milk carton of a house, encircled by trees. To Bird and Sadie, *cabin* calls to mind Abe Lincoln, hewn logs, and howling wolves. The Duchess's cabin is small and simple, but this is as far as the resemblance goes. The wooden floors in the main room gleam like buttery toffee. The big fireplace at its center is made of rounded river stones. Behind it are a pair of small bedrooms, a bathroom. On one wall, a window peeks through a clearing in the trees to the silver sparkle of water in the distance.

I'm trusting you not to drown, the Duchess says. There's not another house for miles, so no one will be coming to save you.

She lifts her wrist and checks a slim gold watch.

So here are the rules, she says. You are not to go off the property, but it's forty-seven acres so I assume that won't be too much of a limitation. You may swim, if you don't mind the cold. You may make a fire, if you're careful. In the fireplace only. I've left you a bag of food that should last until I come back tomorrow. Anything unclear?

Who built this house? Sadie asks. Somehow I don't think it was you.

She grins cheekily at the Duchess, and the Duchess smiles back indulgently.

My father did, she says.

She pauses suddenly and looks around, as if she is seeing the cabin for the first time. Taking in the wooden walls, the planked ceiling, the satiny floor.

Or rather, had it built, she says. That's how he did things. Her voice softens. When I was little, we used to sit on the shore, out there, and fish. He and my mother and I. I haven't been here in many years.

Then she shakes her head, as if shrugging away dust. So don't burn it down, please, she says crisply.

Are you going back to help my mother? Bird asks.

For the first time the Duchess looks uncertain.

You know your mother, she says, and Bird nods, even as he

wonders if this is true. When she gets an idea in her head there's no stopping her. But she's coming to me when she's finished, and we'll be here tomorrow morning to pick you up.

And then what, Bird and Sadie both think, but neither of them dares to ask.

The Duchess checks her watch again.

I'd better go, she says. I won't get back until midafternoon as it is, and if there's traffic—

She picks up her keys from the table and turns back, looks from one of them to the other.

Don't worry, she says, her voice unexpectedly gentle. Bird, Sadie. Everything will be fine.

Of course it will, Sadie says. *We're* here, now.

When the Duchess is gone, Bird and Sadie—suddenly aware of all the months that have passed between them—lapse into bashful silence. Tacitly, they take stock of their surroundings. In the big main room, a table and three chairs, a kitchenette; in the bathroom, a shower and toilet and a small louvered window through which they can see nothing but trees. Two bedrooms, a larger one, cream colored with a big double bed, and a smaller one—pink—with a twin bed in the corner.

Without asking, Sadie kicks her shoes off in the big room, but Bird doesn't mind. It's clear who the house was built for— parents, child—and he is happy to let someone else play the role of adult for a little while longer. He settles on the sofa in front of the fireplace, and beneath him the aged leather crackles.

What is it like, he says. Living with the Duchess. What is *that* like?

Sadie laughs. Domi? she says. She seems super scary, but she's not.

As if a seal has been broken, she begins to chatter away. The first day, she said, she hadn't seen Domi at all. She'd been given a bedroom—up on the top floor, with a huge antique map of the world hung on the wall—and left to her own devices, and she'd spent all day exploring the museum of a house, trying to figure out what kind of place she'd landed in, what kind of woman Domi was. Margaret said she could be trusted, but Sadie was not used to taking things on assurance. Late that night, she'd found her way into Domi's office and was still behind the desk, reading the papers scattered there, when Domi came in.

And just what do you think you're doing? Domi demanded, and Sadie had looked up, studying her with new eyes.

So all these checks, she said, ticking her finger down Domi's ledger. To all these libraries. You know what they're doing. You're—helping.

A long moment, where they appraised each other anew.

Why, Sadie asked, and Domi said: It's one small thing. To start to make things right.

Sadie shut the checkbook. I want to help, she said.

She'd expected Domi to laugh, but she didn't. Instead Domi had sat down in the chair across the desk, as if Sadie were in charge and she was the supplicant, asking for a favor.

Maybe you can, she said.

They'd spent days talking, Sadie telling Domi everything she remembered about the authorities, her host families, the whole system of PACT. How they'd moved her, who had met her, where she'd gone. What she'd seen in the libraries, those months in which they'd hidden her. What she'd wished she'd done, and what she'd wished others had. Domi listening. Learning.

I couldn't go out, Sadie says to Bird. In case anyone spotted me. But Domi found me stuff to do. And she's been looking for my parents. Trying to trace where they've gone.

She pauses and swallows, and Bird knows better than to ask.

She said not to give up *yet*, Sadie says. She says—well, she says you just never know.

The day before Bird arrived, Domi's last lead had come up empty, and she'd broken the news to Sadie gently, the way you'd break news of a death. We'll keep looking, she'd promised, holding Sadie tight.

If you could have anything else, Domi had asked eventually, breaking the silence. What would you wish for.

Sadie considered.

A whole day where I could do whatever I wanted, she said. Without anyone watching or judging or tracing or tracking me. Just one day like that.

Hmm, Domi said. Might be tricky. But maybe there's a way. If you can wait a bit, until the right time.

And now here they were, she and Bird. A day with no one watching or judging. A day to do what they wanted.

She told me, Sadie says. Some of the things she and your mom saw in the Crisis. The things they did—and the things they didn't do. Things she would've done differently. You know that day you came? she adds smugly. I told her what to ask. She came upstairs and said, what would you ask Bird to find out if he really was Bird? And I told her, ask about his bike. Ask about his cereal. Ask about lunch.

Do you know? Bird asks. What my mom's doing.

Sadie pauses.

Domi wouldn't tell me exactly, she admits. Your mom came a few times, to plan. I tried to listen, she adds, rather proudly. But I couldn't hear much.

Together, they pool notes. By their math, Margaret must have hidden thousands of bottle caps, all over the city. At the Duchess's, Sadie had flipped through the newspapers and scanned news reports on television and online: no reports of people finding suspicious devices in bottle caps. No reports of trouble, at least not in the city. Whatever is being set up, it hasn't happened yet. For weeks this has been going on, like a spring being inexorably wound.

It's something big, Sadie says.

Of course it is, Bird says. My mother doesn't do things by halves.

I don't think Domi does either.

Their eyes meet.

Bird, Sadie says, I bet this will change everything. Whatever they're planning.

For a moment they pause, trying to imagine a world after. Inside Bird fizzes with excitement, and he jumps to his feet. Needing somewhere to put it.

Let's go down to the water, he says.

They follow the path through the clearing in the trees and there it is: sparkling in the sunlight, a little inlet stretching out to the blue expanse beyond. Bird scoops up a pebble and tosses it as far as he can. With a satisfying *bloop* the water swallows it in a single gulp, and rings ripple back to his feet at the shore. The Duchess is right: as far as they can see, there are no other houses, no other people, just a dense ruff of trees clustered around this spangle of a cove. From above it must look as if a giant has pressed a thumbprint into the forest, carving this perfect hollow for the cabin right at the water's edge.

He has never been so far from other people before. All his life, there have always been others nearby, watching, listening. Even if you couldn't see them, you knew they were there: just through the window, just on the other side of the wall, just out of sight around a corner. Out here there is no one and he feels himself expanding to gigantic size. Beside him, Sadie gives a sudden whoop, and he gives one, too, and from the nearby trees a cluster of sparrows takes flight, and then they are running, shrieking, churning the rocky shore with their footprints, darting after the velvet chipmunks that whip between the roots of trees and the squirrels that scamper out of reach. When they collapse, exhilarated and exhausted, the hum of silence that settles over them again feels louder than their shouting. For the moment neither of them thinks about their parents. They are simply children, at play.

Let's go in, Sadie suggests. Just up to our ankles.

They pry off their sneakers and socks and roll their jeans to their knees, and as they tromp in, small muddy rings echo outward from their feet. The water is frigid, but they don't notice or care. There are trees to climb, not the thin reedy saplings that ringed the playground, rippling the asphalt with their roots, but tall ones that stretch higher even than Sadie dares to venture.

They spend the afternoon noticing things: the fine white *V*s on each clover leaf, as if painted by a thin-bladed brush. The salmon-colored mushroom caps prodding up through the soil; the delicate lichens that cling to tree trunks like jade fish scales. A slim young birch, too tall for its slender whip of a frame, bowed nearly into an arch, but growing, still growing neverthe-less, sending its jagged green leaves toward the sky. October is nearly over, winter is coming, but things are growing, still alive.

As the afternoon starts to dim, Sadie gives a yelp, and Bird comes running just in time to see a little crab, the size of a quarter, scuttle across the sand. Now that he looks, he spots them everywhere, hiding in plain sight. They've been there all along; he just hadn't looked. For a while they try to catch them, chasing them across the shore, trying to scoop them up in their hands, and once Sadie gets close enough and gets nipped by tiny claws, but every time the crabs escape: down into holes in the sand, among the rocks, out into the vast blue blur of the water.

You need a chicken leg, Sadie says, with authority. She drops to a squat on the sand. That's what you need. To get big crabs, way bigger than this.

She pauses.

My mom took me one summer, she says. You tie a chicken leg to a string and throw it in the water, and when the crab grabs it, you pull the string toward you, really really slow, and the crab follows the chicken, and then you catch the crab in a net.

Bird imagines his own parents teaching him this: mud streaked, wading in the sea. Laughing together, the way he remembers.

Reeling in a line heavy with prey. He wonders, suddenly, what time it is, what his mother is doing right now, if whatever she's planning has already begun. Above them the sky stretches wide and flat and blue, but he scans it anyway, as if they might spot plumes of smoke drifting all the way from the city.

Crabs eat chicken? he asks, pushing the thought away, and Sadie nods. They eat everything, she says.

My mom told me once, she goes on, rocking back on her heels, about this thing that happened where she grew up. Sometimes, like one night a year, all the crabs get confused and run up on the shore. It's like the tide and the phase of the moon, or something. A jubilee, it's called. You wake up in the middle of the night and go down to the beach and the water is just full of them. They practically *crawl* out—you can just reach in and pull them out, bucketsful. She and her cousins and aunts and uncles used to do it. People would fill their trucks. And they'd build a big bonfire and cook the crabs and have a midnight feast, right there.

Wow, Bird says.

She said when she was a girl, she would go to bed in her bathing suit every night in summer and lie there awake in the dark, just praying for a jubilee.

Sadie is lost in thought, her eyes trained on something off in the distance.

She always said we'd go down some summer and visit that side of the family so I could meet all my cousins, but we never did.

Overhead a hawk circles, lazy, in the sky.

We'll find her, Bird says. My mom, Domi—I'm sure they can find her.

They've been looking, Sadie says. I don't know if she's still out there.

He has never heard her sound so uncertain, and this disorients him.

If she's out there, Bird says confidently, they'll find her. His mother, he thinks, always keeps her promises.

This thing your mom is planning, Sadie says, this is *it*, Bird, it's going to change everything.

The tiniest of pauses, before she continues.

I mean, it has to. Right?

The little hitch in her voice, like a splinter, snags Bird's attention. Sadie's eyes appear to be fixed on the horizon, but in the warm afternoon light they shine glass-bright, glazed with tears. His own eyes go liquid and hot. He thinks of everything his mother has told him, of all the years his father has been trying to protect him. Of the man in the pizza parlor, the man at the Common. The woman with her dog. Sadie's parents, his mother's parents. His father's parents retreating from their lives, Mrs. Pollard crouched anxiously beside his computer, D. J. Pierce's spit falling inches from his shoe. Everything that needs to be changed feels immense and immeasurable.

You know, he says. We could build a fire.

It works: her eyes come back from the realm of what if to what is. Right here? she says.

In the fireplace, Bird says. We don't have any crabs, but we can have a fire.

Together, they lay out the wood. A small and concrete thing. My dad showed me how, Sadie says, he was a Boy Scout as a kid. He knew how to do lots of useful stuff, like tie knots, and find north using the stars. You stack it like a log cabin, like this. Dried grass, then sticks, then logs.

Bird flushes. His father has never taught him to do anything useful like this. Like the three little pigs, Bird says. Sadie laughs, and he feels an odd twinge of pride. It feels good, making someone else laugh.

Here goes, Sadie says, and lights a match with a quick grating flick.

The dried grass catches right away, and then the twigs, a burst of gratifying orange. Then the whole thing collapses and goes dark. Huff, puff, Sadie says. With a stick she sweeps the remnants of their fire aside. Let's try again.

They rebuild the crosshatches of wood, and Bird looks for something to help it catch faster, and it's then that he spots the stack of newspapers, set by the hearth. He reaches for one, begins to crumple it, then stops.

Look, he says.

The date on the paper is almost fifteen years old. The middle of the Crisis, they both realize. SIXTH STRAIGHT DAY OF DISRUPTIONS ROIL DC; 400 ARRESTED; 12 RIOTERS, 6 OFFICERS SLAIN.

A photo covers the entire front page: Washington, DC, ablaze, a crowd of people on the run. Attacking? Fleeing? They can't tell, only that from the sharp angles of their bodies—arms and legs thrown wide—they are moving fast, forcefully, instinctively. They wear black, from the hats pulled low over their foreheads to the masks and scarves across their faces, all the way down to the lug-soled boots on their feet; they could be protesters or authorities, it's impossible to say. On the pavement, almost obscured, lies a woman's body, her face turned aside, blood matting her hair. In the background the Washington Monument juts like a single raised finger, dark against a smoldering orange sky.

With both hands Bird crushes the paper into a tight wad, hiding the photograph inside.

Let's try again, he says.

He sets the knot of paper in the middle of the miniature cabin they've built, and reaches for the matches again.

This time, the flame gobbles the paper, flaring up as the newsprint dissoves to ash. Small flames lick hesitantly at the sticks and begin to fade, and this time, Bird remembers something from long ago, something his father once told him. A word, and its story. He drops to hands and knees, sets his face before the flame. As gently as he can, he purses his lips and blows, as if blowing a kiss, or soothing a bruise, and the flames rise, the tinder crumples and shrivels and glows the most intense orange he's ever seen, and then—as he runs short of breath—fades back to gray. Sadie drops down beside him and blows, too, and the glow slowly returns, then grows. It is like watching color return to someone's face, like watching dawn spreading across a darkened sky.

In silence they tend the fire in turns—first Bird, then Sadie, then both together, breathing life into it—until the larger sticks catch, then the logs, and the flames grow steady and calm and hot.

Spirare, Bird hears his father say. *To breathe. Con: together. So conspiracy literally means breathing together.*

They make it sound so sinister, Sadie says, and only then does Bird realize he's spoken aloud. But breathing together, breathing the same air—it's actually kind of beautiful.

They sit for a moment, quiet, and Bird thinks back to the past days huddled with his mother around the coffee table. Piecing together her whispered story, both of them breathing in the same thick air. Sadie feeds a stick into the fire, nudging it closer to the little blaze until it begins to char and glow. Outside, the sun is falling but the night is still warm, and through the window they see the air ignite. Fireflies. In their excitement they have left the door open and a firefly drifts into the cabin, then another, green sparks shimmering in the red glow of the fire.

I used to hate her, Bird says suddenly.

But you don't anymore.

A long silence. Around them, bright flecks swirl and dip.

No, he says, and realizes it is true. Not anymore.

For dinner they eat from the paper bag of food the Duchess has left them. Bird heats water, tips in a packet of angel hair. It's good, Sadie says. You know my foster parents wouldn't let me use the stove? Thought I was a risk. Like I might set the whole house on fire.

They scrape the last dregs of sauce from their bowls.

What do you think she's doing right now? Bird says.

Sadie furrows her brow. She's getting ready, she says. Ready to set them all off.

By *them* she means the hundreds of bottle caps scattered all over the city.

Do you think— Bird hesitates. Do you think she's dangerous? I mean, she couldn't hurt anyone. Could she?

A long pause as they both turn this over in their minds.

I think, Sadie says finally, that anyone could hurt someone, if there was a really good reason.

Bird thinks of his mother, tugging him into the shadows as the police car approached, the sharp-toothed animal that suddenly reared in her eyes. He thinks of his father, that day on the Common, standing over the man who'd pushed him. Of the blood on his fist. They'd been dangerous, he thought; they'd loved him so fiercely it had made them dangerous.

They go to bed early, taking turns in the bathroom, letting their hard-earned fire die down to coals. They are eager for tomorrow. They are full of plans, each building on the other's like a tower of dominoes. Tomorrow, Domi and Margaret will bring them back to the city. Where everything will be different, they are sure, because of whatever Margaret is doing.

It's happening, right now, Sadie says with glee. Bird, just think, it's happening, and Bird has no reply.

A t sundown, she begins.

She opens the old laptop, the one she's scrounged to-gether from parts found on the curb: all those late-night books she'd studied, late at night in all those libraries, put to good use. For the first time she turns on the wi-fi. It is a risk—signals that go out can be traced back. For so long she's muffled her footsteps, muzzling herself. Now it is time to speak.

Her fingers tap the keyboard, running the program she's rigged. She sends out the signal and waits, watching for them to connect. To prick up their ears for her commands. The bottle caps she has been making and planting, four weeks' worth. Every-thing she'd planned so carefully before Bird had arrived.

She has done the math: one every two blocks, all the way down to the Financial District, nearly all the way up to Harlem. Weatherproof in their little plastic shells, small enough to be concealed in places where they won't be disturbed for weeks. Even if one were spotted, it wouldn't be looked at: just a worth-less scrap, a piece of litter to be swept away. No one examined the things in the gutters, in the dustpans, in the street cleaner's bins; those were the things people tried to ignore. By her count, she's planted two thousand and eleven: how many of them have survived and are working, how many will connect and answer her call?

Ten at first, now fifteen. Twenty-five.

She hadn't known, at first, what to do with the stories she'd collected. The first wisp of an idea had formed when one of the mothers clasped her hand, her voice trembling. *Tell everyone what happened to my girl. Tell it to the world. Shout it from the skies if you can.* Later it had crystallized, on a sunny morning in LA, when she looked up and saw it: a cell-phone tower, disguised as an unconvincing tree. Swathed in green leaf-print canvas, right-angled arms held mannequin-stiff. The wrong kind of tree for the climate, an evergreen towering over the palms, head and shoulders higher than the real trees, emitting a faint hum. What kind of messages was it beaming through the air? For a moment she'd closed her eyes and imagined it: all those invisible words made audible, a cacophony of voices crisscrossing the city like a net.

She thinks of it again as she watches the monitor, watching the bottle caps answer her call. Seventy, a hundred, two hundred.

Inside each, a tiny receiver tuned to the precise frequency her computer now emits. And also: a tiny speaker. Reception up to ten miles, Domi had promised her, crystal clear, and you'll hear it from a block away, at least. Her father had made his fortune on this technology, though he'd surely never imagined it put to this use. One by one they wake, the counter ticking upward. Two hundred and fifty. Three hundred. Each a glowing pinprick on the map, spreading northward from the Battery, freckling Chinatown and Koreatown and Hell's Kitchen, dotting Midtown to the Upper West Side and beyond. Over five hundred now, the counter still climbing. When it reaches nineteen hundred, it pauses, and she does a quick calculation. Nearly ninety-five percent, a solid A. Wouldn't her parents be proud.

She lifts the microphone, clears her throat, and across the city, block after block, bottle-cap speakers crackle to life. Picking up the signal she is transmitting. A voice emerging from the knot-holes of trees, the undersides of trash cans, cracks in front stoops and behind lampposts: everywhere and anywhere she has wedged a bottle cap in the past month. Hiding unnoticed until this moment, when from that little round cap her voice would spring, surprisingly loud, startling those nearby. In unison, this voice speaking—slightly scratched, as if from wear—all over the city. Only one voice, but speaking the words of many.

It doesn't have to be live, Domi had said. A recording, maybe. It would be safer. You don't have to be there. She'd said it gently, as if trying to persuade a stubborn child.

Margaret shook her head. I don't have to, she said, but I want to.

She couldn't explain why, but she feels this in her bones: certain things must be done in person. Testifying. Attending the dying. Remembering those who were gone. Some things need to be witnessed. But there was another reason she herself couldn't quite see, could only sense its presence, the way you sensed a ghost. She had not been there to see her parents die; they had died alone, without her, and she should have been there, to see the man who'd pushed her father and sear his face into her mind; she should have been there by her father's hospital bed, among the beeping, blinking machines, to kiss him and send him on his way. She should have been there, that next morning, to catch her mother as she fell, perhaps to save her, but at the very least to give her a loving face to focus on as the light in her eyes faded. She could not have articulated this, but she could feel the shape of this wrong inside her, the way she could feel her own heart kettle-drumming in her chest. They had deserved that kind of caretaking and no one had given it to them and she would, in this small way, give that solemn witnessing and hand-holding to each of the stories she was about to tell.

Alone in the darkened brownstone, she opens the first of the notebooks, a library of stories she has gathered and borne on her body for the past three years. The words of those she's spoken to, faithfully jotted down in microscopic print, entrusted to her to keep and to safeguard and to share. She begins to read the words these families have whispered, letting them speak through her mouth. One by one, child by child, she tells each story.

The outlines first. Only a first name, nothing that could betray anyone: *Emmanuel. Jackie. Tien. Parker.* The city they'd lived in: *Berkeley. Decatur. Eugene. Detroit.* Their age, when they'd been taken: *Nine. Six. Seven and a half. Two.*

And then, shading in those outlines: the contours and textures of a particular life lived, the details that made each child themselves. The smallest and most human moments, that explained who they were. *Keep to the small.*

His smile was so sudden. One moment he'd be laughing, happy. The next, instantly stern. Even playing peekaboo, he took it so seriously. As if he knew even then we might vanish, with the twitch of a blanket, and disappear.

She wouldn't eat any food that had corners. I had to cut her sandwiches into circles. For months, I lived off the cut-off corners she left behind.

At first people stop, baffled. Where is this voice coming from? They glance over their shoulders, searching for the source. Someone behind them? Behind that tree? But no, there is no one. They are alone. And then they begin to listen; they can't help it. One story, then another. Then another. They pause and soon they are not alone any longer, there are clusters of them, then dozens, so many people standing silently together, listening. These steely New Yorkers—people who could ignore a troupe of breakdancers spinning around subway poles, who could swerve around a swarm of camera-toting tourists or a man dressed as a giant hot dog without losing speed or focus, without even a sideways glance—they paused, listening, and the teeming rivers of the city's streets thickened and clogged. The voice comes from all around them, as if from the air itself, and though later a few of them would say it sounded godlike, from the sky, most of those who heard it would insist on the exact opposite: it felt like a voice inside them, speaking somehow both to them and from them, and though it was speaking the stories of strangers, people they had never met, children who were not their own, pain they had not experienced, it was somehow speaking not just to them but with them, of them, that the stories it told, one after the other in a seemingly endless stream, were not someone else's but one larger story of which they, too, were a part.

The night they took you I was angry with you, you'd scribbled on the wall with a permanent pen, you'd scribbled on your hands and your face and part of the carpet, too, angry black scrawls. I'd smacked you and you'd gone to bed crying, and I was scrubbing the wall with a sponge when the knock came at the door.

She wants people to remember more than their names. More than their faces. More than what happened to them, more than the simple last fact that they were taken. Each of them needs to be remembered as a person unlike any other, not a name on a list but as *someone*, someone unlike anyone else.

Do you remember that day we went to the pier? That day the world was full of things to look at, the sea lions gliding through the harbor and the Ferris wheel spinning against the blue sky and the seagulls swooping overhead, and when it started to get dark I said, let's have ice cream for dinner, and you looked at me as if I'd grown wings. You had peanut butter fudge with whipped cream, and I had chocolate. On the way home the Muni was crowded so you sat in my lap and fell asleep and drooled peanut-butter spit down my neck.

296

I hope you remember that day. I hope you remember the ice cream for dinner.

She cannot go on forever; she knows this. Already, somewhere, they are tracking her. They are hunting the speakers, smashing them one by one. She has made it as hard as she can. They will have to follow the sound, elbowing through the crowds of listeners, winding the thread of her voice back to its source. They will need flashlights; they will have only those thin needles of light to probe every crevice and cranny. They will have to feel with their hands, into the gum-crusted undersides of city garbage cans, into slimy gutters and rancid grates and under piles of dog shit, scrabbling to extract the bottle caps that she has so painstakingly concealed. The speakers cannot be turned off; they can only be destroyed, and her trackers will smash them under boot heels, but the sound will continue, from other speakers, just a block or two away; with every one they find, they will realize there are hundreds more, that no matter how far they stretch their net there is somewhere farther that these stories still reach. It is a game of hide-and-seek, and she will draw it out as long as she can. They will never find all the speakers, but sooner or later they will trace her signal, the wi-fi that connects her to those speakers in a trail of tiny digital footprints; they will follow those footprints back to this house, where she sits with a microphone and her stack of notebooks, their covers softened and curved from being carried on her body for so long. By the time they arrive, she will be gone.

She will tell as many stories as she can. She still has time. One family's story. Then the next. What do you want to remember, she'd asked those left behind. What would you want to say to your child. She'd recorded those words and now, as she promised, she says it for them, the words that they're unable to utter aloud.

When I can't sleep I count your freckles in my mind. On your temple, where the skull is thinnest. On your right cheek, just beside your ear. On the inside of your elbow, on the side of your knee, a pair on the knob of your wrist. These marks you have carried since you were inside my body. I wonder if they are still there, or if they've faded with time. If you have more marks on your skin now that I will never see.

At bedtime you used to ask me for something to dream about. Tonight, I would say, you will dream you are a mermaid, exploring a huge sunken city. Or: Tonight you will fly on a rocket and sail past glittery stars. One night, I was tired. I couldn't think of anything. The truth is, you'd been a brat all day and I just wanted you to sleep. I said, Tonight you will dream that you are lying warm and safe and sleeping in your bed. That's a boring dream, Mom, you said, that's the most boring dream I've ever heard. And it was, but now it is the best dream I can think of, the only dream I can imagine.

When they begin to get close, she will abandon ship. She tracks the speakers blinking out one by one on her map, marking how close they've come. Domi is waiting on Park Avenue; the plan is that Margaret, after broadcasting what she can, will smash the laptop and take her notebooks and run.

Is anyone listening, out there? Are people simply rushing by? And how much of a difference can it make really, just one story, even all these stories taken together and funneled into the ear of the busy world—a world moving so quickly that voices and sounds Doppler into a rising whine, so distracted that even when your attention snags on the burr of something unusual, you are dragged away before you can see it, uprooting it like a bee's spent stinger. It is hard for anything to be heard and even if anyone hears it, how much of a difference could it really make, what change could it possibly bring, just these words, just this thing that happened once to one person that the listener does not and will never know. It is just a story. It is only words.

She does not know if it will make any difference. She does not know if anyone is listening. She is here, locked in her cabinet, drawing cat after cat, slipping them through the cracks. Unsure if they will sink even one claw into the beast outside.

But still: she turns another page and goes on.

I saved all the teeth you left under your pillow, in a little tin that once held mints. Sometimes I take them out and tip them into my hand, and let them clink together like beads in my palm. I keep the tin in my jewelry box. It feels like the right place for these fragments of you, the right place for tiny precious things.

I hope you are happy.

I hope you know how much

I hope

Up until the end, she believes she still has time. That she can share every story she's gathered and recorded and promised to pass on, and still make it back to Bird. But she is mistaken. The darkest part of night is over, and far away, just where the sky meets the ocean, the sun is beginning to rise. And then she hears it: a car, then another and another. Another. The squeal of tires skidding to a halt, the sudden ominous silence as engines cut off one by one.

She still has notebooks full of stories that she will not have time to speak. She has miscalculated. She's stayed too late.

They settle on her with their dark wings then, nearly suffocating her: all of her many mistakes of motherhood. Each and every time she'd brought pain to the one she most wanted to protect. Once she'd swung Bird to her shoulders and his head hit the doorframe, a plum-colored bruise blooming on his forehead. She'd handed him a cup, and the glass—invisibly cracked— shattered in his mouth. The catalog of failures in her mind is endless and indelible and each memory digs its talons into her, weighing her down, pinning her in place. She'd pricked him with a needle, trying to dig out a splinter, raised a pearl of blood on his thumb. She'd snapped at him, mid-tantrum, and left him alone to cry. She'd put him in danger, with a line of a poem, and then she'd left him alone for so long, and soon he would be alone all over again. Would he ever understand? Through the feathery blackness she glances down at the notebooks spread on the table. A whole stack of them, lined with the stories of others, all with their own memories and regrets, all their failings and love, all things they wished they could tell the children they might never see again. Maybe, she thinks, this is simply what living is: an infinite list of transgressions that did not weigh against the joys but that simply overlaid them, the two lists mingling and merging, all the small moments that made up the mosaic of a person, a relationship, a life. What Bird will learn, then: That his mother is fallible. That she is only human, too.

She closes the cover of the notebook before her, sets it atop the others. She will take these stories with her the only way she can: she strikes a match and sets the stack aflame.

And then, because she has just one more moment, because they are on their way but not here yet, she begins to tell one last story. An apology, a love letter. A story she has never written down because she knows it by heart. She closes her eyes and begins to speak.

Bird. Why did I tell you so many stories? Because I wanted the world to make sense to you. I wanted to make sense of the world, for you. I wanted the world to make sense.

When you were born, your father wanted you to have my name. Miu: a seedling. He liked that idea, you as our little sprout. But I chose his: Gardner. One who makes things grow. I wanted you to be not only the grown, but the grower. To have power over your own life, turning your energy toward what's to come, leaning into the light.

Except some people have another story for your name. Gar: a weapon. Dyn: an alarm. Gardner, the one who hears the warning call and comes bearing arms. A warrior, shielding what's behind, protecting what's dear. I didn't know that then.

But now, I'm happy you have both in you. A caregiver, tending the future; a fighter, defending what's already here.

There are so many more stories I wish I could tell you. You'll have to ask others—your father, your friends. Kind strangers you will meet someday. Everyone who remembers.

But in the end every story I want to tell you is the same. Once upon a time, there was a boy. Once upon a time there was a mother. Once upon a time, there was a boy, and his mother loved him very much.

When does she stop speaking? When are you ever done with the story of someone you love? You turn the most precious of your memories over and over, wearing their edges smooth, warming them again with your heat. You touch the curves and hollows of every detail you have, memorizing them, reciting them once more though you already know them in your bones. Who ever thinks, recalling the face of the one they loved who is gone: yes, I looked at you enough, I loved you enough, we had enough time, any of this was enough?

She raises the laptop above her head and smashes it to the floor, and behind her she hears the door open.

When Bird and Sadie wake it is sunrise. At first neither of them remembers where they are, and then it comes back to them in a rush: the cabin. The project. Outside the trees are like long straight arrows pointing at the sky. They are certain Margaret's plan has been a success, certain that she will have changed everything, certain that when she and the Duchess arrive they will be whisked back to a city completely transformed, a world set on its axis again.

Only no one comes. They finish their cereal and sit side by side on the cabin steps, waiting. An overcast day with heavy air, dampening the sound around them like a thick quilt. Now and then they swear they hear something—the crunch of tires on gravel, or the grumble of an engine approaching. But still no one comes.

They'll be here soon, Sadie says, confident. I bet there's just traffic. They're coming.

There is no telephone in the cabin, no computer, no internet.

Nothing to tether them to the outside world. It is at this point that Bird and Sadie realize they only have the faintest sense of where they are; on the trip up, they'd stopped paying attention to the road signs the farther they got from the city. It hadn't mattered then, but they think of the forty-seven acres between them and the nearest person. How would you find another person, in such a space? Far off above the trees, the clouds gray and darken.

What if no one ever comes back, Bird says. In the silence they both consider this. They could live here, for a time; it is warm and sheltered; the bag of food the Duchess has left could last a few days, maybe longer. And then?

Maybe we could find a neighbor, and use their phone, Sadie says.

But both of them know this is impossible. Which direction would they head in, and how would they find another house, and once they got there, who would they call, anyway? They try to imagine: they could follow the long gravel driveway all the way back out to the road, and then follow the road. It must lead somewhere: either back to the city, or farther away from it, but it would take them to people. And then? They pause here, stalled, unsure what follows. Whoever found them will surely call the authorities and they will be taken away, and not together. There's a sudden rustling and rattling, and both of them tighten in anticipation, but there is no one there, no movement; it's just the wind, picking up, throttling the trees. Branches whip and thrash in the air. He had never known the forest could be so noisy, or so wild.

Maybe something happened, Bird says.

He doesn't say it, but both of them are thinking it: maybe they were caught, Margaret or the Duchess or both of them, maybe they've been captured, maybe no one will ever come for them again. Or—a much worse thought, one that comes to both of them in near unison though neither of them dares voice it— maybe the authorities are coming for them now, on their way to track them down. The air suddenly cools, puckering goose bumps on their skin.

Sadie shakes her head. As if by refusing to believe, she can will it from the universe.

That could never, she says. They're too careful, they had everything planned. They wouldn't *let* that happen.

Let's go inside, Bird says, pushing to his feet, but Sadie does not budge. Come on, he says, look, it's about to rain anyway. He is right, the air has grown clammy and tingles, teetering on the edge of a storm. But Sadie plants her feet more firmly on the step, hugs her knees.

Go if you want to. I'm staying here. They'll come soon, I know it.

Bird wavers in the doorway, not wanting to leave Sadie alone, not wanting to be alone himself. Neither outside nor in, he scans the gravel drive trailing off into the trees, around the curve and out of sight. Still nothing, and fat drops begin to fall, inking dark blotches on the wooden steps.

Sadie, he calls. Sadie. Come on.

The rain hisses as it falls, like a thousand tiny snakes, and where it hits, the ground writhes. It needles the dirt, punching holes that widen to craters that fill and swell into ponds. It ricochets off the gravel driveway and off the steps, jumping ankle high. Off Sadie, who still sits, faithful, stubborn, eyes fixed on the path to the road, until she is soaked to the skin and finally comes inside.

Bird shuts the door and the quiet that follows, after the whirl and roar of the storm, is deafening. Water trickles from Sadie's clothes to pool at her feet. She doesn't even wipe her face, just lets her hair drip straight down her cheeks, so Bird can't tell if she's crying. He reaches out a hand to touch her shoulder, but she swats him aside.

I'm fine, she says.

She goes into her bedroom for dry clothing, and when she returns she has something in her hands.

Look at this, she says. Look what I found in the nightstand.

A small orange bottle, a white lid. She gives it a shake and inside, pills rattle like hail.

Together they read the faded label: Duchess, Claude. In case of panic attack, take 1 tablet. The date of expiration right in the middle of the Crisis. Sadie twists off the lid.

Only two left, she says. Out of—she consults the label—a hundred and fifty.

Methodically, as the rain thrums overhead, they turn out the hidden pockets of the house. In the dresser: lavender oil, a meditation guide, three kinds of sleeping pills. Letters in a language they can't read, with foreign stamps. In the other nightstand, a broken pencil, a booklet of crosswords—*Easy as Pie!*—an empty bottle of whiskey, an empty carton of bullets. Now they notice the twin sags on either side of the mattress, the worn spots on the carpet where someone must have stood, morning after morning, gathering the strength and the willpower to begin the day again. They notice the crack in the bedside lamp, where it has been broken and then repaired. Burn marks here and there on the wooden floor where hot ash from cigarettes fell.

They have nothing but time. Now and then they think they hear a sound, someone approaching, but when they run to the small front window and peer out, it's always just the wind, the rain rattling against the side of the cabin, the trees creaking and groaning in the storm. In the kitchen, at the back of the topmost cupboard, they find old packages of pasta and beans, with best-by dates from before their births.

For the first time they are able picture it: the long months of waiting, far away here in the woods. Wondering what was happening in the world beyond, worrying about when it would reach them. Dreading what kind of world would await them when they reemerged. They'd had the luxury of retreat, nestled in this cozy house with plenty of food and running water and warmth. They'd been able to bunker down and wait for the worst of the Crisis to pass. Now here they are, huddled together, and finally they understand it, too: the cabin feels like the only safe place, a refuge they clutch with desperate hands. Was someone coming? Who would it be, what news would they bring of the outside world, would they be friend or foe, and when would they arrive? Would they die here, alone and barricaded, sequestered and isolated from the rest of the world? And would that be better or worse than whatever might happen to them if they'd stayed and taken their chances, or did it even matter?

In the middle of the gray afternoon they build another fire, feeling the need for warmth, for heat, for something dancing and glowing and alive. It is easier this second time; now they know how, and they watch the headlines on the crumpled newspapers fade into the flame.

DOW FALLS FOR FOURTH STRAIGHT MONTH; FED WEIGHS BAILOUT CHINESE MARKET MANIPULATION LIKELY A FACTOR IN DOWNTURN, OFFICIALS SAY

Even after the fire has caught, they leaf through the stack of papers, taking in the headlines, the front-page photos. Peeling backward in time. LARGE GATHERING BAN TO REMAIN IN PLACE THROUGH AUGUST. HOUSE WEIGHS MEASURES TO WEED OUT PRO-CHINA SUBVERSIVES. POLLS SHOW OVERWHELMING SUPPORT FOR PROPOSED 'PACT' BILL.

Enough, Sadie says, dropping the papers back onto their stack. I don't want to see any more.

In silence, they feed the fire, slipping it a stick here and there, offering it a log, nuzzling it into the flame, watching anxiously until it catches light. Flecks of rain slither down the chimney, making pops and hisses of steam. Both of them feel, without discussing it, that they must keep this fire burning, that if it goes out something terrible will happen, something precious and irretrievable will be lost, that keeping it burning is their only recourse, that somehow not only their fate but the world's rests on them keeping this fire alight. If they can keep it alight, they are sure, Margaret and the Duchess will come back for them, Margaret will not only be all right but will bring news that her plan has succeeded, that everything has suddenly changed, that all that needs righting has been restored. They will earn this miracle. If they let it go out . . .

They don't think about this, not daring to put those fears into words. That evening they don't bother to cook, subsisting instead on snacks from the food bag, eaten by the handful whenever one of them is hungry. Dried cranberries, crackers, roasted almonds: they nibble their way through the day. As it gets dark, they do not retreat back to their separate rooms. Instead, they sit together by the hearth, watching the flames devour the logs one by one.

When they peek outside everything seems blurred, everything outside uncertain and obscured. No longer trees but an impression of trees: green blurs sliced by wet, dark streaks. No longer the calm water from yesterday but a slate-gray blur, something swelling and churning just at the edge of their sight. They can't see far; a haze hangs in the air, like the spray of salt from the sea, and they pull the curtains shut so they don't have to glimpse whatever terrifying fight is raging outside. The wind grinds against the roof, the windowpanes, the ground— so much rain, it is indistinguishable from an ocean's roar. They are a small boat caught in a squall, everything topsy-turvy. Which way is up? They are no longer sure. The wood-paneled floor might be the deck, upended; the rain scouring the roof might be the waves, lashing and gnawing at the keel below their feet.

I'm scared, Bird says.

Sadie's hand creeps into his, warm and comfortingly damp and alive.

Me too, she says.

Late into the night, they feed the ravenous fire, neither of them ready to give up, nodding off well after midnight, waking up as the fire dies down and the room grows cold, adding another log, coaxing it back to life, rousing it from the ashes again and again until, just before sunrise turns the sky gray-gold, they both fall asleep, side by side beneath the scratchy wool blanket, and at last the fire goes out.

They wake up, stiff-necked and cold, and look at the darkened hearth, then at each other.

It doesn't matter, Sadie says quickly. It doesn't count. It's almost daytime now.

She says this with all her old brash confidence, but he knows she needs him to agree.

He nods. It's okay, he says.

Outside the roar of the storm has stilled. The silence swells and echoes, their ears gradually adjusting to the absence of sound. Now the taps of the slowing rain are discrete, fingers drumming. Instead of an indistinguishable blur, they can make out individual sounds. There is a single drip of rain pattering against the window. There is the single ping of a drop clanging against the gutter like a bell. There, suddenly, is a single bird testing the predawn air, then another bird answering its call.

Though it's still dark, they eat the last of the cereal for break-fast, because even at the end of the world, they think, these things make them feel more prepared for whatever is to come. Then, without discussing it, they take up their posts on the front steps, though they still are not sure what they are wait-ing for. The sky is just beginning to lighten. After yesterday's storm the air feels clean and crisp, the birds shouting at each other from the trees. The rain-damp world seems two shades darker—the rocks changed from pale buff to dark gold, the dirt from gray-brown to near-black—but everything is still here. A squirrel climbs, fusty-eyed, out of its hole, dangles by its rear feet, and stretches itself languidly, first one side, then the other. At Bird's feet an industrious pair of ants lifts a crumb that's fallen from his breakfast and begins the long awkward journey back to the nest.

Perhaps it is possible. Perhaps everything is fine, there was just a delay, perhaps Margaret and Domi are on the way to them, safe and sound and triumphant.

I hear them, Sadie says, jumping to her feet.

She's right: they both hear it, a car crunching up the long gravel drive through the woods. From the front step, they watch it approach. The Duchess's car, so urban and oddly incongruous here, a thin bright bullet boring through the forest in slow mo-tion. It comes slowly, almost reluctantly. Sadie takes Bird's hand, or Bird takes Sadie's hand, they aren't quite sure which, and they watch the car make its way to the cabin with agonizing slow-ness. As it nears they can see two figures in the front, though through the tinted glass they can't make out the faces, only a shadowy shape on the passenger side, another at the wheel. Then it comes to a halt and the engine dies and the passenger door opens, but it isn't her, it's a man, a tall body unfolding itself and turning toward them, and Bird makes a choked sound of recognition. It is his father, the Duchess grim-faced behind the wheel, and they know something has gone terribly wrong.

Dad, Bird cries. Dad. But no sound comes out. Beside him, Sadie begins to cry.

And as if his father has heard him anyway, his father runs to him, runs to them, folds them both in his arms.

She'd waited, the Duchess—waited in her gilded townhouse through the evening and well into the night, waited for Margaret to arrive. As soon as you think they've pinpointed you, she'd said. Don't wait, M. Just get out, before they have time to reach you. Don't cut it close—you always get carried away. And Margaret had agreed.

And then she'd kept speaking, kept on going, past the point where Domi had expected her to stop, past the point where it seemed prudent, then past the point where it seemed safe, then past the point where it seemed possible. By the time it was clear Margaret wasn't coming, that something had gone wrong, the sky had circled from light to dark and was beginning to grow light again, and she got in the car and headed for Brooklyn. Margaret's voice had nearly gone out, the authorities finding and crushing speaker after speaker as they slowly spiraled toward her, but as Domi crossed the bridge, a few minutes after three, there it was again: her old friend, louder now, more distinct, through the speakers they'd missed or not yet found, as if now that she was closer her words came more clearly. Telling the stories that those who needed to tell could not say, now grieving, now angry, now tender, a thousand people shouting through her mouth.

But blocks away she knew things had gone wrong. Suddenly it was eerily silent. The roads were blocked off, starting from Flushing Avenue; she couldn't even get in sight of Fort Greene Park. A cordon of police cars, sirens off but lights flashing, surrounded the whole area, and she turned down a side street and headed home. She already knew what they were there for, and that they'd found it. Still, she waited, watching her phone, still hoping that the screen would light up and it would be Margaret, calling from somewhere, anywhere, to say that she was all right.

When the phone finally did ring it was well into morning, and it was the call she'd expected, and she was ready. Yes, she owned the property in question—*what* had they found inside? No, a complete shock and quite an outrageous one, as they could probably imagine. No, she had *no* idea how—well, wait a moment, there was a keypad at the back; whoever this woman was must have managed to open it and work her way inside. *What* did they say she'd been doing? Absolutely horrifying. No, she never went there herself; her father had bought it during the Crisis intending to renovate it, but it had never happened and he'd passed and it had been sitting there empty ever since. In fact it was a rather upsetting place for that reason; she never liked to go there but hadn't been ready, yet, to sell it. Claude

Duchess, his name was—yes, like the tech company; that was their family. Why yes, of course, she would make it more secure going forward; she would add an alarm system, hire security to keep an eye on it. Given everything happening these days, you really couldn't be too careful. If the authorities could let her know when they'd finished their work . . . ? They were too kind; she so appreciated the service they provided, watching over the community—and this reminded her, she'd been meaning to make a donation to support the officers in their duties. No, no— thank *you.*

In the meantime, she was searching. Margaret hadn't told her much, but the few scraps she already knew were enough. It was surprising how much you could track down with just a name, if you asked the right people. *Ethan Gardner* led her to Harvard, then to the library staff payroll, and then, eventually, to what she needed: a Cambridge address, one of the dorms. No phone number, but of course she couldn't risk a call anyway. It took her nearly five hours to reach Boston, traffic clotting as the afternoon turned to evening, stalling outside of Stamford, then New Haven, then Providence. By the time she reached Cambridge it was just past four, and she parked outside the dorm, waiting. Maybe she'd missed him already, perhaps he didn't work Friday, perhaps he'd already come home from work or he had never left or she was in the wrong place, and she had driven all that way for nothing. She nearly gave up. But finally, just after nine, there he was—a little older, a little grayer, but the same face she remembered from all those years ago. Dressed the same, even: a tucked-in pale blue oxford, a corduroy blazer. She couldn't understand it, at the time, what had fascinated Margaret so, but she thought she saw it now, the softness in him, the promise that there could be gentleness in this world.

As he passed by, she stepped out of the car.

Ethan? she said, and he turned, startled. Uncertain. Scanning her face for something familiar.

It's Domi, she said, and watched recognition flood his eyes. I'm here about Margaret, she said, and then, before he could speak, she added: And Bird.

He'd come home to an empty apartment that Monday, and his chest had seized. So it had happened, he'd thought in a panic: despite everything, they'd taken him at last. Noah, he called out, flicking on the lights in the living room, then the bedroom, circling the apartment again, as if Bird were a misplaced key he'd simply overlooked. Only then did he see the note on the table, the drawing, the scrap of paper reading *New York, NY.* After all these years, he still recognized her writing, quick and pointed and sure, and he understood.

He could not call the police: as soon as they began to investigate they would see the link to Margaret, they would dig gleefully into Margaret's file, and begin one on Bird. He could go to New York, but then what? All he could do was wait. If Bird found Margaret, he assured himself, they'd contact him. He did not allow himself to think *and if not?*

Tuesday morning, he called Bird in sick from school; he called himself in sick from work. If Bird came back, he would be there. He spent the day pacing the apartment, picking up his dictionaries, setting them down again. Again and again he looked at the drawing Margaret had sent: the cats, the cabinet. What had this told Bird? At dinnertime he forgot to eat. Where was Bird? Had he found Margaret? And if he hadn't—? That night, half dizzy, he dreamed himself back in his old apartment with Margaret, the Crisis still whirling around them. In the morning, woozy and sleep deprived, he awoke alone, below Bird's empty bunk, and he called them both in sick again. Exhausted, he half dozed over and over; each time, he woke certain he'd heard Bird's voice, but no one was there.

Friday morning, he headed back to work: he was out of days off. In the library, he wheeled his cart through the stacks, taking extra time to line up the books with care, to restore everything to the precise place it belonged. When his shift was over, he lingered, dreading the empty apartment. Instead he headed to the southwest corner of D level, combing the shelves until he found it: the thin book with a cat on its cover, and a boy who looked something like Bird.

This retelling, he discovered, was different from Margaret's. In this version, the parents had too many children, the boy was sent off to study with priests, the building was not a house but a temple. Perhaps she'd misremembered, or maybe she'd changed the story to suit her own purposes. Or maybe, he thinks, there were simply many versions of this single tale. What did it tell Margaret and Bird that it did not say to him? He read it again and again, until the library closed, looking for the message, for the clue that would unlock everything and tell him where his family was. But the book revealed nothing.

He was still thinking this over as he walked home in the darkness. Whatever the meaning, it was not in the words themselves but somewhere else, and it was then that Domi had stepped out of her car and called his name.

In the small hours, they drove back toward Connecticut, the traffic evaporated, everyone home with blinds drawn. In some places the streetlights were already winking out, but in Domi's car, they sped along the highway, frictionless. For long stretches theirs was the only car in sight, and they glided through the darkness in the small bubble of light cast by their headlights. As if there were nothing and no one else left in the world. For a long while Ethan didn't speak at all, and Domi, as if to fill the silence, chattered away. She had told him the most urgent things already, of course: what had happened to Bird, about the townhouse, the plan. Where they were headed. With these most pressing things covered, though, she found herself coming back to the smallest of details. How Margaret had looked when they'd first seen each other again. I could tell, Domi said, I could tell she'd been happy with you. In the life she'd had. Because she was so sad to lose it. You could see it in her eyes.

She described it all for Ethan, as best she could: Margaret's notebooks, her journeys from one family to the next, until he could almost see it, her tracks like fine lines of stitching crisscrossing the map, trying to suture something torn asunder.

You should've heard it, Domi said, you should've seen it, her voice just—

She waved a hand in the air, and the car wavered over the yellow line and back again.

Just coming out of the air. Everywhere. And people standing there, listening. I looked out the window and I saw them,
just standing. Like statues. It was like she'd turned everyone to
stone.

Except, she thought—and this she could not bring herself
to say aloud, would never manage to utter—except that some
of those stone people were crying. She held on to this fact,
even when the authorities came and searched out the speakers and smashed them under boot heels, even when they ordered
the crowds to disperse, even when there was nothing left to
see from the window but an empty sidewalk and a few strands
of wire and plastic shards on the concrete. Those vanished
people had wiped their tears and retreated back into their lives,
but those tears had been there all the same, even for a moment, and she told herself that this meant something, that this
mattered.

He's a good kid, she said instead. Bird. He's a sweet boy.

After a pause, she added, He looks so much like her. Like
both of you.

He does, Ethan said, and then they both fell silent again, and
outside the road scrolled by, luminous in the reflected shine of
their headlights.

It was like Pompeii, one person would say later. Everyone just
frozen exactly where they were. You just stood there and let it
wash over you. Destroying and preserving you all at once.

Another would carry that moment through her life, and
years later, in the Natural History Museum with her daughter,
she would glance at the dioramas, the animals so lifelike you

could imagine they'd only paused, like burglars caught in a searchlight, that as soon as you turned your back, they would reanimate and scamper off on their way. She would look at that diorama—a lion crouched beside a herd of grazing antelope, the painted savannah air wavering behind them in a honeyed sheen, jackals prowling in the shadows, all of them, predator and prey, transfixed by some invisible force—and she would suddenly remember that evening, as the light dimmed, the voice speaking to all of them, that feeling of being surrounded by strangers who were somehow experiencing the same thing. She would remember the man on the park bench opposite—grizzled and hard, wearing fatigues that didn't fit, slashes of gray sock in the gaps between shoe top and sole—the way his eyes and hers had met, the unspoken affirmation that had passed between them: *Yes, I hear it, too.* She would never see that man again, but standing there in the museum she would remember him, remember that feeling that somehow he was important to her, that they were connected and they'd found each other, that feeling of being conjoined by this surreal moment in time, and she would be frozen again, captivated, staring past the lion and antelope and into the past until her daughter tugged at her hand and asked why she was crying.

I just don't understand, Domi keeps saying. Scrubbing her eyes with the heel of her hand, yesterday's eyeliner smudged to angry dark rings. Sadie's head cradled against her shoulder. Why she cut it so close. We talked about it. She promised. I thought she meant it.

You know Margaret, Ethan says. Now and then, she got carried away. A wild thing.

He and Domi share a pained laugh, everything they found exasperating about her become precious.

They are speaking about her in the past tense, Bird thinks, and he almost smiles at how childish and shortsighted this is. They are so certain that she is gone, but he's not. I promise I'll come back, she had said, but he realizes now: she hadn't said when. Only that she would. And he believes this, still. She will come back. Someday, somehow. In some form. He'll find her, if he looks hard enough. Strange things happened. She might be there, somewhere, in some other form, the way it happened in stories: disguised as a bird, a flower, a tree. If they look closely enough, they'll find her. And as he thinks this, he thinks he might see her: in the birch tree showering its leaves ever so gently down upon them, in the hawk that sails into the sky, releasing its piercing and melancholy and beautiful cry. In the sun that has begun to needle its way through the trees, tinting everything with a faint golden glow.

What now, he says. But already he knows the answer.

What happens now is a choice: they can go back, all of them, to the lives they'd had before. Bird and his father can go back to Cambridge, back to school and replacing books on their locked-up shelves. They can pretend this never happened; they can still say, no, we don't know her, we haven't heard from her in years. We have nothing to do with her, we had nothing to do with it, of course we would never, of course we don't think like that. As for Sadie: the Duchess assures them she can find somewhere safe, but from the look on Sadie's face Bird knows what will happen—she'll run again, she'll keep running, the way she had before she found Margaret, she'll keep searching for her own parents, for a way out of all this, and she'll be gone. So they will all go back to the way they were before, as if none of this has ever occurred, as if it changed nothing, as if it meant nothing.

Or: they can go on. They can keep looking—for Sadie's parents, for the families who've lost children, for the children themselves. For Margaret, perhaps still out there, somewhere, though none of them dare to voice this, even in their minds. They can keep collecting stories, finding ways to share them. Finding ways to pass them on and remember them. They will have to conceal themselves, the way Margaret has all these years, slipping through shadows, moving from kindness to kindness. Listening and gathering. Refusing to let things die. They can let what Margaret has done change them, they can make it change things. They can keep rolling this stone uphill.

Somewhere, maybe, someone is telling someone else: *Listen, this crazy thing happened the other night and I can't stop thinking about it.* Days later, weeks even, Margaret's voice still lodged in the crevices of their brain, the stories they've heard a pin completing a circuit, lighting up feelings that have long lain dark. Illuminating corners of themselves they hadn't known. *Listen, I've been thinking.* Eight million people, all those stories passing from mouth to ear. Would one person be compelled? One out of eight million, a fraction of a fraction. But not nothing. Absorbing that story, passing it on. *Listen.* Somewhere, out there, saying to others at last: Listen, this isn't right.

None of them are sure how this will work, where they will go, how they will find their way, but it is not impossible, and right now that feels like enough.

Before they leave, Domi catches Bird by the hand.

I wish you could've heard it, she says. Her face puffed and pink, swollen with the weight of what she carries. I wish you could have heard her.

And someday he will hear: one day, he will meet someone who, on hearing his story, will say slowly, I remember that, I was there, I'll never forget—who will recite it for him, the very last bit of his mother's broadcast, the one story she did not read but spoke, directly, in her own words, will recite it nearly word for word, because it has been rooted inside them ever since they heard it, all those years ago, that night when out of nowhere, out of everywhere, a voice began to speak into the darkness, carrying messages of love.

Now Domi says: Her poems.

All those years ago, she says, I went to the bookstore and there was your mother's book on the table. I knew she'd write one, one day. I bought it on the spot and read it in one sitting. We hadn't spoken in years. I hated her for a while, you know, I really did. I didn't think I'd ever see her again, until she showed up at my door. But they stuck with me, those poems; I could hear her voice when I read them. I kept thinking about everything we'd lived through. It made me think of who we'd been, back then.

Bird holds his breath. Could it be, he thinks. That she still has it. That she'll take it from her bag and press it, battered and worn, into his hands.

But Domi shakes her head.

I burned it, she says. When they started to go after her. No one knew I had it and maybe no one would ever have known but I did it anyway. I was a coward. That's what I'm trying to tell you, Bird: I'm sorry. It's gone.

Tears clot in Bird's throat. He nods, and begins to turn away. But Domi is still speaking.

There was one poem, she says, speaking softly, almost to herself, as if she is trying to remember an almost-faded dream. One poem that just—

She rubs the spot between her collarbones, as if the punch of the poem still lingers there.

I read it over and over, you know. Because it kept saying something I felt but couldn't hold on to and the words there made it solid, just for a second, while I was reading. Do you understand what I'm saying?

Bird nods, though he's not sure he does.

I think, she says, I think I could write it down for you. The poem, I mean. I might get a word or two wrong. But I think—I *think*—I still know most of it. Would you like that?

And he understands, then, how it's going to go. How he'll find her again. What he's going to do next, alongside everything else his life will bring. Somewhere out there are people who still know her poems, who've hidden scraps of them away in the folds of their minds before setting match to the papers in their hands. He will find them, he will ask them what they remember, he will piece together their recollections, fragmentary and incomplete though they may be, mapping the holes of one against the solid patches of another, and in this way, piece by piece, he will set her back down on paper again.

Yes, please, he says. I would like that, very much.

Author's Note

Bird and Margaret's world isn't exactly our world, but it isn't *not* ours, either. Most of the events and occurrences in this book do not have direct analogues, but I drew inspiration from many real-life events, both past and current—and in some cases, things I'd imagined had become realities by the time the novel was done. Margaret Atwood once wrote of *The Handmaid's Tale*, "If I was to create an imaginary garden I wanted the toads in it to be real," so what follows is a list of just a few of the real toads—and conversely, the beacons of hope—that shaped my thinking as I wrote.

There is a long history, in the U.S. and elsewhere, of removing children as a means of political control. If this strikes a nerve with you—as I hope it does—please learn more about the many instances, both past and ongoing, in which children have been taken from their families: the separations of enslaved families, government boarding schools for Indigenous children (such as that in Carlisle, PA), the inequities built into the foster care system, the separations of migrant families still occurring at the U.S.'s southern border, and beyond. Much more attention needs to be brought to this subject, but Laura Briggs's *Taking Children: A History of American Terror* gives an invaluable overview.

The pandemic that began in 2020 brought a sharp increase in anti-Asian discrimination, but this isn't a new phenomenon, either: such discrimination has long and deep roots in American history. As I wrote this novel, real-life examples were never far from my mind—including Japanese American internment during World War II, Vincent Chin's 1982 murder, and the Department of Justice's long-running "China Initiative," among many others. If you're new to this subject and want to learn more, I hope you'll look at *The Making of Asian America*, by Erika Lee; *Yellow Peril!: An Archive of Anti-Asian Fear*, edited by John Kuo Wei Tchen and Dylan Yeats; *Infamy: The Shocking Story of the Japanese American Internment in World War II*, by Richard Reeves; and *From a Whisper to a Rallying Cry: The Killing of Vincent Chin and the Trial that Galvanized the Asian American Movement*, by Paula Yoo, as a few starting points. New books on Asian American experience are being written every year, and I'm grateful to those illuminating the many facets of this complex and ever-expanding topic.

I'm fascinated by the way folktales and language are both remembered and slowly altered as they're passed between generations—and how we find different meanings in them depending on the circumstances we're in. The version of "Sleeping Beauty" that Bird recalls is from *The Illustrated Junior Library's Grimms' Fairy Tales*, the volume I had growing up, and throughout the book, Margaret tells Bird a mix of Western and Asian stories that I remember from my own childhood. The Japanese folktale at the center of this novel was popularized in English by Lafcadio Hearn in 1898 and has been retold many times over the years; the version in this novel, with all its variations, is my own. On the language side: the Online Etymology Dictionary, various message boards on linguistics, and my father's research on the history of Chinese characters were invaluable in inspiring Ethan's etymologies, though any errors Ethan makes are of course mine alone.

Inspirations for some of the protests in the novel came from widespread sources—in general, the concept of guerrilla art was a guiding light, as were Gene Sharp's writings on nonviolent protest. The knitted web in the Common is based on various pacifist yarn-bombings around the U.S. and the U.K., while the ice children in Nashville have their seeds in the surprise overnight installations of statues, such as the nude Donald Trump statues created by INDECLINE to protest his policies, and the haunting depictions of caged children that were planted by the Refugee and Immigrant Center for Education and Legal Services (RAICES) to draw attention to migrant family separations at the U.S.-Mexico border. In particular, the nonviolent protests of the Serbian Otpor! movement, Syrian anti-Assad protestors, and other groups, especially as described so vividly in *Blueprint for Revolution*, by Srdja Popović, sparked the ideas for the cement block and crowbar in Austin, the ping-pong balls in Memphis, and Margaret's bottle caps, as well influencing the overall spirit of all the art protests. The struggles of prodemocracy Hong Kongers, particularly against the recent China-imposed "national security" legislation, were always on my mind as well. I am also deeply grateful to Anna Deavere Smith, whose work I discovered only after completing this book but who nevertheless is clearly one of the foremothers of Margaret's project.

Several real people make appearances in this novel: Anna Akhmatova arrived in my life, clicking various pieces of this story together, with the kind of fortuitous timing that makes you believe in fate. *Poems of Akhmatova*, selected and translated by Stanley Kunitz and Max Hayward, gives a wonderful intro-duction to her work and life story. I was honored to name a character—one who bravely speaks out about injustice—after Sonia Lee Chun, as thanks for her family's generous support of Immigrant Families Together. Margaret thinks of the legacy of Latasha Harlins and Akai Gurley; may we remember your names and your lives. Last but not least, after finishing the novel, I discovered that there is a Facebook group using the hashtag #ourmissinghearts, dedicated to raising awareness about missing persons. I'm grateful for the work they do in try-ing to bring peace to families hoping for answers.

Finally, it was all too easy to imagine PACT, the justifications for it, and the impacts it might have on society: there are far too many instances of free expression being stifled—and discrimi-nation rationalized—under the guise of "protection" and "secu-rity." Over the course of writing this novel, the news provided a slew of contemporary examples in both the U.S. and abroad, and in the time between my typing this note and your reading it, there will doubtless be more. It is hard to analyze your own era, but looking to history provided some helpful perspective. Writ-ings on McCarthyism, including *Naming Names*, by Victor S. Navasky, and *The Age of McCarthyism: A Brief History with Documents*, by Ellen Schrecker and Phillip Deery, provided a chilling glimpse into how all-pervasive fear can become; *Perilous Times: Free Speech in Wartime*, by Geoffrey R. Stone, cataloged dozens of historical examples with eerie resonances to our current times; and books such as Ronald C. Rosbottom's *When Paris Went Dark: The City of Light Under German Occupation, 1940–1944* helped me consider the blurry overlaps between resisting, tolerating, and colluding. More generally, Timothy Snyder's *On Tyranny* was a powerful reminder about how quickly authoritarianism can rise (as well as what can be done about it), and Václav Havel's classic 1978 essay "The Power of the Powerless" changed my thinking about the impact a single individual could have in dismantling a long-established system. I hope he's right.

Acknowledgments

No one does anything alone, and I owe more thanks than I can say to the many, many people who have helped along the way.

I'm still not sure what I did to deserve my agent, Julie Barer, but I sure am grateful. My undying gratitude to you, Nicole Cunningham Nolan, and everyone at The Book Group. Full stop.

Thank you, as always, to my editor, Virginia Smith Younce, for your unflappable calm and unerring guidance (and for providing ice cream exactly when I most needed it) and to Caroline Sydney for keeping everything running smoothly. Once again, Juliana Kiyan, Matthew Boyd, Danielle Plafsky, Sarah Hutson, Ann Godoff, Scott Moyers, and the whole team at Penguin Press have shepherded this book into the world with such thoughtfulness and love; I can't imagine better hands for my work to be in. Jane Cavolina, my copy editor, continues to have the patience of a saint and the eyes of a hawk.

In the UK, huge thanks to Caspian Dennis and Clare Smith for their ongoing championing of my work, as well as to Grace

Vincent, Celeste Ward-Best, Hayley Camis, Kimberley Nyam-hondera, and everyone at Little, Brown UK; and to Nicole Winstanley and Deborah Sun de la Cruz at Penguin Random House Canada. Thank you to Jenny Meyer and Heidi Gall for helping my books find such good homes abroad, and to all my overseas editors and translators for sharing my words with readers.

Thank you to Ayelet Amittay, Tasneem Husain, Sonya Larson, Anthony Marra, Whitney Scharer, and Anne Stameshkin for your invaluable reads and feedback along the way, and to my writing group, steady guiding lights and unflagging supports. Conversations with Jenn Fang and Dolen Perkins-Valdez shaped my thinking and made this book immeasurably stronger (and Jenn, thank you for Marie's family tree).

Thank you to Jenni Ferrari-Adler, Marissa Perry Stuparyk, Ariel Djanikian, and Anne Stameshkin (again) for that weekend in the woods, the sofa by the fire, and almost two decades of thoughtful conversation; to Catherine Nichols for making my brain fizzy over ramen lunches and for graciously loaning me the name Bird; and to Jermaine Brown for his advice on the legality of child re-placements and the chilling comment "With a sympathetic judiciary, anything is possible." Huge thanks to Peter Ho Davies for his wisdom and mentorship, and immense gratitude for sharing that story about his father—I hope this revision of it resonates.

The Guggenheim Foundation provided support for this project and, even more importantly, an early vote of confidence without which I would probably never have attempted this book. The Cambridge Public Library provided me not only writing

Acknowledgments

space but also endless inspiration in its books, patrons, and librarians; thank you for all that you do, and thank you to Kate Flaim for arranging that behind-the-scenes tour that sparked my imagination.

Most importantly, thank you to my family. My mother and my sister continue to indulge me in This Creative Writing Thing, forty-odd years along. It's not easy to have a writer in the family, so thank you for letting me be one and for sharing your stories with me. I hope I'm making you proud. Thank you to my husband for bringing me lunch when I forget to eat, patiently listening while I ramble about plot points and research, taking on more than your fair share of house and family duties while I write, and having faith in my work even when I've misplaced my own. I'm so lucky, and grateful, to be on this journey with you. Finally, thank you to my son: you're still the best thing I've created.